ALREADY DEAD

A Chase Adams FBI Thriller

Book 9

Patrick Logan

Prologue

DEATH IS A CURIOUS STATE of being.

Or, more accurately, it would be if you had some alternative state to compare it to. Unfortunately, 22-year-old Ruth Pierce never had that luxury.

While it was true that she breathed, and occasionally ate, albeit sparingly and only when explicitly directed to do so, Ruth wasn't truly alive.

Not by her estimation, anyway.

And perhaps this was one of the reasons why nobody paid any attention to her. That, and the fact that she was filthy, with stringy dark hair covering most of her face, and she reeked of urine and feces. Ruth sat alone on the sidewalk, her rag-covered back pressed up against a brick wall. The building upon which she rested was unoccupied, but this had nothing to do with her presence.

That honor was bestowed upon the nightclub not thirty feet away. While this particular hotspot catered to some of the wealthiest Columbusite clubgoers, the music was loud and obnoxious.

If Ruth had had any thoughts about the building outside which she loitered, she may have concluded that it was likely to remain vacant for some years to come.

Contributing to Ruth's anonymity was that when most patrons exited the club and left the comforts of the neon lights above — ironically, or perhaps idiotically, spelling out the club's name, which happened to be NEON — they turned right. Then they would walk, stumble, trip, and fall their way to the taxi/Uber/Lyft/hooker pickup area. Then they would get in their ride, and annoyingly shout at their driver that they were going to the rich part of town—no, not *that* part, with the stuffy old people with their ancient money, but the *new* part. The part where the crypto-millionaires lived. Where tact and tacky had somehow become reversed.

Nobody turned left outside of NEON—nobody headed toward the parking lot and unwittingly came across the foul-smelling dead girl.

Well, maybe not *nobody*. There was one person who had driven to the club tonight. A man who typically used a car service, but tonight had taken it easy. Dr. Wayne Griffith III had surgery scheduled for the morning—he was performing breast augmentation on the wife of a local congressman, and he wanted to be fresh. It wasn't just that he was friends with both the congressman and his wife, but doing an exceptional job would lead to more work from high-profile clients. Business was good, great even, but just in case things with Mrs. Griffith III didn't come to a sanguine conclusion, Wayne needed to make sure he was flush enough to support both of their habits—or at least fifty percent of them.

Unfortunately, the woman who hung on Wayne's arm suggested that a resolution to their marital strife wasn't trending in a positive direction.

"I'm parked over here," he said, leading Julia toward the abandoned building.

Unlike some of the men who left NEON with one or multiple female companions, Wayne knew the name of the girl on his arm: Julia Dreger. She was someone he really cared for, which made tomorrow's surgery even more important.

He wasn't positive he wanted things with Mrs. Griffith III to become copacetic.

Besides, they both needed a fresh start—it was long overdue. Things just hadn't been the same since Rebecca left.

And that was two years ago.

"You okay to drive?" Julia asked. Her lips were painted a deep red, and when she spoke, they never quite touched. She'd imbibed quite a bit more than him.

"I'll be fine. I only—"

A cross between a grunt and a moan cut him off mid-sentence. Most people may not have even noticed it or assumed that it was just one of those sounds generated by the night, but not Wayne.

He'd heard it before, years ago, back when Wayne had been resident in the Emergency Room. Twice, to be exact. But both experiences were haunting enough to have stuck with him for more than two decades.

It was a death rattle.

"Wayne?" Julia asked as she adjusted her white blouse. The top two buttons were undone, revealing large, round breasts. Most men who didn't share Wayne's professional experience would have assumed that they were fake.

He knew them to be very real.

Death rattle or not, Wayne was distracted, if only for a moment.

"Did you hear that?" he asked, drawing his gaze from Julia's chest and scanning the surrounding area. Only one of the three nearest streetlights worked and the sad yellow light that it emitted revealed nothing but an empty sidewalk.

"I didn't hear anything," she glanced over her shoulder. "Except the music."

She tried to move Wayne forward, but he remained rooted.

"Wait, just hold on a second."

As Wayne's eyes adjusted to the dim lighting, he scanned the dark building next to NEON.

After nearly thirty seconds, he finally spotted the source of the sound: someone was huddled in what could have been either dirty towels or a blanket and leaning awkwardly up against the brick wall.

"Hello? Are you okay?" he asked tentatively.

"Wayne, let's just go," Julia urged. "Please."

The small hairs on the back of Wayne's neck were standing at attention, and he felt an odd sense of unease wash over him. There was something strangely unnatural about the situation and, whatever it was, had primed his autonomic nervous system.

Wayne overrode the fight or flight response and approached the person slumped against the wall. It was his duty as a physician to see if they were okay, if they needed help, which was undoubtedly the case.

Julia felt no such compulsion and remained a few feet back.

"Hello?" The closer Wayne got to the figure the stronger the smell became. There were the odors characteristic of vagrancy—sour urine, putrid feces—but there was something else, as well. Something far worse.

Wayne was forced to cover his nose and mouth with the crook of his elbow.

"Excuse me?"

He reached out with his free hand to touch what he thought was the figure's shoulder and as he did, the moan recurred.

The sound was so laden with pain and anguish that it gave Wayne shivers.

One of what he now saw were rags slipped down, revealing a bare arm.

Wayne had seen a good many things in his time that would have made other men vomit, but this was the first time that he'd nearly succumbed to the urge.

The smell that seemed to accost not just his nose, but all of his senses at once, derived from rotting human flesh. The bare arm was covered in weeping pustules, most of which were encircled by dark areas of necrotic skin.

"Jesus Christ," Wayne whispered as he drew back.

The figure moved, just a minor tremble, but this was still startling—it was nearly inconceivable that someone with this degree of putrefaction and gangrene could still be alive.

"Julia?" When Wayne got no response, he turned his head. Julia had clearly caught a whiff of the stench because she'd backed up a considerable amount. "Call 9-1-1. Tell them—" he stopped when the woman raised a hand and pointed not at Wayne, but behind him.

"Wayne! *Wayne!*"

Movement out of the corner of Wayne's eye drew his gaze back to the rotting corpse.

He saw a flash of greasy hair, and rheumy, lifeless eyes. What he didn't see until it was too late, was the knife in the hand that wasn't exposed.

"You need to stay still," he implored. "Help is—"

The figure, which he now saw was a woman, lunged. It was so unexpected that Wayne toppled, even though his attacker couldn't have weighed more than a small dog.

One side of his neck was still covered with the crook of his elbow, but the other was exposed.

The woman didn't hesitate. She jammed the knife into the soft pocket of flesh just below Wayne's jawbone. He instinctively shoved her backward, which turned out to be a mistake.

Before the blade came free, it raked from his jaw to beneath his chin, filling his mouth and esophagus with blood.

"Wayne!" he heard Julia scream from somewhere behind him. He tried to rise to his feet but staggered. Blood was everywhere, all at once.

Wayne desperately tried to put pressure on his throat, using both hands, but the hot, viscous fluid sprayed from between his fingers. It was like trying to stem a leak in the Hoover Dam with a tiny ball of plasticine.

"Julia," he attempted to say, but the word became a sloppy, wet mess at his lips.

Wayne experienced a single moment of clarity before darkness swarmed in.

He saw his assailant raise the blade covered in his blood. He saw her glance skyward and flick tendrils of oil-saturated hair from her face.

Then he glimpsed the sickly woman drive the knife that had taken his life into her own throat and drag it across without a single moment of indecision.

PART I – Grief

Chapter 1

"GEORGIE, YOU NEED TO GET ready earlier," Chase nagged. "You can't be late all the time."

She shoved her niece's lunchbox into the rainbow knapsack. The zipper protested loudly as it struggled to contain the bag's contents.

Jesus, did I really have to bring this much crap to school when I was a kid?

"I had trouble sleeping," Georgina Adams said as she turned to face Chase.

Even though they were running behind—*again*—and despite the bus driver Mr. Edwards' threats that if they weren't standing at the bus stop at eight-fifteen, he'd leave without them, Chase wasn't about to let this comment pass.

"Why not? Bad dreams?" she asked as she observed Georgina.

The girl wasn't lying, that much was certain; there were dark circles beneath her eyes, which stood out on her pale skin. The eyes themselves were glassy.

The first thought that came to mind was that Georgina was being bullied, that somehow, they'd found out about her past and were teasing her.

Chase shook her head.

That was unlikely. Not only did Bishop's Academy have a one-strike policy on bullying, but Lawrence and Brandon had taken the girl under their wing and looked out for her.

They wouldn't let something happen to her, else face Louisa's wrath.

"I don't know," Georgina said with a shrug. "Think so, just can't remember them."

When the girl looked away, Chase suspected that she was lying. But instead of challenging her on it, which would only cause her to put up a more fortified wall, Chase softly asked, "You want to talk about it?"

When she saw the conflict on Georgina's face, Chase almost wished it had been bullies. Bullies, she knew how to deal with. Whatever psychological stress that Georgina was experiencing, she did not. Yet, the girl's unwillingness to discuss the base of her problems, frustrating as it was, was something that Chase could relate to.

"No," Georgina said, her voice just a step above a whisper. "I can't remember."

She needs help, Chase thought. *And as much as I want to, I'm not qualified to give it to her.*

While her time with Dr. Matteo had been a far cry from a panacea, Chase couldn't deny the man's influence. He'd astutely identified her triggers and offered her suitable coping mechanisms.

The good doctor had also empowered her with techniques to prevent descending into degeneracy, as well.

It wasn't his fault that Chase chose a different path.

But perhaps Dr. Matteo, or someone like him, could help Georgina before her stubbornness became entrenched.

Now, already ten minutes late for the bus, however, wasn't the time for psychoanalysis.

"All right, sweetie. Just hurry up, okay? We don't want to miss the bus."

Georgina nodded and showed her back. As she tied her shoes, Chase slipped the backpack on, which was so heavy that it nearly brought the girl down.

With a grunt, Georgina rose and together they hurried to the door.

It came as no surprise to either of them that the bus was waiting at the top of the street. As she squinted into the early morning sun, Chase saw the familiar outline of Mr. Edwards through the front windshield. The man was constructed like a snowman, made of mostly round shapes. Instead of snow, he was covered in a dew-like layer of gray fluff.

Chase couldn't see the man's expression at this distance, but she knew what face he was making.

"Shit," Chase grumbled. She put her hand on Georgina's back and guided her onto the gravel road.

"You owe me a dollar," Georgina said, her tone suddenly jovial.

"No, you're going to owe me a dollar if I have to drive you in today," Chase shot back.

They broke into a run when the bus started rolling. Chase wasn't sure if Mr. Edwards had seen her, but the timing seemed awfully suspicious.

"Let's go! *Hurry!*"

Mr. Edwards either spotted them or decided not to punish them further and stopped the bus.

Huffing, Chase made it to the door before Georgina.

As predicted, Mr. Edwards looked as if he'd swallowed a handful of porcupine quills.

"I'm sorry," Chase said between breaths. She held up one hand. "My fault—I'm sorry."

Her preemptive apology did nothing to dissuade Mr. Edwards from chastising Chase as if she were an unruly occupant of his sacred yellow bus.

"Every day this week."

"I know, it's just—"

"You've been late every single day this week, Mrs. Adams," Mr. Edwards continued as if she hadn't spoken.

Mrs. Adams.

It wasn't 'ma'am', but it was nearly as bad. Perhaps even worse.

What Mr. Edwards didn't, and couldn't have known, is that Chase's estranged husband Brad had sent her divorce papers earlier in the month.

Divorce papers along with a request for sole custody of their son, Felix.

In true Chase Adams fashion, her initial response had been one of rage. But after that passed—*live in the moment*—she realized that the man she'd once loved was trying to do the right thing.

He'd moved on—literally. With her permission, Brad had relocated to Sweden for work and had taken Felix with him. The man had made numerous attempts to contact her over the ensuing few years, mostly to try to foster what little relationship she had left with her son, but Chase had refused contact.

She'd told herself it was to protect them from her, but that was probably a lie.

More likely, it was because of her guilt, the seed of which had been her sister's abduction decades earlier. But that had been a long time ago. The seed had since sprouted, and a tree had grown. The roots were her drug abuse, the trunk her sister's death, and the main branch Stitts' near-fatal injury. Other branches included Drake, Beckett, Floyd, Hanna, Louisa, Tom, Georgina... the list went on and on.

If you don't forgive yourself, Chase, then you will never be able to move forward, Dr. Matteo had told her.

But she didn't want to move forward—whatever that meant. Chase just wanted to live in the moment, which just so happened to be a cesspool of guilt and pity.

That was her, and she could not be changed.

"I'm sorry, it won't happen again," Chase said, as she ushered Georgina onto the bus. "Bye, sweetie, love you."

Georgina turned on the second step, a genuine smile on her face.

"Love you too, Chase."

"No, it won't," Mr. Edwards grumbled. "Because next time, I won't wait."

Chase bit her tongue until the dust from the bus's tires swirled around her.

"The fuck you won't."

She felt a pang in the pit of her stomach as she watched the bus disappear through a haze.

Mr. Edwards didn't matter. The fact that they were late every morning didn't matter. The divorce papers didn't matter, either.

What mattered was that Georgina was out of Chase's sight.

And that meant that there was a possibility, no matter how remote, that someone might take her.

Chapter 2

CHASE HAD JUST FINISHED HER morning five-mile run and was about to hop in the shower when her phone rang.

She was no longer afraid of the thing after what had happened in New York City, but it was still tucked safely away in the table by the front door. Chase walked over to it and opened the drawer. The first thing she saw wasn't the cell phone—it was her gun case. Inside that was not only her pistol and FBI badge but also the last Cerebrum pill.

Perhaps the last of its kind on earth.

The phone rang again, and she grabbed it and slammed the drawer closed. Normally, Chase would inspect the number before answering, but she needed to take her mind off the pill and even a telemarketer could serve that purpose.

Besides, it could be Louisa calling or the school.

Something might have happened to Georgina.

"Hello?" she asked desperately.

"Yes, I'm... I'm looking for Special Agent Chase Adams?"

It wasn't Louisa, and the school, like Mr. Edwards, only knew her as Mrs. Adams. This wasn't starting well.

"Who is this?"

Chase pulled the phone away from her ear and looked at the screen. The number was unlisted.

"This is Terrence Conway of the TBI." The man, who had a mild, soothing southern drawl paused, clearly expecting his name to ring a bell. When it didn't, he continued, "Is this... is this Agent Adams? Because we worked together on a case a couple of years back."

Chase's vision suddenly narrowed.

Terrence Conway... Terrence Conway...

It didn't ring a bell.

"Sorry," she replied dryly. "I'm not with the FBI anymore, but this is Chase. If you need someone to testify, please get in touch with—"

"No, I don't need anyone to testify. I just wanted to talk to you about the Jalston Brothers."

Chase's breath caught in her throat and the phone slipped from her fingers. The corner struck the floor sending a spiderweb of broken glass across the screen.

She made no move to pick it up.

"Agent Adams? Chase? Are you still there?"

Chase took a deep breath and squeezed her eyes closed.

Live in the moment.

But when Brian Jalston's fat face and his iconic aviator sunglasses appeared in her mind, the moment that she existed in wasn't the present. It was in the past.

And her past was dark.

Chase set her jaw and picked up her phone.

"Yeah, I'm here," she said, her voice full of anger.

It had been so long since Chase had heard the Jalston name being uttered out loud that it sounded foreign to her. But the feelings it roused deep inside her did not.

They were uncannily familiar.

"And I remember you."

Adjacent to images of Brian Jalston in her mind were those of Terrence Conway. The two men couldn't be more opposite in nearly every respect. Terrence had dark skin as opposed to Brian's sunburned pink, and he was thin instead of fluffy.

Terrence had also been instrumental in helping Chase find the two men responsible for Georgina's abduction. Then there was the fact that the man had conveniently looked the other way when Chase had exacted her revenge on one of the brothers.

"Chase, I've got some disturbing news that I thought you should know."

Chase had been holding out hope that Terrence was calling to tell her that the man was dead. That Brian had either offed himself in prison, or that someone had murdered the child-molesting piece of shit.

"What?"

It wasn't the friendliest form of inquisition, but her jaw was clenched so tightly that it was all she could manage.

"I don't know any other way to put this, but…"

"Just say it."

Terrence cleared his throat.

"Brian Jalston is being released next week. I just thought you would want to know."

For the second time in a minute, the phone threatened to fall from Chase's hand. This time, she managed to adjust her grip and then squeezed the sides hard enough to extend the cracks on the screen.

"You're fucking kidding me. You've gotta be *fucking* joking."

"I wish I was—sorry, Chase. This is no joke. Brian's getting out."

No amount of measured breathing was sufficient to calm her down now.

"That piece of shit kidnapped how many girls? Four? And that doesn't count the others… that doesn't count my sister. How the fuck is he getting out, Terrence? Tell me how the *fuck* that sick bastard is getting out."

There was a short pause, and she could hear what sounded like Terrence's ear rubbing up against the phone as he shook his head.

"He was initially charged with four counts of especially aggravated kidnapping with a minimum sentence of fifteen years for each. DA was prepared to go to trial, but things got... complicated."

"What do you mean, complicated?"

Another pause, this one extending for twice as long as the first.

"His brother, Chase. Brian started talking about his brother, Tim, about how... well, he started to raise a stink."

Terrence didn't need to say the words—Chase knew what he meant now. She remembered almost being raped by the skinny bastard. She also remembered slitting his throat from ear to ear.

"Yeah, but it's only been..."

How long had it been, Chase wondered? *Two years? Three? Four at most.*

So much had happened in the interim—from her sister's murder to finding and adopting Georgina.

"Two and a half years—nearly three. DA cut a deal, knocked the especially off because of the man's brother. Aggravated went, too, when the..." Terrence sighed. "When the women came forward and spoke on his behalf."

Chase was crestfallen. There had been a time when Georgina had been one of those women. Maybe she still was, in the end. Either way, her fate was probably worse.

"Then, after serving two years, Brian came forward with information about—"

"Stop," Chase whispered. "Just stop. Please."

Her anger had transitioned into sadness, and she felt tears welling in her eyes. Terrence remained quiet while she collected herself.

"I'm coming to see him." Chase took a shuddering breath. "I'm coming to Tennessee to see Brian Jalston."

Terrence grunted.

"You said you're not with the FBI—"

"I don't care. I'm coming."

"Chase, it's—Listen, I-I think somehow Brian anticipated this. He's refusing to speak to anyone, not even his women until—"

Chase added incredulous to her tsunami of emotions.

"They're *still* coming to see him? After everything?"

"Fuck," Terrence said, clearly dejected. "Yeah, they've been seeing him every week since he was locked up."

None of this made sense to Chase. She'd freed them—she'd broken whatever spell Brian and Timothy Jalston had on them.

And, yet, they'd stayed.

Why?

"I'm so sorry, Chase. Anyways, I just thought you should know."

Feeling that Terrence was winding down the conversation, Chase perked up.

"I'm coming," she stated defiantly. "I'm coming down."

"He's not talking to anyone. Not even his lawyer. You'll just be wasting—"

Chase snarled.

"Oh, he'll talk to me all right. You bet your fucking ass he'll talk to me."

"Chase, I'm not—"

Chase felt bad for hanging up on Terrence because she genuinely liked the guy.

But there was a time for making friends, and there was a time for squashing your enemies.

And there was no bigger enemy in this world to Chase Adams than Brian Jalston.

Chapter 3

"**WHAT WE GOT?**" **FLOYD ASKED** as he plopped down in his chair and sipped his coffee.

Tate Abernathy peered over the case file in his hands. The space between the man's hazel eyes was always pinched, but while Floyd thought it made him look like he was perpetually scowling, Tate claimed that he appeared naturally inquisitive. What Floyd didn't say, was that it also made him look older than his forty-seven years, and well into his fifties.

"What we got?" Tate repeated, his words staccato. "What we *got*? Is that how we refer to the crimes that we investigate, Agent Montgomery?"

Floyd chuckled and leaned back in his chair.

This was their shtick—had been ever since they'd been partnered up about six months ago.

Floyd teased Tate for being old and curmudgeonly while Tate countered that everything Floyd said originated from Tik-Tok. The irony was, that Floyd was fairly certain that his partner spent more time on social media than he did.

Close, anyway.

"All right, Sherlock, what crime pray tell might we be investigating this f-f-fine morning?" Floyd mocked in a British accent.

Instead of answering, Tate tossed the folder at him. With one hand holding his coffee mug—which Tate had bought him and was emblazoned with the word 'MILF' in huge letters on one side—Floyd fumbled the catch and photographs spilled onto his lap.

The gaiety was sucked out of the room faster than the air from a punctured 747. The first photo Floyd saw was of a man lying on his back with his throat slit. The victim's eyes were open and blank, and the front of his collared, button-down shirt was matted with blood.

"That's what we got," Tate said. "Dr. Wayne Griffith the third, forty-four years old, wealthy plastic surgeon out of Columbus, Ohio." As the man recounted additional case details, Floyd put the photographs back in the folder in the appropriate order and followed along. "He was out clubbing when he ran into a vagrant. Girl slit his throat, and then," Tate indicated that Floyd turn the page, which he did, "she did the same to herself."

At first, Floyd wasn't sure what he was looking at. There was a person in the photo, but their—her?—face was so dirty that it took him some time to orient himself. Even then, identifying the wound proved difficult, what with all of the grease and filth that coated her skin.

"Yup, yup." This was one of Tate's favorite things to say, a throwback to some TV show, apparently, one that Floyd had never and had no interest in seeing. "I couldn't tell either." Tate also had an uncanny way of knowing exactly what Floyd was thinking. Not that it was all that difficult—Floyd's emotions always showed on his face. It was an endearing quality... most of the time. Occasionally, like when he was playing poker, it was a massive disadvantage. "Initial autopsy revealed that the girl was extremely malnourished, but they couldn't find any trace of drugs in her system. The ME isn't even sure how old she is—but confirmed that the Jane Doe is indeed a female."

Floyd made a face.

"Couldn't tell how old she is? Don't they measure bones or something like that? Surely, she's not a child, right?"

Tate shrugged and played with his mustache.

"Couldn't say. I mean, she's not a baby, she's, *uhh*, of child-rearing age, but the doc said her nutrition was so poor that he couldn't tell if she was sixteen or twenty-six."

"What about fingerprints?" Floyd asked, his own brow furrowing in confusion.

"Nope—not in any system." Tate cocked his head. "Although, the ME wasn't completely certain about that, either. Said Jane Doe's skin pretty much just sloughed off her hands."

"Jesus," Floyd remarked. "Chemical burns or…?"

"Nope, nope," Tate said, taking a sip from his coffee. "Nothing like that. He just said that her skin was all fucked up, on account of her being so filthy and malnourished. He said the smell was so bad that he almost vomited. But, hey, get this: the ME once had a victim, a male victim, whose balls were—"

"Sheesh, okay, okay, I get it," Floyd said, and Tate chuckled.

Even though Tate pretended to be prim and proper, he was always bringing up the strangest and vilest cases to gross Floyd out.

"So, what are we thinking? Random act of violence? The woman just snapped? I mean, it's rare for a female to murder someone by slitting their throat, even more so to commit suicide that way," Floyd glanced down at the photo once more, "But this girl doesn't seem normal."

Tate shrugged.

"Random… yup, yup, that's what the woman who was with Dr. Griffith at the time said."

Floyd raised an eyebrow and flipped back to the case file. He hadn't noticed a mention of someone being with Dr. Griffith when he was killed.

"Yeah, it's there, but Dr. Wayne Griffith III wasn't out with his wife that fateful night. Apparently, the powers that be decided to make the fact that he was hanging out with a stripper a footnote."

Floyd found the note near the bottom of the second page. The 'stripper' in question was Julia Dreger and her brief statement indicated that they'd come across Jane Doe and Dr. Griffith attempted to help her. The girl attacked Wayne and then slit her throat.

Floyd was still a junior agent, but his time working for his uncle in Alaska had taught him that those with privilege could alter the facts to suit their needs.

Even post-mortem.

"As rare as this type of crime might be, I'm not really sure why we—the FBI—are looking at it. So, what gives?"

Floyd's first instinct was that they were being called in as a favor, that whoever had reduced Julia's statement to a footnote also wanted the FBI to investigate. He asked as much, but Tate, who loved to play this sort of guessing game, shook his head.

"Keep trying there, Kemosabe."

Floyd swirled the coffee in his MILF mug.

"Because you're also seeing this Julia girl?"

Tate smiled and his brown eyes twinkled. He reached back, grabbed another folder off his desk, and tossed it at Floyd.

He was ready this time and caught the file with a deft touch of a first baseman scooping a ball out of the dirt. Floyd's question was answered with the first photograph. Still, Tate felt the need to speak up, if for nothing more than to put another 'teaching' notch in his belt.

"Because the same thing happened two days earlier near Charleston, West Virginia—that's why, Tonto."

Chapter 4

CHASE WASN'T A FAN OF flying, not because she had any fear of it, but because she preferred the flexibility of having her own car. But in this case, driving to Franklin, Tennessee would take more than twelve hours while the flight was under three.

It just made sense.

And when she landed at Nashville International Airport, she wasn't surprised to find the Director of the Tennessee Bureau of Investigation Terrence Conway waiting for her. The man hadn't changed a day since they'd first met. He was still slim, but not wiry, with a mustache and short, dark hair.

Even though Chase cared little about her own appearance, she wondered briefly if she, too, looked the same as she had back then.

She severely doubted it, and one of the first things that Terrence said confirmed this fact.

"Chase, it's good to see you," Terrence said. The man must've remembered Chase's stance on handshakes because he didn't offer his palm. Instead, he just nodded politely. "I like what you've done with your hair."

Chase casually massaged her scalp, remembering how Cerebrum had given her hair a pale gray appearance.

"Thanks," she said absently.

And that was the end of the formalities.

"I'm parked just over here," Terrence said, indicating an unmarked vehicle about thirty feet away in a taxi spot.

They walked in silence, with Chase enjoying the fact that Terrence didn't feel the need to fill the dead air with chatter. After all, they weren't friends. They were one-time colleagues and acquaintances and although Terrence had seen Chase near her very worst, that didn't make them buddies.

Still, it was thoughtful of the man to call her up and let her know about Brian's pending release.

He didn't have to do that.

"Brian Jalston is being held in Franklin County Jail," Terrence said once they were inside his car.

"County? The man's being held in *County*?"

Terrence nodded.

During the flight, Chase had tried to research what happened to Brian Jalston post-arrest, but details were scant. This was likely due to the deal that the man had struck with the DA. She'd tried to access more information using her FBI credentials, but her login had been deactivated. Chase had considered contacting Floyd and going through him but had decided against it.

Too many questions, not enough answers.

She was still trying to wrap her mind around the idea of Brian getting out of prison. While this was frightening enough on its own, what made her angry was the idea that the three remaining members of his harem—Sue-Ellen, Portia, and Melissa Jalston, or their given names, Anastasia Blackwood, Kim Bernard, and Teresa Long—visited him in prison. That meant that there was a high probability that they had everything set up for Brian's release.

All so that he could repeat the vicious cycle of kidnapping young girls and drawing them into his sadistic fold.

Chase pictured her late sister's face.

And then he would brainwash them, impregnate them, and strip them of any sense of self.

"Chase?"

She shook her head and turned her attention to Terrence.

"Yeah?"

She hadn't realized that the man had been speaking, but judging by his expression, Terrence had been deep into a one-sided conversation.

"You said on the phone that you weren't with the FBI anymore, but what about your partner? He still with the Bureau?"

"Floyd?"

Terrence pursed his lips and raised both eyebrows.

"No, I think his name was Jeremy."

"Ah, Stitts. No, he's—" she was about to say that he's not with the FBI either, but then she remembered what Floyd had told her about seeing Stitts's teaching at Quantico. "Yeah, he's still there but working a desk job now."

Terrence grunted an affirmative, and she suddenly felt bad for the man. They might not be friends, but he had gone out of his way to help her out. The man was practically begging for answers, and as much as it pained her, a little small talk was warranted.

"I left," Chase said quietly. "I left the FBI shortly after my sister was killed."

Chase went on to tell Terrence, in far greater detail than she ever thought she'd be capable of, what happened to Georgina after they both fled Tennessee. She spoke about Stitts too, about how he'd been shot in New Mexico and then resigned to teaching profiling at Quantico. Chase glossed over what happened in New York with Father David and Cerebrum and concluded the rather long-winded tale by describing her new life looking after her niece.

She made no mention of Brad or Felix, and for a long while after she'd finished her story, Terrence remained respectfully quiet.

"I'm sorry about what happened to your sister, Chase," the man said at last.

"Thank you."

Social graces decree that it was Chase's turn to ask about him now, but she couldn't bring herself to do it. Not only did she fear that her interest would come off as disingenuous, but it might also be construed as insulting.

Terrence didn't press her, though, and in less than ten minutes Franklin County Jail loomed large before them.

The building was a flat structure, blue-gray in appearance, and segmented into pods reserved for different types of inmates. The entire area was surrounded by massive stretches of concrete walls broken by short sections of chain-link fence. The front gate was guarded by two booths, one on each side, and Terrence slowed as he approached.

"Terrence Conway, Tennessee Bureau of Investigation," he said, flashing his badge.

The guard took note of it, then looked over at Chase in the passenger seat.

"That's FBI Agent Chase Adams," Terrence offered.

"ID?"

Chase silently thanked Floyd for getting her badge—she still didn't know how he'd done that—and she held it out to the guard. The man jotted something on a clipboard and then gestured at his partner to lift the gate.

"You can park over there," he said, indicating a small secondary lot reserved for law enforcement. "Head's up, you're going to have to give up your service weapons, though, so feel free to leave them in your vehicle, if you prefer."

Terrence thanked the man and then parked the car. Chase remained seated, even after the man had gotten out.

Her breath was coming in shallow bursts, and her hands had started to tremble.

With everything that had happened over the past year, year and a half, Brian Jalston had been the furthest thing from her mind.

And being back here was the last place she thought she would find herself—back in Franklin, Tennessee, close to where she grew up and close to where the lives of everyone in her family had been destroyed.

"You're okay, Chase?" Terrence asked in his smooth, even tone.

Chase swallowed hard and forced herself out of the car.

She'd come all this way, and Chase was damned if she was going to let someone like Brian Jalston dictate where she went or what she did.

"Yeah, I'm okay."

But Chase's heart was beating so fast in her chest that her body was rocking back and forth, and they both knew that she was lying.

Chapter 5

THE SIMILARITIES BETWEEN THE CRIMES in Columbus, Ohio and Charleston, West Virginia were uncanny. It didn't take an FBI Agent to see that.

Two affluent men are out for a night on the town when they are confronted by a vagrant. The vagrant promptly murders them with a knife before slitting their own throats. Not only were the manners and causes of death identical, but even the knives used were similar.

Both crimes were vicious, violent, and seemingly random.

"Wow," Floyd muttered as he stared at the photograph of the second vagrant. She—he assumed it was a she—was even more decrepit than the first.

"Wow? That's all you have to say? *Huh.* Anyway, the ME couldn't even come close to getting prints off of her—said her skin was too, uhh, *macerated.* Slipped right off like fleshy gloves."

Floyd cringed.

"Really?"

Tate nodded.

"Yep, just sinew and bone beneath."

"That's horrible," Floyd remarked, to which Tate shrugged.

"I mean, I don't feel that bad for her. She is a murderer, after all."

Floyd flipped the photograph of the woman around and pointed at her ragged neck.

"She was sick, really sick."

Tate pursed his lips.

"She's dead, really dead."

Now Floyd rolled his eyes.

He liked Tate—they had a good back and forth relationship. It wasn't just that, though. It was also the fact that while Tate had years of experience, he didn't make Floyd feel like an idiot when he said something wrong. Well, he did, but in a fun-loving sort of way.

But sometimes, the man could act like a child rather than a man. Floyd supposed that this was Tate's coping mechanism, which, while it could be annoying at times, was better than the way he dealt with things: deer-in-the-headlights-style freezing.

"The thing I still don't understand is why the FBI is getting involved? I mean, we have two unrelated murders—similar yes, but no concrete links. Now, I'm no veteran here, but to me, that doesn't warrant the FBI's involvement."

Tate didn't hesitate.

"Two reasons: one, we've already deduced Wayne Griffith has some important friends; and two, the brass wants to make sure these aren't the start of a series of murders across the Midwest."

As he said this last part, Tate put his arms out to his sides as if to say I don't get it either.

"Strange," Floyd muttered.

"Sure is, but guess who's going on a road trip. This guy," he pointed at his chest with one hand and Floyd with the other, "and this guy."

Floyd sipped his coffee.

He'd just gotten back from a case in South Florida involving a man who was raising crocodiles in his backyard with the intent to—get this—*militarize* them, and the last thing he wanted to do now was travel again.

"The real question is, where to first, Floyd?"

Floyd thought about it for a moment and then mumbled, "Wherever's closest, Tate. Whatever's closest."

***

Unfortunately, 'the brass' as Tate referred to Director Hampton and his inner circle, had decided that Dr. Wayne Griffith III was a more important victim than no prefix Roger Evans. Charleston was out, Columbus was in. Upon touchdown in Columbus, Floyd wished he'd spent a little more time researching the weather. He'd assumed that it was warm based on the fact that Dr. Griffith hadn't been wearing a jacket at the time of his murder, but this was not the case. The weather was dreary, windy, and cold. Floyd was used to cold—it was nearly always cold in Alaska—but this was different.

Columbus was wet and soggy, and more uncomfortable than the dry subzero temperatures of Alaska.

Floyd wrapped himself tightly in his overcoat, tucked his chin, and hurried across the street toward the mass of waiting taxis. He didn't look to see if Tate was following, he didn't have to. Tate was like Stitts in this regard, he liked to hang back, watch things unfold in front of them. That's where their similarities ended, however; whereas Stitts liked to keep his mouth shut and let others fill the void, Tate was the complete opposite.

"Yo, Floyd! Over here!" Tate shouted and Floyd turned. His partner was indicating a pickup spot in front of the taxis. "Lieutenant Lehner is going to grab us here."

"Lieutenant?" Floyd asked as he joined Tate. It seemed odd for a man that high up in the organization structure to be on a case that is, or most likely will soon be, marked as closed.

"Yep—Lieutenant Lehner of Homicide division. As I said, the good doctor had some important friends."

"Hmm."

Floyd shivered for a full minute before an unmarked car slowed as it neared. There was no doubting who the man driving it was. If you were to look up Columbus Police Lieutenant in the dictionary, you would see this man. Big, red cheeks, gray goatee, and a thick torso, but he wasn't obese. More like an ex-college football player who would let himself go a little bit, and with age and neglect came a layer of fat.

Floyd raised his hand, but Tate was stepping in front of him, waving wildly. The car pulled over and the big man behind the wheel got out.

"Lieutenant Lehner," Tate said, his tone suddenly proper. "Tate Abernathy and this is my partner, Floyd Montgomery."

Lieutenant Lehner thrust his meaty hand out, which engulfed Tate Abernathy's, even though Tate wasn't a small man himself. When the lieutenant went to shake Floyd's hand next, Floyd prepared himself by flexing his fingers to avoid them being crushed. Nevertheless, each digit ached as soon as Lehner released his hold.

"Get in," Lehner said. "I assume you want to see the bodies first?"

Floyd was about to recommend they go to the station beforehand, maybe for a coffee or something equivalent to help warm him up, but as usual, Tate chimed in first.

"Yeah, let's go see the bodies," he said, casting a tentative look over his shoulder at Floyd. "Both of them."

Chapter 6

"**WEAPONS IN THIS BOX,**" THE security guard instructed. "All other metal belongings in this one."

Chase and Terrence did as they were instructed, and the latter passed through the metal detector first.

It remained silent.

As luck would have it, when Chase stepped through, it started beeping.

"God damn it, what is it now?" she grumbled.

"Ma'am, can you please—"

His eyes shot up.

"Don't call me ma'am," she snapped.

"I'm just—"

"Chase, your belt," Terrence said, intervening before things got out of hand.

Chase looked down, cursed again, then tore off her belt and put it in one of the boxes before striding through the metal detector a second time.

It didn't dare beep again.

"Satisfied?"

Terrence put his hand on Chase's shoulder and guided her down the narrow hallway leading to the non-contact visit rooms. They reached a simple chain-link fence manned by a thin guard standing behind a computer terminal.

"Do you have an appointment?" the man asked, never raising his eyes from the monitor.

"No appointment, but we're here to see—"

"Brian Jalston," Chase interrupted Terrence. She suddenly had an uncanny urge to spit on the floor. Just moving her lips in the way necessary to form those two words caused a foul taste to develop in her mouth.

The man typed something and then finally looked up. His eyes were the lightest shade of gray Chase had ever seen.

"Brian Jalston is eligible for visitors, but he has made it clear that he doesn't want to see anyone."

"I know, it's just—"

Once again, Chase cut Terrence off mid-sentence.

"Why is that?"

The thin man frowned.

"Don't know. But he's stated several times that he is not interested in seeing anyone until he's released. Even turned back a couple of his regulars."

"Regulars?"

The man typed something as he said, "Regular visitors."

Chase sucked in the corner of her lip.

"I know what it means," she spat. "Who are his regular visitors?"

Chase was confident she knew who these people were, but she wanted names and addresses.

"You have ID?"

Chase produced her badge and set it on the counter. While most people are impressed by the presence of such a badge— thank you, cheesy prime time television—but the man with the gray eyes seemed unfazed. Given his profession, he'd probably seen every badge imaginable, and even some that weren't.

"Normally, it takes a while to compile a visitor list, but given the fact that Mr. Jalston is due to be released, I'll try to get it to you as fast as possible." The man typed furiously on the keyboard, then added, "I'll also pass your name," he glanced quickly at her ID, "Chase Adams onto Mr. Jalston concerning your request for a visit, but as I've already stated, it is highly unlikely that he will agree to see you. Now, if this is related to a crime, I can contact the warden and we can work on—"

"That won't be necessary," Terrence piped in.

Chase looked at him for a moment, her frown now etched. She understood the man's position, but if left to her own devices, she would have traipsed back there and dragged the fat bastard out by the collar.

"Okay, then I'll put the request in."

"Wait," Chase said. A thought had suddenly occurred to her, something that might help increase her chances of getting Brian to agree to the visit.

The man's fingers rose from the keyboard like a bank teller had been instructed not to touch anything else he be shot by a potential robber.

"Change your mind?"

She shook her head.

"No, just don't put in the request from Chase Adams."

"All names have to be—"

"Yeah, I get that, but could you please put the request in from *Georgina* Adams?"

The man looked at her then Terrence.

"Mrs. Adams, I'm required to use the name from your identification."

"Please—he's leaving in a week... what does it matter if you accidentally misspell Chase?"

She could feel Terrence tense behind her and figured that the only time that the man had broken or even bent the rules was when he was with her.

Well, Chase thought, *you're back with me now, Terrence Conway, ol' buddy, ol' pal.*

"Misspell Chase as... Georgina?" The man asked.

"What can I say, sometimes the C and the G... you know, get mixed up."

Chase wasn't used to putting on the charm, and it wasn't her strong suit—wasn't even close.

Pale gray eyes bored into her, and Chase expected the next series of questions, if there were any, to be concerning the reason for her visit.

The guard surprised her.

"You know what? I've never been good at spelling," he said under his breath, then he hammered the backspace and typed what Chase suspected was Georgina. When he was done, the man sighed and leaned forward. "Now, would you two please take a seat, and I'll call you as soon as Brian Jalston rejects your visit."

Terrence said thank you and then started to walk back towards the area where they'd dropped off the weapons. He made about five paces before Chase stopped him.

"You know what? I think I'll wait right here," she said. Before the guard could suggest otherwise, Chase leaned up against the wall.

Terrence joined her.

"I hope you know what you're doing," he said in her ear.

"So do I," Chase replied. She hesitated, then added, "Terrence, I know you're not comfortable with this. I'll tell you one thing, though; I *will* see Brian today. Beyond that? Who knows? But it's probably better if you aren't around when I do. I can just get a cab back to the airport when I'm done."

Terrence looked at her as if he were constipated.

"Chase, after what you told me, after what you and your sister went through... I can't even imagine—"

Chase wasn't in the mood for more placation or condescension or whatever this was devolving into.

"To be honest, I'd rather go in alone."

Terrence's expression did not change.

"What you prefer, and what's best for you, are rarely the same thing," he retorted. "I'm coming with you, Chase."

"I really don't—"

"Agent Adams? Agent Conway?"

Chase pushed herself off the wall and looked at the security guard.

"Yeah?"

The man was shaking his head a little and had an odd look on his face.

"I just got word that Brian agreed to your visit... *Georgina*. Now, please, come with me."

Chapter 7

"I'M GLAD YOU GUYS COULD make it down," Lieutenant Lehner said as the three men walked toward the morgue. "It's a sad day when a piece of shit vagrant takes the life of a good man. A doctor no less."

"I hear you," Tate remarked. "It's definitely not fair."

Floyd lagged behind as the lieutenant and Tate discussed Dr. Wayne Griffith III as if they'd both been best friends with the deceased. Floyd's decision to hang back wasn't just because the two other men had much in common, including their upbringing, color, and age, but he liked to watch his partner at work. While Chase had her special talents, so did Tate Abernathy. He might not have her insight into the dead, but he was infinitely better with people than she ever was. In short, Tate was a chameleon. Within seconds of meeting someone, he would know exactly how to speak to them in order to make them comfortable. It went even beyond words and extended to mannerisms and figures of speech. Anything to disarm the suspect, victim, or, as in this case, law enforcement.

To Floyd, watching this happen was like observing a method actor seamlessly fall into a new role.

And he made it look so easy, too. On a few occasions, when Tate was conveniently indisposed, Floyd had tried to mimic his partner.

The results had been disastrous. Floyd's attempts came off so disingenuous that the suspect had called him out. He'd tried to stay cool, keep up with the act, but a second challenge, this time riddled with curses, and Floyd broke down into a stuttering mess.

So, for now, he was relegated to observing.

And that was fine by him.

"Yeah, I get that, but you said that this was a one-off, random event," Tate reminded the lieutenant.

"True, true." Lehner shook his head as he reached the door with *Morgue* stamped on it in faded blue letters. "I just wanna make sure that ain't like a new bath salt thing, you know what I mean? The last thing we need is another drug making people lose their fucking minds, run around killing good people."

Floyd was familiar with the bath salt case down in Florida a number of years back. He also knew that drugs had nothing to do with it. And, if he'd been the one in conversation with the lieutenant, he might have said as much. Which was why he remained in the background and let Tate do his thing.

"Anything come up on tox?"

Lehner shook his head as he opened the door.

"Nope, but I think we both know that sometimes the real good stuff doesn't show up, know what I mean? Not in Columbus, anyway. Now, the FBI, on the other hand…" Lehner let his sentence trail off and then concluded it with something that might have been construed as a wink.

And some things don't even show up for us, Floyd thought, his mind turning to Cerebrum. *And even when they do, God only knows what these new compounds do to your brain.*

"After you," Tate said, gesturing towards the interior of the morgue.

"I don't think so," Lehner replied. "I'm going to wait outside."

Both Tate and Floyd raised eyebrows at this. Even with Floyd's limited insight, the big man didn't strike him as someone who got squeamish around death.

"Trust me, boys, you'll want to cover your noses before heading in."

"Cover our—"

It was the first thing that Floyd had said since their introduction at the airport and he wasn't even able to complete his sentence.

The smell was that bad.

Floyd gagged.

"Jesus Christ," Tate said, covering his nose with the inside of his elbow.

"More like Satan's breath," the lieutenant countered. "I'll wait for you here."

"After you," Tate repeated, this time indicating Floyd.

Floyd, grimacing and dry swallowing rapidly, stepped into the morgue. Every single one of the dozen or so fluorescent lights seemed to be on its last legs and flickered madly. This wreaked havoc on Floyd's eyes, and he found himself squinting one and blinking uncontrollably with the other. That, combined with his scrunched nose, must have made quite a sight. But if the medical examiner noticed, he didn't say anything.

The man was wearing a heavy green smock that was covered in grease-like stains. A plastic shield covered his face and a nose clip, which was probably designed for swimming, pinched his nostrils closed.

The whole look was bizarre, but also appropriate.

What Floyd would have given for a nose clip at that moment.

"Dr. Barnaby," the man said, holding out a gloved hand.

It was covered in grime, and at the last second, Floyd resisted the urge to shake it. There was something uncannily human about being handed something, be it a person's hand or a random object, and just taking it without any forethought.

"FBI Special Agent Floyd Montgomery," he said in all one breath.

Floyd was forced to inhale after speaking and was glad to discover that his nose had already adjusted to the smell... somewhat. It was still highly unpleasant, and he could feel a slight burn somewhere in the back of his throat.

"Special Agent Tate Abernathy," Tate announced from behind Floyd.

Oh, now you're sitting back?

Dr. Barnaby offered them both nods before leading them over to a cadaver lying on a metal gurney. The man's torso was bare, whereas a white sheet covered him from the waist down. He looked healthy if you ignored the six-inch gash in his throat that ran from one ear to just past his chin.

"I assume you're here to see Dr. Griffith."

Floyd was actually more interested in seeing the vagrant, but he kept this to himself. There was something about the way that Dr. Barnaby had said the victim's name that suggested they knew each other. This wasn't all that surprising given that they were both physicians, but they worked on very different ends of the spectrum. Dr. Griffith was a plastic surgeon who enhanced life while Dr. Barnaby deciphered death.

Maybe Tate is rubbing off on me after all.

"Such a shame," Tate offered.

"Indeed," Dr. Barnaby said curtly, confirming Floyd's theory. "As you can see, Dr. Griffith took care of himself. He's in excellent shape for his age—for *any* age," the doctor quickly added as if his comment had been challenged. "As you can see, the initial entrance wound completely severed his carotid artery. He bled out in a matter of minutes."

Dr. Barnaby grabbed an evidence bag off the table behind him and held it up for both agents to see.

"This is the knife."

It was old, with an eight-inch blade and plastic brown handle.

"Run of the mill hunting knife," Dr. Barnaby informed them. "Available from just about any Walmart or Target in the country."

Floyd nodded but took a cell phone out and snapped a picture just in case.

Remembering Lieutenant Lehner's comment, Floyd asked, "Anything in Dr. Griffith's system?"

This got a glare from both Dr. Barnaby and Tate. Floyd gave the latter a subtle shrug as if to say, What? We both wanted to ask it.

"Dr. Griffith went out for a few drinks and that's all I found in his system—a reasonable level of alcohol."

Floyd thought it strange that the ME didn't mention the exact blood alcohol percentage, but then he remembered from the report that Dr. Griffith was most likely heading to his car when he was attacked.

Yeah, Floyd thought, *they definitely knew each other.*

"Thank you, Dr. Barnaby. Now can we…" Tate signaled to the gurney beside Dr. Griffith's cadaver. Floyd noted how his partner didn't mention the perpetrator by name or by anything other than a gesture. This was probably by design.

Or maybe it was just a consequence of not having an appropriate title at the tip of his tongue.

After all, what do you call the disheveled vagrant who killed Dr. Griffith? His killer? A psychopath? A deranged homeless person? Or do you follow Lieutenant Lehner's lead and go with the piece of shit vagrant?

Dr. Barnaby's upper lip curled.

"Of course."

Dr. Barnaby covered Dr. Griffith's upper body and face with the sheet, and then moved to the next table.

"You, *uhh,* you might want to plug your noses."

Floyd didn't know how it could possibly smell worse in the room, but when the man peeled back this sheet, he nearly vomited on his own shoes.

Bile filled his mouth and he had to gulp back down.

He was embarrassed, but when he saw Tate doing the same thing, he felt a little better.

In the head, not so much in the stomach.

There was some sort of slime, reminiscent of what was on the front of Dr. Barnaby's apron, coating the underside of the sheet.

What the fuck is that? Floyd wondered. Then, when he looked at the corpse, he thought, *What the fuck is that?*

"I thought—" Tate gagged. "I thought Lieutenant Lehner said the body has only been here for two days." The words came out in a single rush, clearly by design; he wanted to limit the number of particles of putrefaction that entered his mouth and throat.

"Yup, two days. Like I told the lieutenant, I have never seen anything like this before in my career. I've been working in and around Columbus for near thirty years. Seen a lot of strange things, let me tell you, but this? Nothing like this."

Floyd squinted one eye and tilted his head away from the corpse to avoid unseen fumes creeping into his body.

On the table was what could only be described as a skeleton covered in a thick layer of oily sludge. If he were forced to determine sex, he would go with female, but he wouldn't bet more than a dollar on it. The only discernible thing was the jagged gash in her neck. It was similar to Dr. Griffith's wound but appeared more jagged.

It looked like hesitation marks—a manifestation of someone not sure if they wanted to go through with the heinous act.

"Are those hesitation marks?"

"I don't think so," Dr. Barnaby replied. "Impossible to tell for sure, but I think what happened was her flesh was already rotting, and when she tried to cut her throat, it was like using a butter knife to cut a piece of paper... it just kept crumpling and folding."

Jesus.

"All right, all right," Tate said. "Cover her back up."

The ME didn't need to be asked twice. He swept the sheet back on top of the corpse, and it suctioned to it with a hideous slurp.

Floyd opened both eyes and took a shallow breath with his mouth. There was still a foul odor in the room, but it had become manageable.

"What makes a person..." Tate shook his head. Now, Floyd couldn't tell whether the man's incredulity was genuine or part of his act. "How did this happen? Was it long-term drug abuse? Neglect? A rare condition? Infection? What?"

Tate was just spewing out scenarios now, which was another thing that the man did from time to time. Floyd still wasn't sure if this tactic was meant to inspire or confer a sense of superiority to the other party. Nor did he know if Tate favored one idea over another.

"Could be all of those things, could be none of them. I don't know for sure. Lieutenant Lehner is worried about some sort of drug epidemic, so I ran what little blood I could draw through a tox screen. No drugs in her system. She was suffering from multiple organ failure—kidney and liver, primarily—and her heart had a reduced cardiac silhouette and decreased left ventricular mass. Symptoms of anorexia and/or chronic intravenous drug use. I just—I couldn't find track marks, because of the condition of her skin. I'll tell you this, there are going to be a lot of 'inconclusive' remarks on my pathology report. Like, I said, I've never—" Dr. Barnaby paused to scratch the top of his head. Floyd saw some of the sludge from the man's glove transfer to his thinning gray hair and cringed. "Come to think of it, I *have* seen something like this. Back when I was a pathology resident, I spent time at a body farm up in New York, run by this strange Dr. Swansea guy. Anyway, you guys familiar with a body farm?"

From his brief time with Dr. Beckett Campbell, Floyd knew what a body farm was, but before he could say as much, Tate jumped in.

"No, what's a body farm?"

"A place where they set up donated bodies in unique scenarios, trying to understand what happens over time. They can use the data to compare it to different crime scenes to understand wildlife predation, more accurately predict time of death under different conditions, that sort of thing. In this case, it reminds me of a body that was left in soft mud for weeks. Extreme maceration occurs, and the epidermis starts separating from the layers beneath. *That's* what this reminds me of: a corpse in the mud for days on end."

Floyd tried to wrap his mind around what the ME was saying and failed.

"Thanks for taking the time, Doc," Tate said. "Really appreciate it."

"And I appreciate you guys coming out here. I think this was just a sad person who lost their mind and Wayne was just in the wrong place at the wrong time."

Tate nodded and as he thanked the man one last time Floyd hurried out of the morgue.

Back in the hallway, Floyd put his hands on his thighs, retched once, twice, and then had no choice but to spit on the linoleum floor.

It was all too much.

"Yeah, I told you you might want to cover your face," Lieutenant Lehner said with a chuckle. Then he slapped Floyd on the back as if they were old football buddies instead of FBI and CPD. "Don't worry, kid, I did the same thing—the exact same fucking thing."

And then, as Floyd struggled to collect himself, he realized that Tate hadn't followed him out and that his partner was discussing something with Dr. Barnaby in hushed tones.

Chapter 8

CHASE HADN'T BEEN IN LAW enforcement long enough to witness anybody who she'd helped put behind bars make the long walk from death row to the execution chamber. But she likened what she was doing now to something similar. Not the gravity of the situation—she wasn't so naïve to think that meeting a man whom you loathed with every ounce of your being was the same as walking to certain death—but she imagined that the feeling in her chest was similar.

It didn't help that the trek from check-in to the non-contact visitor room was bordering on infinite in length.

Chase realized that she was slowing, and this allowed Terrence to come up behind her.

"You want me to—"

Chase straightened and picked up her pace.

"I'll be fine."

"I thought that he would refuse your visit," the security guard mused out loud. "You must really mean something to him."

Not me, Chase corrected in her head, *but Georgina.*

The thought made her sick to her stomach.

The security guard led them to a thick door and started to unlock it. Chase sucked in a breath, and then Terrence gently nudged her.

"He's not here yet," he whispered.

Terrence had done his best to keep his voice down, but the guard must've heard because he followed this up with, "They're bringing Brian now, so it'll be a few minutes. You want me to sit in with you guys?"

"No," Chase said dryly.

"Okay. Well, if at any point you need me, all you have to do is holler, stamp your feet, pretty much do anything and I'll be right in."

This was the one time in recent memory that a man's promise to protect her offered Chase comfort.

"Thanks," she muttered and then hated herself for saying the word.

To compensate, Chase strode defiantly into the small room. It was an eight-by-ten-foot space, with a blue metal table in the center that was bolted to the floor. On the table was a welded metal ring. There were also two chairs sitting across from one another, also bolted to the floor.

High up on the wall in the corner opposite the door she'd entered sat an old video camera. There was no light indicating whether it was on or off, but she assumed the former.

I can get them to turn it off—if I ask the guard, I bet he'll do it.

"You want to stand or sit?" Terrence asked.

Chase thought about this for a moment, and then jumped when she heard the door behind her close. She looked through the glass and saw the guard nod at her.

"I'll stand, for now."

"Is there anything…" Terrence let his sentence trail off when he caught a glimpse of her stare. "I'm here if you need me."

The humbleness of the man's comment, as the Director of the TBI no less, reminded Chase that he was the one doing her a favor and not the other way around. It might have been her idea to use Georgina's name, but his influence got her in the door. And his call had alerted her to the fact that Brian was set to be released.

"Thanks, Terrence. I really appreciate—"

The sound of a door opening cut her off.

A man she didn't recognize shuffled into the room. He was wearing an orange jumpsuit and his hands were cuffed in front of his waist. His chin was down, revealing short brown hair with a thinning spot near the crown of his head. He was of medium build with considerable musculature—Chase could see veins in both biceps and his shoulders were round and thick.

Every mental image she had of Brian Jalston was of him cowering, his massive belly quivering, his greasy ponytail flapping in the breeze, as the women in the white dresses threw themselves in front of her gun.

And that grin...

Head and eyes still down, the man in the orange jumpsuit was guided to the table. There, the guard who had brought him in, not the man with the gray eyes, Chase noted, undid one cuff, and attached it to the ring on the table. The prisoner sat and adjusted his chair, still not raising his eyes. It was all strangely ritualistic.

The guard left the room and closed the door behind him. Then he locked it.

Chase's heart was thudding in her chest and sweat broke out on her forehead. Her pits also felt damp. Still, something felt off.

They brought the wrong guy, she thought. *This isn't the man who kidnapped me and my sister, not the one who raped and impregnated her. He isn't responsible for the death of my entire family. It can't be him. It isn't Brian Jalston aka Bobby Jenson.*

True to his word, Terrence was there for her when she needed him. Even though she couldn't ask for help, he must have sensed it. All it took was the man to clear his throat and the spell was broken.

Chase opened her mouth to speak, to say something along the lines of *this isn't him* when the prisoner finally looked up.

Brian Jalston smiled. If he was surprised to see Chase and not Georgina waiting for him in the visiting room, it didn't show on his face.

Nor his eyes.

And it was him, Chase saw. He was slimmer, fitter, had less hair, but that fucking lecherous grin... it was *him*.

"Well, you ain't Georgina," Brian said in a slightly thicker southern drawl than Chase remembered. "Still, I'm sure as hell glad that I decided to take this visit. But judging by your face, girl, I doubt you feel the same way."

Chapter 9

"**WHERE TO NEXT, AGENTS?**" **LIEUTENANT** Lehner asked as they piled into the man's unmarked vehicle.

Floyd was desperate to ask Tate about what he and Dr. Barnaby had spoken about in private but didn't dare do it in front of the lieutenant. In time, he knew his partner would let him in on the secret conversation, but that knowledge did nothing to quell his curiosity.

"Well, the way I see it, we can do one of two things: we can dig a little deeper into Dr. Griffith's life, see if this was a random act; or we can try to figure out where this vagrant came from, and see if there a more like her waiting in the wings." Out of respect for the late doctor, the first part of the sentence took roughly twice as long for Tate to say compared to the last.

And Floyd noticed something else about this planned speech. It was something minor, and if he hadn't been paying close attention, he might not have noticed. Hell, if Floyd didn't have a history of stuttering, he probably wouldn't have caught it, either.

The first part of the word vagrant sounded a lot like *vi*-grant.

For a moment, Tate's chameleon act had lifted, just enough to show his true colors.

Based on their many discussions during long hours on flights, Floyd knew that Tate shared some of his opinions about the perpetrators that they hunted, which were very different from those that his previous partner, Chase Adams, held.

While what happened to Dr. Wayne Griffith III was undeniably horrific, there was another victim here.

This victim just happened to look like a living corpse and wielded a knife that was used to take the doctor's life as well as her own. But she was still a victim, and it would take some digging to find out exactly why she'd done what she did. That was her pathology. Or, in this case, *pathologies*.

And Tate had nearly said *victim* instead of *vagrant*.

"I think the decision is easy then, *innit*?"

The lieutenant took a hard left, dramatic enough for Floyd to physically shift in the backseat, and gunned it.

"There are only a handful of places that a piece of shit like that would fit in, but you know what? I think I know just the place she might hang out."

Lehner's words had a finality to them and there was nothing either of the agents could say to change the man's mind.

They sat in silence as Lehner drove through Columbus proper and toward the suburbs. Gradually, the size and overall state of the homes lining the road were on the decline. Eventually, the number of broken windows that Floyd spied from the backseat exceeded those intact.

They reached a junction consisting of several highways, but the lieutenant didn't merge onto any of them. Instead, he continued along a small service road that led beneath an overpass.

"And this, my friends, is called Junkie Row."

There was an element of pride in Lehner's voice that Floyd didn't quite understand, but the moniker was clear enough.

There were makeshift tents and tarp coverings as far back as Floyd could see. There were also several barrel fires going, which, even though it was the middle of the day, made sense due to the chill in the air.

And then there were the people. Some were sitting in lawn chairs, while others just staggered about. Floyd saw at least a handful of people carrying open liquor bottles and at least two who appeared to be injecting something into their veins.

They made no attempt to move, let alone to scatter, even when the lieutenant pulled over to the side of the road. Lehner drove an unmarked car, but anyone who had any experience on either side of the law, and Floyd suspected that many of these people did, would have identified it immediately.

"Geez, it can't be like this all day?" Floyd couldn't help but ask.

"All day, every day."

"And they don't care that you're here?"

"Oh, they care all right," the lieutenant said as he got out of his car and adjusted his belt. If they didn't know he was a cop before, they must now; Lehner was wearing his uniform, after all. "There just ain't nothing I can do about it. At least, not at the moment. Every fucking jail we got is over capacity. Normally, junkies from Junkie Row stay here, where they can inject whatever toxic compound into their veins without being bothered. But if this... if *she* came from this place? Then we might have to clear them all out, overcrowding or not." Lehner took two steps forward and aimed a finger at a man in a faded baseball cap and a stained muscle shirt. "Hey, you!"

The man was rail thin, and there were red sores on his face that extended down his neck and onto the part of his chest that was exposed.

Floyd was suddenly struck by the realization that he couldn't tell how old this man was. Puberty pimples were indistinguishable from drug sores in this case.

"You seen this woman before?" Lehner asked gruffly, producing a cell phone, and holding it out.

The man looked at the photo and then immediately shook his head.

"Naw, never seen her."

The lieutenant shoved the phone right into his face.

"You sure?"

"I'm sure."

"The fuck you are," the lieutenant grumbled.

The vagrant muttered something incoherent and then stumbled off. Floyd suddenly felt uneasy and wished they'd gone to investigate Dr. Griffith's private life rather than coming here.

Tate either felt the same way or picked up on Floyd's apprehension, because he said, "Lieutenant Lehner, why don't you go take a breather in the car. Let me and Floyd ask some questions around here."

The lieutenant wasn't happy about being told what to do, and it showed on his face.

"They know you here," Tate quickly added. "That guy was scared shitless. They don't know us—they might just slip up, you know? We'll meet you back at your car in about half an hour."

A compliment disguised as an order. Clever.

The lieutenant still didn't look one hundred percent pleased, but he accepted.

"Half an hour—I'll meet you right here."

Floyd and Tate waited until the big man was tucked away inside his vehicle.

"Thanks for that," Floyd said after their backs were turned.

"You thought that was for you? I can't stand that guy," Tate hissed. The admission was so surprising that Floyd chuckled.

"All right, let's move. I really doubt we're going to find anything, but you never know. You still have the picture of the woman on your cell?"

Floyd opened his phone and pulled up the cadaver photo. Then he pinched the image and zoomed in so that the ragged neck wound was just out of the shot.

Tate cocked his head.

"I mean, she probably didn't look that different when she was alive, am I right?"

They canvassed some of the junkies, moving from tent to tent, person-to-person, but they got nowhere fast.

No one had ever seen the woman, heard of her, and no one had any idea who she was.

It was almost as if everyone in Junkie Row had the same lawyer, and they were conditioned to answer in the same way.

No, sir, never seen her. Don't know who she is.

"What did you talk about with Dr. Barnaby, anyway?" Floyd asked as they moved to an adjacent tent.

"About you, my son," Tate joked.

"Very funny. Seriously."

"I asked him about some of Dr. Wayne Griffith's extracurriculars—I got the feeling that they were more than just acquaintances if you know what I mean?"

"I do—I had the same feeling."

Tate stopped a woman wearing a bikini top and cutoff jeans despite the frigid weather.

"Hey, have you seen this girl before?"

Usually, they would add more information than just the picture to such a query, such as age, hair color, eye color, that sort of stuff. In this case, they just didn't know these details.

The woman's response suggested that they could have had a DOB, name, and social security number and that wouldn't have mattered.

"Fuck you."

"Cute," Tate said, and then lowered his phone as the woman walked away. "As I was saying, I asked the ME about Dr. Griffith and his regular trips to the nightclub."

"And you thought he wouldn't be comfortable answering in front of me?"

Tate shrugged.

"Pretty much. You're too young and naive to know about women of the night."

Floyd thought back to the small footnote on the file about Dr. Griffith being with one Julia Dreger, not his wife, at the time of death.

"And?"

"He admitted that Dr. Griffith was a regular, but only with one woman in particular: Julia Dreger. Not only that, but he said it wasn't much of a secret, and went as far as to suggest that Wayne's wife was probably aware of the affair."

Bingo. Motive.

Alarm bells went off in Floyd's head, but he quickly stopped them from ringing too loudly. He had to remind himself that a vagrant had stabbed Dr. Griffith in the throat and then killed herself.

Hardly what one would describe as a revenge killing.

"Hey, you ever seen —"

This time, Tate didn't even finish his sentence before the hunched man with a long white beard streaked with dark brown nicotine stains told him to fuck off. At least, that's what Floyd thought he said. It was difficult to work out based on the man's mouth being completely devoid of teeth.

"You know what?" Floyd said, his mood perking. "I think that this here is maybe one place you can't fit in."

Tate looked around.

"And you can?"

It sounded like a challenge, and Floyd didn't back down.

"Skinny, young black man? Sure, I blend right in."

"Wearing a Brooks Brothers suit?"

Floyd couldn't resist and glanced down at himself. He wasn't wearing a suit, but an overcoat, pale blue button-down, and slacks.

"More like J. Crew."

Tate laughed.

"Okay, let's see what you got."

Floyd nodded and started away from his partner. As he walked, he pulled his secret weapon out of his back pocket: a handful of ones and several five-dollar bills.

And in less than ten minutes, he'd not only found someone who said he saw their vagrant but that he'd also spoken to her.

Chapter 10

"THIRD TIME WE'RE MEETING, YOU and I," Brian said with a leer.

Even during times of high stress, when challenged, Chase's responses were automatic.

"Only this time, you're the one chained up and not me."

Brian raised his hands and the chain connecting him to the table rattled on the metal.

"I don't recall tying you up. I mean, I *woulda* if you wanted me to."

The man continued to grin at her, but it had transitioned into something downright sinister.

Chase glowered.

"What do you think your brother would have wanted?" she shot back. Brian's eyes immediately narrowed, and his lips became a thin line. "Do you think he wanted me to tie him up? I mean, before I slit his fucking throat, that is."

Brian tensed and started to rise from his chair, fury plastered all over his features. But then he shook his head and sat back down.

Chase had nearly had the man. Not quite, but almost. And, if nothing else, this proved one thing: Brian Jalston could be goaded. So long as she pushed the right buttons, Chase could get him to react. This realization made the monster human again.

"I guess we're even," she muttered. Chase wasn't even sure why she said this, but she had. And once the words had left her mouth, there was no way to get them back.

"What are you talking about?" Brian snarled.

Chase raised her eyes and stared at the man across from her.

It suddenly dawned on her that he didn't know. Brian Jalston had no idea what had happened to Georgina. And how could he? The man who had had a child with Georgina Adams didn't know that she was dead.

Chase had enlisted Drake and NYPD friendlies to keep what had happened at the Butterfly Gardens under wraps to protect little Georgina. She hadn't once thought about the implications for this piece of shit locked in a cell.

Chase simultaneously felt revulsion and a surge of power.

"What are you doing here, Chase?" Brian asked. His tone and drawl were still harsh, but less so than when she'd first entered.

"Just walking by," Chase said. "Sizing you up, trying to figure how I can make sure you don't ever get out of this shithole."

Brian laughed.

"Hmmm, c'mon now, sweetie, I'm getting out in four days. *Four.* And there ain't nothing you could do about it."

Chase stepped forward and placed her hands on the table.

That's where you're wrong, Brian. There are a lot of things I can do to keep you in here, and there are even more ways that I can send you to the morgue.

"I just want you to know that when you get out of here, you'll be looking over your shoulder for the rest of your measly, pathetic life."

Brian laughed again.

"From what? From *you?*"

Chase jutted her chin.

"Did you forget about little Timmy? About how much he bled?"

Brian Jalston's expression hardened.

"I don't need to look over my shoulder," the man said flatly, "because I'll have my wives to do that for me."

While Chase had figured that she could get to Brian, he knew how to get to her too. She bared her teeth and reached across the table, intending to grab him by the throat, but the man raised his large hands and she touched them instead.

And then it happened.

The same thing that happened when she'd come in contact with Father David.

Chase was transported into the man's shoes, living his life… living his despicable, disgusting, reprehensible —

But that wasn't it. Chase felt something, sure, but it wasn't what she expected from a man like Brian Jalston.

Calmness washed over her. There was a sunrise behind a blue house and white dresses in tall grass. There was laughter and smiling faces.

Chase's mind rebelled against this imagery. This couldn't be Brian's life. Brian existed in one of Dante's nine rings of hell.

This was… relaxing. Soothing.

A hand came down on her shoulder, and Chase pulled back so violently that she would have fallen if not for the chair. Trembling, she took a seat.

"You okay?" Terrence asked softly.

Before she could answer, Brian spoke up.

"What's wrong, Chase? You don't like my silky-smooth hands? They take good care of me in here. They take such good care of me that—"

"Georgina's dead," Chase breathed. "She's dead."

Brian Jalston pulled back as far as his chain would allow.

"What are you talking about?"

Chase stared blankly at a spot over Brian's left shoulder. She realized that there might be some confusion as to who Brian thought Georgina was: her sister or her niece. So, she did the man a favor and clarified the situation.

"My sister, the one you called Riley, but who was actually Georgina Adams was murdered. She was shot and killed."

"You lie," Brian hissed.

Chase hated using her dead sister as leverage in a conversation with the devil, but she knew that what she was about to do next was even worse.

"I'm not lying, you piece of shit. She was shot and killed." Brian's face turned a deep shade of red and he started to hiss.

"Oh, upset you, have I? Well, how about this for upsetting: your daughter? Yeah, little Georgina, my niece?" Chase looked at Brian's hands and saw that they were clenched into tight balls of hate. "I adopted her. Your daughter is *mine*."

"You lie!" Brian screamed.

Both doors, the one behind Brian and the one behind Chase, opened at the same time.

But Chase wasn't done yet.

"My sister's dead and it's all your fault! And even if you get out of here, you will never see your daughter again!"

Brian jumped to his feet, only the chain caught when he was halfway up and yanked him back down. Chase seized the opportunity and grabbed the back of the man's head and slammed his forehead against the metal table. There was a resounding thump and Brian cried out. Chase, still gripping his scalp, went to repeat this action when someone grabbed her by the waist and spun her around.

It was Terrence, and he was holding her back.

"You're the one who needs to look over your shoulder, Chase!" Brian said.

There was blood coming from a cut on his forehead, but the man was smiling again. That fucking grin of his.

"Fuck you!"

Chase tried to get to the man, but Terrence was too strong, and he dragged her to the door.

"I have my people, my wives, looking out for me, but who is looking out for you, Chase? Anyone? Anyone at all?"

Then, as Chase was pulled out of the visiting room, Brian Jalston began to laugh.

Chapter 11

THE MAN IN THE PLEATHER overcoat and not much else pocketed the two five-dollar bills that Floyd gave him.

"Yeah, I recognize her. I saw her."

Floyd immediately raised his arm and snapped, looking over the tents for Tate. He spotted the man and gestured for him to hurry over.

"Just a second."

When Tate arrived, Floyd said, "Repeat what you just told me."

The junkie who had thick lips that seemed too big for his face and eyes far too small, blinked, then said, "Yeah, I saw the girl."

To reinforce this point, Floyd turned his phone around and showed him the image of the rotting woman in the morgue.

"You saw *her*?"

The vagrant curled his fat upper lip, making it look like a fleshy banana.

"Yeah, like I said I fuckin' saw her. Hard not to see her... or smell her."

The mention of the smell clinched it for Floyd. All of Junkie Row reeked—piss, shit, sweat, you name it—and if this particular woman stood out, then it had to be the one.

Floyd was transported back to the morgue and was reminded of the sheer visceral reaction he'd experienced when the sheet had been pulled back.

He shuddered just thinking about it.

"All right, all right. When did you see her?"

The man shrugged.

"You don't remember? Too much—"

Floyd hushed Tate and pulled out another five. This time when the man's chapped fingers reached for it, he held it back.

"This is for all our questions, not just one."

The man licked his lips, never taking his eyes off the money.

"Yeah, sure. All the questions you want."

Floyd held the money out of reach for a second longer, then gave it over. It disappeared even faster than the first two.

"All right, so you said you saw this girl. When did you see her?"

"Three nights ago. I saw her in Junkie Row three nights ago. Never saw her again."

Floyd internalized this information.

"So, she was only here one night?"

Another shrug.

"You said you'd answer our questions," Tate warned, his voice escalating. Floyd looked around and saw that they were starting to draw a crowd.

This was not a good sign. They may be FBI agents, they were also carrying guns, but to be attacked by a dozen or more of these people with nothing to lose was something that Floyd wanted to avoid at all costs.

"I did answer," the man said, the timbre of his voice equaling Tate's. "I said, *I* saw her here one night. I 'on't know how long she was here."

Oh, great, Floyd thought, *we have Capt. Literal before us.*

"Okay, okay, let's just calm down. You said you saw her and also spoke to her?"

The man nodded.

"Yeah."

"What did she say?" Floyd was starting to get annoyed, as well. This was like pulling teeth and given the general paucity of the little white cubes in the vagrant's mouth, he was particularly keen on keeping them.

"Nothing."

Tate threw his arms up in the air.

"This is a fucking waste of time," he said.

"Nothing," the vagrant countered. "She didn't say nothing."

If it hadn't been for the mention of the smell, Floyd would have been certain that they were getting played.

Bribery was a lot like torture in that way: show enough money or cause enough pain and people will say whatever they think they want you to hear.

"Nothing at all?" Floyd asked.

"Naw, she wouldn't speak. I tried—I tried to talk to her... but she didn't say nothing. After I got used to the smell, she was... I dunno... cute. Tight little ass, know what I mean?"

Floyd's stomach did a flip.

Cute?

Even potty mouth in the bikini and Daisy Dukes would have been a more palatable choice than a walking corpse.

"You sure she didn't say anything?" Floyd pressed.

"*Nuh-uh.* I don't even know if she could speak."

"Why? Was she high?" Tate asked.

Floyd made a face, wishing that, for once, Tate let him run with this part of the investigation. This was his witness, after all.

But Tate was his superior, and he had much more experience.

"No. She *wasn't* high."

Of all the answers that the man had given them thus far, this was the most definitive.

"How can you be sure?"

The man looked at his toes then, as if he was ashamed of himself.

"I just know," he said quietly.

"How?" Tate demanded.

Floyd reached out and put his hand on his partner's shoulder, silencing his inquest. He already had a pretty good idea of how things had gone down between Jane Doe and this man. The junkie had seen her, a new face in Junkie Row, and had approached. Maybe his intentions had been decent at first, but when Jane refused to respond to him, the vagrant tried to rob her. When he came up empty, he probably attempted to have sex with her. Given that the ME hadn't mentioned anything about recent sexual activity in regard to Jane Doe, that too was likely unsuccessful.

"Okay," Floyd said. "Can you tell us anything else about this woman? Did she do anything strange? Did she have any belongings with her? Anything?"

"Naw, man. She didn't have nothin' and didn't do nothin'. She just sat right over there." The vagrant indicated a corner of the fence near the very back of Junkie Row. "It started to rain, but she still didn't move. Was weird, man. Like, she didn't try to get under one of the tarps or tents or nothin'. She just got soaked. Then I fell asleep, never saw her again. I didn't see nothin'."

This was a signal that the conversation was over if there ever was one.

I didn't see nothin'.

"Okay, thanks."

As Floyd and Tate walked back toward the location where Lieutenant Lehner had dropped them off, the man grumbled something about pigs—likely to save face with his fellow vagrants.

"Well, that was a complete and utter waste of time," Tate remarked.

True to his word, Lehner was waiting for them. The big man was no longer in his car, however; he was now leaning up against it, dozens of spent sunflower seeds scattered on the ground around him.

"It told us something," Floyd said to his partner.

"Like what? That our killer was fucking weird? That she didn't eat anything and didn't do drugs? That she liked the rain?"

Floyd said nothing. He felt as if they *had* learned something, something important, he just wasn't sure what.

"Hey, don't worry about the five bucks, I'll expense it," Tate said.

Floyd chuckled and didn't bother correcting him on the amount spent.

"You guys done?" an unsmiling Lehner asked. The man spit sunflower seeds dangerously close to Floyd's feet.

Tate took the lead, and this time Floyd let him.

"All done... here, anyway. But I think we need to explore option two."

The lieutenant's round face, which was already twisted in displeasure, became even more tortured.

"Option two?"

And for the first time since meeting this rotund lieutenant, Tate broke character.

"We need to visit Julia Dreger, the woman who was sleeping with Dr. Wayne Griffith III and who was with him when he was murdered."

Chapter 12

"**Fuck!**" C<small>HASE</small> <small>SHOUTED AS SOON</small> as they were outside the walls of Franklin County Jail. Then she looked skyward and screamed the word.

Aware that Terrence was staring at her, she slowly brought her breathing under control. Still fuming, she waited a few more seconds before looking at the man.

There was pity in his eyes. Or maybe it was compassion. Either way, this would typically be the ignition point for the powder keg that was Chase Adams, but she managed a herculean feat of self-control that surprised even her. Chase didn't understand why Terrence had this effect on her, but he did. Maybe it was his demeanor, or that he'd been present when she'd found her sister, or perhaps it was the fact that he'd reached out to her when others rarely did.

"I'm sorry," Chase said from between clenched teeth.

Surprisingly, Terrence didn't appear to need anything else from her, which was a good thing, because Chase wasn't prepared to offer more. In her experience, an apology was just the tip of the iceberg, a stepping-stone. People wanted multiple apologies, then they lauded it over you, expected reparations, debts to be repaid, that sort of thing.

But not with Terrence. Because Terrence was different, but exactly how, Chase wasn't sure.

They walked in silence toward the man's car. And as they did, Chase's thoughts started to swirl.

That piece of shit. He thinks he can control me? He thinks that I should be the one looking over my shoulder? Really?

When they got to the car, they both got in without saying anything.

Chase was so lost inside her head that she didn't notice that Terrence made no move to start the vehicle.

Stay in the moment, Dr. Matteo whispered. *Stay in the moment, Chase.*

"I can't," she said out loud. "Because this moment… it's too fucked up."

Realizing that she wasn't alone, Chase looked over at Terrence and her face immediately turned red.

"I said, I'm sorry—that's it, that's all you're getting."

"I didn't even want that," Terrence said. "I just want to know if you're going to be okay?"

It was a loaded question and Chase didn't understand the motivation behind it. Was Terrence concerned that he would be responsible now if she did something crazy? Or was he genuinely worried about her?"

"No, I'm not okay. But I will be fine. I've gotten through worse. I've *survived* worse things than Brian Jalston."

Terrence nodded.

"You want me to take you back to the airport?"

Chase guffawed. She wasn't sure if she'd ever made a sound like this before, but if there had ever been a time for it, it was now.

"No fucking chance. I've got a friend looking after Georgina and she won't mind another four days."

Terrence finally started the car and left the Franklin County Jail parking lot.

"Four days?"

The man's intonation suggested that this was a question, but he wasn't stupid. Terrence knew exactly why she needed four more days.

Because that's when Brian Jalston was scheduled for release. And when he stepped through the door in the chain link fence, Chase would be there, arms crossed.

What she planned on doing next, even she wasn't sure.

"I don't understand how he only got two years," Chase said absently. "It doesn't make sense."

Terrence sighed.

"It was complicated. Things—"

"You said that already," Chase snapped. "But it doesn't make sense! Brian and his brother kidnapped girls and raped them. Kids. And then they brainwashed them so they could rape them over and over again." Her anger about everything finally reached a boiling point and spilled over in spectacular Chase fashion. And this time, even Terrence's presence couldn't stop it. "For years! For *fucking* years! My own goddamn sister! They kept her and it ruined everything! My mom, dad… *everything*! And when I finally found her, she was gone. Before Mark Kruk killed her, she was already dead. And the man responsible for all of this gets two fucking years in a country club."

Terrence suddenly pulled the car to the side of the road. Then he hammered it into park and glared at Chase.

"You done yet? You done accusing me? You done blaming me like I'm the fucking judge, jury, and executioner?"

Chase recoiled, surprised by the sudden aggression from the man. She'd never seen this in Terrence before.

"You—"

"No, you had your chance, Chase. Now it's my turn. You wanna know why he got two years, Chase? The real reason?"

Chase remained silent.

"Because of you. Because of what you did to his brother. Brian told the DA about how you killed him, about how you slit his throat. About how you murdered him."

"Murdered?" Chase was aghast. "They fucking—"

"I know!" Terrence shouted, tapping the center of his chest aggressively with two fingers. "I *fucking* know! But those women? *His* women? They were prepared to testify against you, and they told one hell of a story, Chase. A twisted fucking tale about how you had grabbed Timothy Jalston, how he was begging for his life, and how you cut him. The DA... he wanted to press charges. Not against Brian, but against *you*."

"W-what?"

Terrence nodded.

"Yeah, they wanted to get *you* up on charges. I couldn't fucking believe it. And don't get it wrong, I know what you did in that house, and goddamn it, I would have done the exact same thing. It wasn't anything like what Brian said, but they had... they were... they had the perfect story and the perfect appearance. I was scared it was going to stick." Terrence started to calm down a little. "I don't—I don't blame you, Chase. But the only way I could get Brian to shut the fuck up about what happened to his brother was to offer him this half-assed reduced sentence plea. I don't blame you, but please, *please*, don't fucking blame me for this."

By the end of the man's revelation, Chase's eyes were wide, and she felt an unusual sensation.

She felt like she was going to cry.

It had been a long time since anybody had spoken to her like this, a long time since anybody had put things so bluntly and succinctly. People liked to use kid gloves with Chase given her past and what she'd been through over the years. Despite her best efforts to get others to treat her like an equal, it was a rare occurrence.

Even more infrequent for this to come from someone like Terrence.

Chase choked back her tears and straightened.

"The bar."

"What?"

Chase shook her head.

"Don't bring me to the airport, Terrence. I want to go to the bar."

Terrence threw his arms up.

"The bar? It's in the middle of the—"

"Take me to the bar, Terrence. I owe you a drink. Maybe even two."

Chapter 13

"I DON'T KNOW WHY YOU want to talk to this Julia chick," Lieutenant Lehner said. "I can tell you exactly what she said in the interview because I was there."

Floyd knew what Tate's rebuttal was going to be even before he opened his mouth. He'd heard it many times before.

"I know, I know. I'm not questioning your work, lieutenant, it's just... it's just I have this thing."

"This thing? What thing?"

Tate nodded.

"Yeah, like when someone tells me something new, I just have to look it up. It doesn't matter if it's just a random fact, or who tells it to me, I *have* to research it for myself. It's annoying, even to me, but..."

Floyd couldn't tell from the lieutenant's expression if the man understood what Tate was saying or if he thought he was batshit crazy.

It didn't really matter.

The only thing that Floyd was presently concerned with was the fact that they didn't have their own car — and that there was no way in hell he wanted to speak to Julia with Lehner present.

"I know you're probably really busy," Floyd began, taking a page out of Tate's book and appealing to the man's sense of authority. "So, if you could just take us to the nearest car rental joint, we'll be out of your hair."

The lieutenant looked to Tate, who backed Floyd up with a nod.

"It would be more convenient for all of us, I think," Tate said.

Lehner grunted, which Floyd was beginning to recognize as the man's preferred form of communication. Then he said,

"Rental? Naw, I can't let the FBI drive around in a rental. I'll get one of my boys to lend you their car. How long do you think you'll be in town for?"

"As long as it takes," Tate said, and this was something that the lieutenant could get behind.

The man grunted again.

"All right, I'll drop you off at Julia's and then have one of the boys leave a car for you."

"We can just meet your officer at the station or —"

The lieutenant pulled into the driveway of a large house with a manicured front lawn.

"Too late, we're here."

Floyd peered out the window at the modern home.

"I thought you said that Julia was a hooker—excuse me, a prostitute?" he asked, confused.

"Well, that's not what it says on her tax return, but that's what she is."

Floyd squinted.

He figured that real estate in Columbus wasn't as expensive as New York City or Richmond, Virginia, for that matter, but this wasn't a home that he pictured a prostitute living in any part of the country.

"Looks like I picked the wrong career," Tate muttered as he got out of the car. Floyd followed, but the lieutenant did not.

He turned back and saw Lehner leaning out of the window.

Without prompting, he said, "I don't know if it's a good idea for people to see my car here again. They're going to start asking questions."

Floyd wasn't sure if Lehner was referring to questions about Dr. Wayne Griffith and his involvement with the prostitute or the lieutenant's own.

He was just glad that they didn't have to convince him to stay back. Questions or not, Lehner's presence wasn't going to inspire fluid conversation with Julia Dreger. Floyd had already seen the lieutenant in action back at Junkie Row and tact was not the man's strong suit.

"I'll have one of my men drop off a car."

"Thanks," Tate said, as the lieutenant drove off.

Floyd turned to his partner.

"Well, that was interesting."

"Sure was. Just glad to be rid of him."

"Me too. How do you want to handle this?"

Tate grinned.

"The same way I always do."

And then he was off, heading up the front walk, and knocking on the door.

Floyd didn't expect Julia to answer. After all, women of the night, as Tate had referred to them, usually didn't like their visitors wearing identical suits and carrying FBI badges, irrespective of the profession listed on their tax returns.

But he was surprised when the door opened, and a petite blonde woman peered out at them. She wasn't wearing makeup and the skin beneath her eyes was red and chapped.

She'd been crying.

"Can I help you?"

"I'm very sorry to bother you, Mrs. Dreger, but we're with the FBI. We just have a couple of questions for you."

Julia nodded.

"Do you have ID?"

Tate and Floyd took their badges out, and Julia gave them a casual look over before inviting them inside.

"Come on in. And just call me Julia, please."

The interior matched the exterior: nice, but not extravagant, tastefully decorated.

"You guys want a coffee or something?"

Floyd, who never really drank coffee before starting at the FBI opened his mouth to say yes but he was too slow.

"No, thank you," Tate answered for them.

Speak for yourself, Floyd thought.

"I hope you don't mind if I make one for myself, then," she said.

"Of course," Tate said.

Floyd looked around while Tate kept his attention locked on Julia. He wasn't sure what he was looking for, but this was of no consequence; he never really was. It took an additional few moments to discard further misconceptions and generalizations—*Chase would have slapped me silly for this*—based on Julia's profession.

Julia's home was clean and neat and could have belonged to a suburban housewife for all he knew. Everything seemed in order.

Julia finished making her coffee and turned around, holding a mug in both hands as if to warm them even though the house, unlike the outside, had to be seventy-two degrees or more.

She looked terrified. And why shouldn't she be? Floyd didn't think it likely that Julia worked the rough areas of town, giving hand jobs for promised crack rocks that never materialized.

In addition to her house, there was also the fact that the only client they were aware of was a prominent plastic surgeon.

"Julia, we just have a couple of questions about Wayne."

Julia nodded and sipped her coffee.

"I… I liked Wayne. Really liked him. I…" she paused to sip her coffee and while they gave her ample opportunity to continue, she never did.

Floyd wanted to point out that the man was cheating on his wife with her but bit his tongue. He didn't want his comment construed as victim-blaming, because he was not suggesting anything Wayne might have done justified his murder.

"Well, I'm very sorry for your loss," Tate said, toeing the party line. "We are aware that you've already spoken with Lieutenant Lehner."

There was a slight twitch at the corner of Julia's mouth when Tate said the lieutenant's name.

"I can't—" she shuddered. "It was horrible… so horrible…"

The recollection sparked tears that she tried to hide by drinking more coffee. This vulnerable moment dashed the idea of Julia Dreger as a prostitute from Floyd's mind. This was just a woman, a woman who was leaving the club with a man she cared about, and he was murdered, viciously murdered, right in front of her eyes.

And then, as she tried to save his life, Julia was forced to witness the perpetrator commit suicide.

"I don't want you to have to go through all the details, again, Julia," Tate said sympathetically. "We're just trying to figure out why this happened to Wayne."

Julia sniffed, wiped her nose, and nodded.

"Did—did she say anything?" There was no need to further describe the vagrant as anything other than *she*. Everyone in the room knew who Tate was talking about. "Before she attacked Wayne? Did she say anything at all?"

Floyd saw fear flash in Julia's eyes.

"No—nothing. Wayne… he thought she was sick, you know? Thought maybe she'd had an overdose. I'd been drinking, and I told him to leave her alone. He didn't listen. And she just… she just stabbed him."

This was the final straw. Julia broke down and started to sob.

Floyd's instinct was to go to her, to hold the distraught woman, but he knew that was inappropriate.

It had been a long time since he'd felt this helpless. Since Chase, maybe.

"I'm sorry," Julia said after she'd regained some semblance of control. "I'm sorry."

"No," Tate said, moving forward and doing what Floyd wanted to do but had decided against: offering the woman a comforting touch by placing his arm over her shoulders. "Don't be sorry, this isn't your fault. None of it is your fault."

"I know… but… why would anyone want to hurt Wayne?"

"That's what we're trying to find out."

Tate did an about-face.

"You guys came from the club, right? Was it busy that night?"

The question set Floyd's mind down a path. He began to wonder what the killer was doing outside NEON nightclub. The man at Junkie Row had said that the woman had sat in the rain, hadn't even moved when it began pouring. If his instincts were correct, no guarantee there, then she didn't even budge when someone had attempted to rob and rape her.

But the killer had traveled a considerable distance from Junkie Row to NEON. The real question was the same as the one that Julia had just verbalized.

What was her motivation?

"Yeah, it was packed."

"What time did you leave the club?"

"It was late. Around two, maybe. Not completely sure."

"And he was driving you home? Is that correct?"

"Yeah. Wayne had surgery in the morning. He only had a couple of drinks. We were coming back here."

The question, *Where did Wayne's wife think he was going that night*, was on the tip of Floyd's tongue, but he was only the observer here.

"I just have one final question for you, Julia," Tate said. "It's personal, and I know that based on your —"

Julia lowered her mug and stood up tall.

"If you promise that you'll tell me why this happened to Wayne, whenever you find out, I'll answer any question."

Floyd knew that this was a difficult agreement for Tate to make. His partner was a realist, through and through. He believed strongly that sometimes bad things just happened to good, and even bad, people. Random accidents, horrible occurrences, but events that had no discernible preceding factors that could have been altered.

And this particular case was looking more and more like a psychotic break by a very sick person, and Wayne was just the unfortunate victim.

The problem lay in the fact that most bereaved widows, children, and even mistresses, were often unsatisfied with this result. It clashed with the intrinsic human need to place blame.

If Tate agreed to Julia's proposition, there was a very real risk of pushing too hard, of making links that weren't there and generating false leads that always ended up being red herrings. In and of itself, not such a terrible thing, but their time and resources were limited.

And there were bad people out there that needed to be stopped, as of yet unrealized crimes that could be prevented.

But this is where Floyd came in—he didn't have to share his partner's lack of faith, in a greater power or in humankind. If it came back the way he thought it would—Wayne's death was completely random—he'd be the one to break the news to Julia.

And it would end there.

"When we find out, we'll tell you," he said, producing his card and handing it over. "You can even call me to check up if you want."

Julia appeared surprised by this but took the card.

Then Tate grabbed the reins again.

"Did Wayne have any other partners? Besides you and his wife?"

There are many ways that Floyd would have approached this question, but this wasn't one of them. It was blunt, to the point, and seemed callous at best.

But it worked.

Julia seemed unfazed when she replied, "No. Just me. Things with his wife... they were rocky at best. We were close. I don't want to make up a fairy tale story about a doctor leaving his wife and saving a hooker from the streets, because it wasn't like that. But," she sighed, "I know how this is going to come off, but our relationship was different than it was with others."

She left it at that, and it was enough.

"Thank you for your help," Tate said.

They were nearly at the door when Floyd couldn't resist.

"Julia, I'm sorry again that you went through this. Please, call me if you have any questions," he said.

The woman nodded and Tate and Floyd left.

"You looking for a date?" Tate asked once the door behind them had closed. "Or a service?"

Floyd grimaced at the joke made in poor taste.

"What?" Tate asked, feigning hurt.

"Talking about service," Floyd said, grateful for the segue when he noticed the car waiting across the street. "I guess they dropped it off while we were inside."

The doors were unlocked, and the keys were in the ignition, but the vehicle was off. There was a short note in terrible handwriting on the dash.

Agents Abernathy and Mongomery please return the car to 11 Division before leaving. Officer Larry Holten

The smell of stale cigarettes and old fast food that struck Floyd once he opened the door made him quickly forget the misspelling of his surname.

"Yeah, about that service," Tate muttered as he got behind the wheel. "At least we didn't have to pay for it."

Chapter 14

"SCOTCH, NEAT—SOMETHING PEATY," CHASE said as she sat at the bar.

Terrence sidled up next to her.

"Just a beer, whatever you have on draft."

The bartender performed the universal signal for order received—a healthy one-handed slap on the bar—and then turned around to prepare the drinks.

The two of them sat awkwardly, both staring straight ahead not saying anything, until the drinks were delivered. Even then, it took several sips before Chase broke the ice.

"That was… fucked up."

Terrence licked the foam from his mustache.

"Yeah."

More silence, more drink sipping.

"Do you—"

"We—"

They both tried to speak at the same time and Chase smirked.

It reminded her of a first date, even though they were far from compatible. Terrence was handsome, but he wasn't damaged enough for her taste.

"Go ahead," she said.

Terrence shrugged as if to preemptively diminish his statement.

"We've been through some shit, Chase, but there are a lot of things I don't know about you, and there's stuff you don't know about me."

"I—"

He held up his hand.

"Wait, just let me finish. I just wanted to say that I know enough to consider you a friend."

It was strange to hear these words. They sounded childish, cliched, even, but Terrence was real. And his revelation touched her.

"Me too. And I appreciate what you've done for me. All of it."

Terrence looked down at his beer and that's when Chase realized that there was more to this than a simple ode to friendship.

"I hope you don't find me stepping out of line for asking this, but—"

"Yeah, I have people."

Chase had anticipated what the man was gonna say because it was the same thing that was on her mind.

I have my people, my wives, looking out for me, but who is looking out for you, Chase? Anyone? Anyone at all?

Brian Jalston had shouted those words at her as she'd been pulled from the visiting room.

"Good," Terrence said, going back to sipping his beer.

Chase was mildly perturbed that he didn't ask who, which got her thinking.

Do I have people looking out for me?

At one time, she'd had Stitts—she trusted him with her life on many occasions. There had been a time when Floyd was constantly watching her back, too. But both of them had since moved on. There was always Louisa, who was as dependable as they came.

But Chase couldn't forget where they'd met and the fact that there was always a chance of relapse.

For both of them.

Chase finished her first drink and then ordered a second.

With this beverage came another thought.

Do I need anyone else?

She wasn't scared of Brian.

But there was one person who Chase was terrified of.

Herself.

"I'll be fine," she whispered.

"What's that?"

When Terrence turned to look at her, Chase averted her eyes and stared out the window.

And then she stood up so quickly that she dropped her glass of scotch.

"Chase?"

Chase was already on the move, rushing toward the door. She shoved it open and squinted into the sun. Shielding her eyes, she looked up and down the street, trying to locate what she'd seen from inside the bar.

There was only a man walking his dog.

"What the fuck?"

Terrence appeared at her side, breathing heavily.

"Chase? What's wrong?"

Chase shook her head as she continued to search the street.

"I thought... I thought I saw something," she mumbled.

"What?" Terrence asked.

Chase looked at him.

She knew what he was thinking: Terrence thought she was going nuts. That she'd imagined Brian Jalston walking the streets of Franklin, Tennessee.

She didn't blame him.

Terrence was right about one thing: there were a lot of things that he didn't know about her.

A lot.

But Chase hadn't seen a mirage. She hadn't seen Brian, either.

She'd seen a woman in a long white dress. Not just any dress, but one of *the* dresses. The creepy flowing dresses that Brian made his women wear. The ones that Chase had also worn.

"Nothing," Chase said. But the time between question and answer had drifted into the strange zone.

"You going to be okay, Chase?"

Chase picked up what was left of her drink and downed it.

"Yeah."

Terrence was uncomfortable. He checked his watch, then said, "I gotta get back to work. You wanna meet up after I'm done? Six-ish?"

Chase considered the offer. Terrence wasn't qualified to deal with her issues, but the man was trying—was he ever trying. But Chase knew that if she stayed here, this close to Brian, she might lose her mind.

She also knew herself, and that she would be driven crazy, counting the hours until Brian was released. With nothing else to do, temptation was destined to rear its ugly head.

This simple thought was enough for her to sense an itch on the inside of her left arm. Imagined, certainly, but did that matter?

After a dry swallow, Chase looked at Terrence, *really* looked at him.

No, I can't do that either.

That left only one outlet for her own special brand of insanity.

Fuck you, Dr. Matteo. Fuck you for being so right.

"I can't," she said, shaking her head. "I can't stay."

Chase hugged Terrence, and he hugged her back.

"Thank you. Thanks for everything."

Terrence eyed her suspiciously but let her go.

"Take care of yourself."

"You, too."

And then he was gone, and Chase was once more alone.

"I need another fucking drink," she said, and the bartender obliged.

I can't stay here, but I can always come back.

With this in mind, Chase pulled out her phone and dialed a number she'd hoped she never had to call again.

"Fuck you, Matteo."

Chapter 15

"**WHAT IS WITH COLUMBUS AND** the smells?" Floyd asked.
"First the morgue, now this."

Tate chuckled as he started the car.

It sputtered before turning over.

"Looks like the lieutenant didn't take kindly to your words," Tate said with a grin.

"My words?" Floyd demanded. "Why is it always me? I barely said anything!"

"Because it is. Anyways, you got the address?"

Floyd pulled out the case file and found Dr. Griffith's address. He relayed it to Tate who put it into his phone and started to drive.

"Alright, Sherlock," Tate said once they were on the road. "I know you picked up something back there, why—"

"Oh," Floyd teased. "The wise one doesn't know?"

"Of course, I know," Tate shot back. "I just want to know if *you* know what *I* know."

Floyd chuckled.

"Alright, well, here's the thing. She doesn't move, right? If we believe the ME and the guy at Junkie Row, this girl doesn't move for anything. But for some reason, she finds herself miles away at NEON."

"Maybe she was zonked out from some Special K and when she came to, she realized what pleather jacket man had or tried to do to her and fled."

"No drugs in her system, remember?"

"The ME didn't seem all that confident," Tate reminded him.

"Okay. But there's more. She's outside this club, right? Packed club. How many people walked by her after leaving the club? Dozens? Hundreds? And only Dr. Griffith was the one to stop to see if she was okay?"

Tate shrugged.

"Do you interact with vagrants on a regular basis, Floyd? When you see someone lying on the street, do you stop and have a little chat? Especially one that smells like *death*? Oh, and let's not forget that you just left the club, and the six, twenty-two dollar each vodka crans you sucked down are making you feel mighty good about yourself."

Floyd thought about this for a second.

"I don't drink vodka crans, but what you're saying... that's kinda my point, right? Most people are gonna walk right by. But not a doctor. They're always going to stop."

The only sound in the car from the next minute or so was the rattle of the engine.

"All right, all right. I'll give it to you," Tate relented. "It's possible that this *wasn't* random. Let's just see how this plays out, though, before we make any rash decisions, shall we?"

"I'm not doing anything. I was just telling you —no, wait, *educating* you," Floyd said with a grin.

Tate laughed again.

"Okay, Sherlock. Maybe you want to lead this next interview, then?"

Floyd stopped smiling.

Tate was joking, of course, but the idea of him speaking to a bereaved wife? The thought alone brought back memories of him in the disaster that happened in New York City when he'd spoken to Mr. Bailey. Or had attempted to.

"Hell, no," he said.

"That's what I thought."

Tate pulled up to the late Dr. Wayne Griffith's house, and Floyd was struck by how similar it was to Julia Dreger's. It was slightly bigger and in a better neighborhood, so far as he could tell, but he could've seen the doctor living in Julia's place had he been a little younger and just starting out.

How strange it was for two people with completely different careers to have such similar lifestyles.

As usual, Tate led the way up to the house and Floyd followed. He felt a twinge of anxiety as he approached, but he was comforted by Tate's presence.

The similarities between Dr. Griffith's women's houses ended there. The women were very different. Julia was blonde, whereas Meredith Griffith was a brunette. The latter was also on the heavier side. Not fat, but the woman had a little extra flesh around her middle. Most of Julia's extra flesh was located a little higher and had a specific firmness to it. But Meredith was pretty with full lips and bright eyes that were visible even behind her designer glasses.

"Mrs. Griffith, my name's Tate Abernathy with the FBI. This is my partner, Agent Montgomery."

The women's differences were further accentuated when considering their attitudes toward visitors on their doorsteps.

"I've already told the police everything I know."

There was no *call me Meredith*, no *please, come in*, no *would you like a coffee?*

"Yes, I understand that, and we're very sorry for your loss," Tate said.

He sounds like a broken record, Floyd thought.

"But we just have a couple of questions for you," Tate finished.

Meredith crossed her arms over her chest but didn't say anything. Tate took this as a cue to continue.

"Mrs. Griffith, can you think about anyone who might want to hurt your husband?"

Meredith's expression did not change when she answered, "Yeah, the homeless bitch who killed him."

Okay, she's got a point, Floyd thought. *I'll give her that.*

"Of course, but what about someone else? Can you think of anyone else?"

Meredith's expression became hard.

"My husband was a respectable plastic surgeon. Nobody wanted to hurt him."

"Again, I'm sorry to ask these difficult questions, Mrs. Griffith. And as of now, we are treating your husband's murder as a closed case. We just want to wrap up some loose ends."

No response.

"Can you think of a recent patient, maybe, who wasn't happy with their surgery results? And I recognize that you aren't—"

"No," Meredith said sharply.

Sensing that Tate was nearing the end of this line of questioning, Floyd chose this moment to speak up.

"Thank you, Julia."

Everyone froze. Meredith, Tate, and time itself seemed to come to a standstill.

Then Floyd's phone started to buzz, and he scrambled to pull it out of his pocket. He was positive that he'd turned it on silent before the interview.

"Sorry," he grumbled. This comment, or perhaps it was the phone ringing, seemed to restart time.

"My name is Meredith."

"Yeah, I'm sorry about that," Tate said, shooting Floyd a look. "My partner's terrible with names."

Floyd barely noticed because he was staring at his cell phone. Taking your phone out during an interview was one thing, answering it was another.

"Yeah," he mumbled, his eyes locked on his phone. "I have to take this. Meredith, I'm very sorry for what happened to your husband."

Both Tate and Meredith said something, but Floyd didn't hear them. He was already moving toward the stinking car, his heart pounding in his chest with the same authority as when Tate had joked about him talking to Meredith on his own.

The last time he'd spoken to her, they'd been sitting on church steps, discussing what had happened to Father David. In the end, no definitive conclusion had been agreed upon.

With a sigh, Floyd finally accepted the call.

"Chase? Everything okay?"

There was a short pause, during which time he heard Chase breathing.

"Chase?" he asked again, alarm creeping into his voice.

"Floyd, it's nice to hear your voice."

Floyd allowed himself a small breath. Chase sounded lucid, normal.

Normal for her, anyway.

"What are you... what are you up to?"

Even the awkwardness of Chase's attempt at small talk was normal.

"On a case."

"Need any help?"

Floyd raised an eyebrow and then looked back towards the house. Meredith had since closed the door and Tate was hurrying toward him.

"Naw, I don't think so."

"What's the case about?"

"Chase, you sure you're okay?" Floyd knew that this sort of conversation was torture for Chase.

"Fine, just... just need someone to talk to."

Floyd cleared his throat.

"I'm in Columbus. Vagrant murdered a prominent doctor and then immediately slit her own throat."

There was a pause during which Chase expected Floyd to add more. He resisted.

"Why are you guys there, then? Why is the FBI involved?"

"Because there was another killing like this over in West Virginia just a couple of days ago. Same MO: seemingly random vagrant murders someone with a knife and then kills herself."

"Right."

Floyd smiled. Time had apparently stopped when his phone had rung and then worked itself backward when he'd answered the call.

Chase had said the same thing when Floyd had called her and asked for help on the Suicide Girls' case. The only difference here was that Chase was calling him, asking to help, and not the other way around.

"What can I say, I don't make the rules, I just follow them."

Chase grunted.

"And you don't need any help at all?"

Floyd finally grasped the notion that Chase wasn't asking him if he needed help on the case but stating that she *wanted* to help.

No—not wanted but *needed*.

Tate caught up to Floyd and waited patiently for the call to wrap up.

"Well, I'm in Columbus and—"

"I heard it's beautiful this time of year."

"I'm not sure it's beautiful any time of year," Ford remarked. "Where are you?"

"Tennessee."

Floyd's concern returned with fervor. He could only think of one reason why Chase would be down south, and it didn't bode well for her.

"You know what? Why don't I talk to my partner and then give Director Hampton a call? If—"

"Already called Hampton. He cleared it. So long as you're on board, I can fly down and meet you today."

Floyd looked at Tate who appeared lost in thought. He knew that he should probably ask him if this was okay, but then Floyd remember the man's joke in the car.

About him interviewing Meredith Griffith alone.

Besides, it was about time the two met, given how much Floyd had talked about Chase with his new partner.

"It's fine by us."

Tate lifted his head and Floyd smiled.

"I'm looking forward to it."

"See you soon, Chase."

Floyd hung up, and Tate was immediately on him.

"Oh, was that the famous Chase Adams? The only FBI Agent in the Bureau's illustrious history to have been killed and resurrected?"

"Yeah, that was her."

"And did I hear you say, see you soon, Chase?" Tate teased as he opened the door to their foul-smelling car and got in. "Does this mean that I'm finally going to get to meet her?"

Floyd massaged his temples. Maybe this wasn't such a good idea, after all.

"Yeah, I guess that's what it means."

Tate clapped his hands together.

"Goodie! I'll make sure to have my *Sharpie* at the ready for an autograph. Maybe I'll get her to sign my chest. What do you think, Floyd? Think she would like that?"

"She would love that, Tate," Floyd said with a sigh. "Just fucking love it."

What in the world have I just done?

PART II – Disease

Chapter 16

CHASE PULLED HER SUNGLASSES DOWN her nose as she entered the cafe. There had been a time in her life when these shades would have been designer but that had been long ago. She still enjoyed good-quality fashion, but most of her gear had been highly impractical for living in the country.

As for her sunglasses, well, she had no idea where those had gone. Lost either during her travels or in the course of the move.

When she spotted Floyd, Chase took her no-name brand glasses off completely and tucked them into the V-neck of her white shirt.

"Floyd," she said with a smile. He rose from the booth, and they hugged.

"I like what you've done with your hair," Floyd remarked when they separated. "Makes you look distinguished."

"Distinguished or old?" she asked with a halfhearted grin.

Floyd shrugged.

"Both, I guess."

"Fair enough."

Chase peered over Floyd's shoulder at the other man seated in the booth. He was in his late forties, maybe even older, and was clearly going for early Tom Selleck vibes: dark mustache, short hair, slightly unkept. The only thing he was missing was the dimples.

"That," Floyd said, following her gaze, "is my partner, FBI Special Agent Tate Abernathy."

Chase cocked her head.

Tate Abernathy? Sounds like a discount men's clothing line.

"Nice to meet you," she said. Tate stood and held out his hand. "Yeah, I don't really do that."

Instead of being offended, Tate held up his hand as if to say, no problem. Then he opened his arms, offering a hug.

"I don't do that either," she remarked, knowing and not caring that she'd embraced Floyd but a few seconds ago.

Tate didn't appear to mind this, either.

"Okay, well, how about this, then?" Tate turned, grabbed a napkin and a pen off the table, and held it out to her. "An autograph?"

"Sure," she said. Chase scrawled FUCK YOU in capital letters on the napkin, folded it, and then handed it back with a warm smile.

Tate, who had seen what she'd written, nodded and put the napkin in his pocket.

"Thank you, and I do apologize for all my fangirling."

"No problem," Chase said as she slid into the booth. There was half of a hamburger on a plate with some French fries and she helped herself to the latter, dipping a fry into ketchup before tossing it into her mouth. "So, what's this case we're on?"

Floyd and Tate sat.

"Go ahead, Floyd." Tate took a big bite of the hamburger that was in front of Chase. "Let Chase in on our crazy mission to save the world."

Chase was normally excellent at reading people, but Tate was impossible. He seemed half-goofball, half-serious, half-sarcastic, and a whole lot of strange.

The worst part is she thought she was gonna like him.

"So, we have two murders…" Floyd began, taking out the folders and laying them out on the table. He gave Chase a quick rundown of what had happened, including interactions with the vagrants in Junkie Row, the girlfriend, and the wife.

Afterward, several things stuck in Chase's mind.

"This girl—the killer—how old is she?" Chase asked, dropping a finger on the image of the vagrant from the morgue.

"That's the thing, the ME couldn't tell us. Just gave us a range. Sixteen to twenty-six, something like that," Tate said.

"What do you mean? Can't they tell by her femur size?"

"Yeah, usually," Tate confirmed, "but in this case, all he could tell us is that she hit puberty and stopped growing. Her growth plates were fused, but beyond that… impossible to tell. Just too malnourished and neglected."

Chase just stared at the man, confused.

"I don't think I did an adequate job describing what kind of state this girl or woman was in," Floyd said.

"Clearly not," Tate agreed.

Both Chase and Floyd shot the man a look, but he was already back to eating the hamburger.

"The doctor said he'd never seen anything like it, that she was basically dead before she was dead. Smelled like…" Floyd shuddered and let his sentence wane.

Chase frowned.

"What about the other girl?"

Floyd flipped through the photographs before he found one of the woman who had murdered Roger Evans in West Virginia. They all inspected it and then Chase said, "It looks like the same person."

"Yeah, but it can't be, because they're both dead in different states."

On closer inspection, the two perpetrators weren't exactly twins. They did have several things in common: both were women of an indistinguishable age, Caucasian, although this was concluded based on bone structure and not skin color, and both were covered in a thick layer of filth.

The list went on: sunken eyes, chapped lips, weeping sores on the face and neck. Hair like grease-soaked spaghetti.

Then there was the gash in their necks. They, too, looked eerily similar.

"What about the murder weapons?" Chase asked, turning her eyes away from the haunting images. She was no longer interested in the fries, but Tate continued to munch on his burger as he answered.

"Not the same, but similar." He swallowed. "Generic knives primarily used for hunting."

Chase banked this information.

"What about," she slid the photographs aside and read the case report, "NEON? You guys head over to the club?"

Tate shook his head.

"Me and Floyd here are more NASCAR than rave types. Local PD, led by this super nice guy, just all class, Lieutenant Lehner, reviewed security tapes, asked employees. Nobody saw the girl outside."

Chase found this hard to believe but had no basis to contradict and didn't think there was any value in going to the club herself.

"It's freezing here," she remarked, eying Floyd who was tucked into his overcoat. "Who's up for a road trip to West Virginia?"

"I am!" Abernathy said. "And I'm driving."

He stood but neither Chase nor Floyd followed.

"What?" he asked, drawing out the word.

Chase and Floyd just stared at him.

"Oh, come on," Tate whined, stomping his foot. "I wanna go with mommy and daddy to West Virginia."

"I think it's better if one of us stays here," Chase said. "If we discover something in the Mountain State and want to check on this case, it's best if we keep someone local. It can't be me because I need to be partnered up at all times. Director Hampton says that I'm something of a loose cannon."

"Ain't that the truth."

Chase expected the remark from Tate, but it had been Floyd who had said it.

"Okay," she said, nodding. "And it obviously can't be you, Floyd, because you wet your pants if you have to do anything on your own."

Tate burst out laughing.

"Floyd, a joke! You never told me she does jokes!"

"She doesn't," Floyd growled.

Chase flicked her hair.

"New hair, new me. In all seriousness, though, you're the odd one out, Tate."

It wasn't that she didn't like him—on the contrary, while his shtick was a bit schlocky, Chase thought that Tate would be a good partner... for anyone else but her. Chase knew that she could be difficult—*could, ha! Look, another joke*—and she didn't want to fuck things up for Floyd with his new partner when she went back to her house in the woods.

"Guess I'm riding the short bus."

Tate was taking this surprisingly well. Not the fact that he was staying behind by himself, per se, but that Chase had immediately taken over since walking through the cafe doors. Not only did she have no jurisdiction, but Tate had more experience in the FBI than both she and Floyd combined, *and* she'd just come on the scene. On her way to Columbus, Chase had told herself to just let things happen, to mostly observe and bide time until her date with Brian.

But a zebra can't change its stripes and the scorpion is always going to sting the toad.

Fuck it, she thought. *What can they do? Fire me?*

"To be honest, we're just here to ask a few questions, then wrap things up. Gimme your number and we'll call you if anything interesting pops up."

Tate held up a finger and then retrieved the napkin that Chase had written on. He scribbled on it, refolded it, and handed it back.

"I'll stay here with the fart car and discuss the historical merit of the Confederate Flag with Lieutenant Lehner."

Chase wasn't sure what any of this meant, so she ignored it. They said their goodbyes and went to their separate vehicles, with Floyd joining Chase in hers.

Only then did she unfold the napkin that Abernathy had given her and read it out loud.

"Fuck you, too."

Chase grinned, balled up the napkin, and tossed it to the floor of her rental car.

"Let's take us some country roads, Floyd. West Virginia, here we come!"

Chapter 17

"I'M NOT GOING IN THERE, Chase. Been there, done that."

Chase's gaze drifted from Floyd to the morgue door.

"It's that bad?"

The officer standing behind Floyd, the one who had led them here, nodded emphatically.

"Oh, it's worse. Trust me. You're going to want to cover your face."

Chase ignored the suggestion and knocked once. The door opened and she was confronted by a prepper. Gloved from fingers to elbow, thick black apron, dark green gas mask.

"Sorry about the mask—you want one?" the ME's voice was muffled, but Chase was able to understand.

"No, I'm—*Jesus*."

The smell was so cloying that it coated the inside of her mouth. Chase clucked her tongue, but that only made it worse.

The ME chuckled.

"Here, take this."

Chase accepted the offered gas mask and slipped it on. Even with it on, it took a handful of breaths to rid herself of the taste of rot and decay.

Wow, that was… fierce.

"Can I see the body?"

"*Bodies*," the ME corrected.

"Sure, bodies."

"Over here. But even with the mask, I suggest standing back a little."

This time, unlike in the hallway, Chase listened. The ME peeled back the sheet covering the cadaver and Chase inhaled sharply.

She'd already seen the woman on the gurney's photograph, but that, as horrible as it had been, did not do it justice. Before her was more a pile of decomposing flesh than it was a corpse.

Chase, who was a good three feet from the table and was wearing what looked like a Chernobyl level mask, still felt sick from the smell.

"Why didn't you clean her?"

"I did. Believe it or not, this is *after* I cleaned the cadaver. There's just only so much I can do... it's hard to tell where the dirt ends, and skin begins."

Chase wasn't well versed in forensic pathology, but she would have bet a significant sum of money that what this man was saying was the absolute truth.

"How old is she?"

"The body is in such a state of decomp that I can't tell for sure. Best guess: between fifteen and thirty."

"Broad range. Is there any test we can do to narrow that down?"

"There's something called the Horvath clock, which uses DNA methylation to determine age. Usually, it can get within three years or so. That's on normal samples though. Not sure of the accuracy we're going to get from her tissue. I sent a sample out anyway, just in case."

"Sounds expensive," Chase remarked.

The ME shrugged.

"My lab is covering the cost. We'll write this case up when we're all done here. Rare to see this degree of decomp—"

"Yeah, you said that," Chase interjected. She wasn't interested in this man's publishing plans or career aspirations. "What would make someone do this to themselves?"

"Not sure. Could be a psychiatric disorder, I suppose although I've never seen self-destruction to this level before. If we had a psych history…" As the ME spoke, Chase stared at the body, silently asking the corpse the very same question she'd posed to him. "Another possibility is that she didn't do this to herself."

This was something that Chase had considered. The girl was kidnapped and held without food, water, no access to personal hygiene. She escapes and hunts down her captor and exacts revenge. Ashamed of what she'd done, or perhaps just unable to suffer her own body odor, she then takes her own life. Except that Dr. Wayne Griffith III was a plastic surgeon and Roger Evans ran an electronics store—hardly the kidnapping types. They also had no connection to each other and lived in completely different states.

"…drugs."

Chase turned to face the ME.

"What was that?"

"I said long-term drug abuse can induce psychotic episodes, delusions, and hallucinations."

Don't I know it, Chase thought grimly.

"Did she have drugs in her system?"

The ME shook his head, which made his mask slip a little. He adjusted it before answering.

"Ran the standard tox-screen, nothing came up. No drugs, no alcohol."

This guy really thinks that this is some sort of academic exercise.

"Run a full panel, everything you can. I want to know what was in her system no matter how obscure or unrelated."

"On a murderer? Who's going to pay for—"

"It'll make the article better, don't you think?" Chase recalled something Leroy had said when they were investigating possible motives for the Suicide Girls' case and how Cerebrum hadn't shown up on any normal test. "Check for monoclonal antibodies, too."

Instead of waiting for a reply, she moved closer to the body.

"I'm not sure you want to—" the ME let his hands fall to his thighs. "Fine, go ahead."

Chase felt the stench physically pushing up against her, so she pushed back. She pulled the leather glove off her left hand and extended it toward the gurney. It was trembling slightly, but Chase wasn't sure why.

Was it her fear that if she touched the body, nothing would happen? Or was she scared that if she did, the contents of her stomach would evacuate themselves and fill the mask? That would necessitate removing the mask, which would only make things worse.

Just do it, Chase. Touch the body.

Her thoughts turned to what happened when she'd come in contact with Brian Jalston.

What was that? Why did it seem so fucking peaceful? There was the tall grass, the flowing dresses... is that why I saw the woman in the white dress outside the bar in Franklin? Was Terrence right? Did I imagine it?

For most people, what they saw was reality. But Chase knew that this was not necessarily true. What you saw was what your brain interpreted as reality—*your* reality. Drugs, alcohol, physiological state, experiences, memories, superstitions, and biases, they can all change what you see.

But that didn't make it real.

"Ma'am? Are you alright?"

The voice startled Chase.

It was the motivation she needed. Chase extended her hand and felt slime against her palm as she came in contact with the decrepit corpse.

Chapter 18

DARKNESS.

No, not darkness. The notion of darkness suggests the presence of light.

There is no light.

There is nothing.

"I do not eat, for I am dead. I do not sleep, for I am dead. I do not bathe, for I am dead."

Her liver is decomposed, her brain encephalitic. Her lungs, fibrotic. Her skin, ulcerative.

"Kill."

The word comes from nowhere and everywhere and it fills every putrid pore and every fetid cavity.

"Kill."

There was something in her hand.

"Kill."

Something sharp.

"Kill."

A knife.

"Kill."

A promise.

"Kill."

A way out.

"Kill."

The word had come from the nowhere and everywhere, but now it came from her.

Chapter 19

CHASE PULLED HER HAND BACK and gasped. Her stomach was in knots, but it was no longer because of the smell.

What the fuck was that?

She moaned and doubled over.

"It's okay, you're gonna be okay."

The ME put a hand on her shoulder, and she swatted him away.

I do not eat, for I am dead. I do not sleep, for I am dead. I do not bathe, for I am dead.

Chase forced herself straight and then, like a reverse ink blot, the darkness receded, and her vision cleared.

"I'm fine," she said, but her voice betrayed her. It was hoarse and dry.

Thankfully, the mask muted most of this change.

Chase stepped back from the gurney. Her eyes happened on the corpse, and she immediately averted her gaze for fear of becoming nauseous again.

She had no idea what had happened. There had been a time that her subconscious had value. It was helpful. A useful tool.

But now? Now, she touched a dead body and she just felt death. She touched a pedophile rapist and felt joy.

"Fuck me," she whispered.

"Do you want to see the other body? Roger Evans?"

Chase shook her head.

"I understand. Listen, uhh, I'm pretty much immune to what I see in here, day in, day out, but it can be quite alarming, even to an FBI agent such as yourself."

The condescension in the man's voice was thicker than the smell in the air. And both elicited the same urge to puke.

"Sure," Chase muttered, unwilling to even justify the man's comment with an argument. "I gave the secretary my card. Let me know what the drug screens pick up and how old she actually is."

Chase walked to the door and started to remove her mask on the way.

"You can keep that on until you leave. Just put it outside the door and I'll grab it later."

As much as she wanted to rip the mask off and throw it at the ME, she knew that this would cause her more pain and discomfort than him.

She wore it until she was outside and then tore it off.

Floyd took one look at her and started to laugh.

"What's so funny?"

Perhaps it was her tone, perhaps it was her expression.

Floyd immediately stopped laughing.

"Come on, let's go," she said and strode down the hallway. Floyd and the confused officer followed.

"Where we going?" Floyd asked.

"I want to see where she was killed," Chase said.

She and he, a voice in her head reminded her. *Roger Evans is the real victim here.*

Chase agreed with the ethereal voice, but she also knew that the key to finding out what really happened lay with *her* and not with *him*.

***

Chase placed her hands on her hips and looked around.

They were standing outside a strip mall that consisted of a mattress shop, a dentist, and an electronics store. The latter had been co-owned by the victim, Roger Evans.

"He was killed here?"

For some reason, perhaps due to the bizarre nature of the murderer herself, Chase expected the scene to be equally as strange.

This was mundane, however, and bordered on boring.

"Just around the corner," the police officer confirmed. "He was killed in the alley. The killer stabbed him in the throat, then slit her own. Both bodies were discovered by the owner of the mattress shop when they left for the night."

Chase found the spot almost immediately: a dark stain on the ground next to the dumpster. She squatted and then looked up and down the alley.

The way it was angled was odd.

"You can't see the electronics store and you can barely see the parking lot from here. Was his car here?"

"Yeah, we found it parked directly in front of the shop."

"So, Roger couldn't see the alley from his car, either."

Chase stood and then scratched the back of her head.

"Why would he come down here?" she asked absently. "Why would Roger leave his store and come down the alley?"

"Taking out the trash?" Floyd suggested. "Or maybe she called out to him?"

The beat cop was less interesting and less helpful.

"Nobody saw him leave the store. All we know for sure is that this is where they died."

"We can't be sure that this is where they first met, though," Chase remarked. It was an innocent enough comment, but full of implication. Normally, this idea would have come sooner — a man meeting a woman in an alleyway for carnal reasons — but the condition of the killer made this seem repulsive. But so was necrophilia, and countless other equally pathological sexual perversions.

"Was Roger married?"

The officer shook his head.

"No."

Chase moved toward the mouth of the alley and let her eyes bounce from the store to the parking lot, to the dumpster.

Why did you come down here, Roger?

Her gaze settled on Roger's store, *E-Tronics*. There was a CLOSED sign hanging from the door—more evidence that the man was indeed leaving for the night when he was murdered—and numerous stickers on the glass announcing one sale or another.

"Did Roger have any employees?"

Even though the lights were off, Chase could see inside well enough to conclude that it was a small store and that the shelves didn't appear fully stocked.

"No employees," Floyd said, after consulting the case file. "The store was run by Roger and his partner Henry Saburra."

"Looks like another visit is—"

Just as Chase was turning her head, something flashed in her periphery. At the back of the alley, she thought she spotted a woman in a white dress.

"Did you see that?"

It wasn't just *a* woman in a white dress, but *the* woman in *the* white dress—the same one that she'd seen outside the bar in Tennessee.

"See what?" Floyd asked.

Chase pushed by him and started to walk briskly back down the alley. She thought it ended at a fence that was sprouting hedges to protect the privacy of the adjacent residential backyard, but it didn't. It continued behind the building. There were loading bays, and additional dumpsters, but no woman in white.

"What?" Floyd asked, breathing heavily. "What is it, Chase?"

"A woman in a white dress," Chase said as she continued to scan the laneway behind the strip mall.

There was nobody there—not a person or a car. Nothing. Not even a rat.

"You sure?"

Chase was sure. She was as sure as she had been back in Tennessee. Or was she? That was before the incident at the morgue.

Chase grimaced.

"She must've gone over the fence into someone's yard." But there was no indication of this, no depressed sections of shrubbery. "I saw her. She was here."

"You want me to go around the front?" Floyd asked.

She looked at him then. His stark naivety was both pathetic and endearing.

"Yeah, go—"

"What's happening?" The officer appeared confused and out of breath. "Did you see something?"

"Agent Adams saw—"

"Nothing," Chase interrupted. "I didn't see anything."

"Then why'd you rush back here?" the cop asked.

"No reason," Chase repeated, shaking her head. "Floyd, let's go pay Henry a visit."

The cop exhaled and looked confused, but he wasn't Chase's concern. Floyd was. And Floyd didn't look confused, he looked uncomfortable and anxious.

"Don't worry," she added, "I'll do the talking."

Chapter 20

"I CAN SEE WHY YOU left the FBI," Floyd muttered under his breath. "All we do is drive around going to people's houses that we can never afford."

Chase pulled into the driveway of Henry Saburra's two-story house on the outskirts of Charleston.

It was nice, but Chase disputed her partner's claim that they would never be able to afford it. She, for one, was fairly certain she could afford two or three such houses. But that wasn't worth commenting on.

"Getting disgruntled already, Floyd? You only just started your career."

"Yeah, but some of that time was with you," Floyd replied. He was ducking down and looking up at the house through the windshield when he said this, but when he continued, his gaze went to Chase. There was a grin on his face, but she wasn't confident that it was one-hundred percent genuine. "That's worth at least double."

He's just nervous. Nervous because he's going to have to interact with someone grieving. He's not nervous because he's with me.

Maybe.

Chase turned her entire body so that she was square with Floyd. To his credit, he managed to hold her gaze for a few sentences before looking away.

"I know this is hard, Floyd. But you have to try. You have to try to get over this."

"I know."

Floyd interlaced his fingers in his lap and cracked his knuckles in sequence.

Pop, pop, pop.

His PTSD ran deep.

"When I have to give people bad news, I take the band-aid approach. Just say it and get it out there. As emotionless as possible." Chase took a deep breath. "I treat them as victims, put the widow or father or whatever in a silo. They're just—"

"I can't do that," Floyd whispered.

"You can. Disassociate what you're doing from the people—why are you shaking your head? Floyd?"

He looked at her again and she saw that there were tears in his eyes.

"I can't do that. Chase, I've tried. I've tried to look at those girls in the subway as just a collection of skin, blood, and bone. I tried to compartmentalize, to pretend that these... bodies aren't *people,* they're victims or unsubs or whatever the fuck you want to call them. But I can't do it. I just can't."

Chase opened her mouth to speak then closed it again. She knew that Floyd—hell, most people—couldn't do what she did. They hadn't been through what she had.

There was no pride in this understanding.

There was shame.

Chase nodded continuously as she said, "Okay. Okay, follow my lead. Find what works for you. But you have to find something. You *have* to. Because what you're feeling isn't just about giving someone bad—no, not bad, the worst news you can ever imagine. It's about you dealing with the absolutely vile things that humans are capable of. It's about you being able to live without being so haunted by what you see during this job that you find yourself descending into a pit that you can never—*never*—crawl out of."

Darkness.

No, not darkness. The notion of darkness suggests the presence of light.

There is no light.

There is nothing.

Floyd wiped his eyes and nodded.

It wasn't a *hoorah, thank you for the pep talk, coach,* that Chase might have expected, but it was something.

Truthfully, she wasn't even sure where the words had come from. It hadn't been a planned speech but, boy, had it been a speech.

I've spent too much time alone with Georgina, Chase thought. *Louisa is right… I need to spend more time around adults.*

She got out of the car and walked up to the door.

Adults that aren't pedophiles, murderers, and parasites.

The door was opened by a man with short, thinning blond hair and wireframe glasses. He held a black and white spotted cat to his chest, and he was stroking it gently.

"Can I help you?"

Chase and Floyd showed Henry Saburra their badges and introduced themselves.

"Is this about Roger?"

What else would it be about?

"Yes, I'm afraid it is. Do you mind if I ask you a few questions?"

"That's fine," the soft-spoken man replied.

"Thank you. You co-own *E-Tronics* with Roger Evans, correct?"

Henry nodded.

"And your partner was killed in the alleyway beside the store?"

Henry's eyes widened behind his glasses.

"Yes. That's—" he paused and then nodded. "Yes."

"I know this is hard, but we're just trying to make sense of this, okay?"

Another nod.

"Why would… do you have any idea why Roger would be down the side alley? Would he regularly go down there?"

"I don't—usually, we take turns running the store. We aren't often there together."

"Right, but would he maybe be taking out the garbage? Getting a delivery, maybe?"

"Yes. Garbage, maybe. After we close up, we usually dump the garbage in the bin down the side alley."

Chase looked at Floyd to make sure that he was getting all of this.

"Just a few more questions, Mr. Saburra. Did Roger have any enemies? Do you know of anyone who would want to hurt him?"

"The cops said that this was random. You don't—you don't think that someone purposefully targeted him, do you?"

"No," Chase said quickly. "We are just trying to get an accurate picture of exactly what happened to your partner, that's all."

Henry's eyes narrowed.

"But you're the FBI. Why is the FBI—"

"Please," Chase interrupted. "I understand that you want answers, and we will give them to you, but let us ask the questions."

Henry looked upset but, in the end, acquiesced with a nod.

"So, did Roger have enemies?"

"No. Everyone loved Roger."

Chase once again looked at Floyd. If he hadn't been there, she probably would have just thanked Henry and gone on her way. But she needed to show him.

"Floyd, your phone?"

Floyd appeared confused but started to hand it over. Chase refused.

"Show him the photo."

The photo—the photo of the murderer.

Floyd's hands started to shake as he scrolled through his images. They were trembling even more strongly as she watched him pinch and zoom.

"Show him," Chase urged.

Floyd shot daggers at her as he slowly turned the phone around.

"Oh, oh, Jesus," Henry grunted, partially turning his head away from the phone. Chase was pleased to see that Floyd didn't lower it—he held it up until Henry looked down. "Is that—is that who killed Roger?"

Chase's attention was on Henry again. She ignored his query.

"Have you ever seen this person before?"

The corners of Henry's lips pulled downward.

"No. I don't think so. What's wrong with—"

"Thank you for your time, Henry."

Chase indicated for Floyd to head back to the car. He started to turn, then stopped.

"Do you know a Wayne Griffith? A Dr. Wayne Griffith III?" Floyd asked suddenly, surprising both Chase and Henry.

"Wh-who?"

"Dr. Wayne Griffith III," Floyd repeated.

"No. Is he involved in this? In Roger's murder?"

Floyd shook his head.

"No. Thanks again."

Back in the car, Chase asked, "What was that about?"

Floyd shrugged.

"I'm not sure. It just kinda came out."

Chase's first instinct was to chastise him, but she stopped herself. Who was she to condemn someone for acting on instinct?

"But did you—did you see his face when I mentioned Griffith's name?"

"I wasn't—I didn't see."

I was looking at you, Floyd. Trying to figure out if you were okay, if you were going to break.

"He looked... I dunno. He looked surprised to me."

"Surprised?"

"Yeah. But why? I mean, just a random name to him, right?"

"He's grieving." She raised one shoulder. "Grief can make you act strange."

"Maybe," Floyd hesitated. "What was their relationship, anyway? Roger and Henry's?"

"Business partners."

"You think maybe—"

A knock on Chase's window startled them both. It was the police officer, their loyal chaperone.

"Yeah?"

The officer looked embarrassed for some reason.

"Are you guys—you guys done here?"

Chase glanced at the house then back at the officer.

"Here? Yeah."

"In town, I mean?"

"What's this about?" Chase demanded.

"There's something I need to do, something personal. If you don't mind—"

"We'll be fine on our own."

Chase actually preferred it this way. The less interference on a case, the better.

Case… this isn't even a fucking case, she thought. *This is a crime. The killer's dead*—definitely *dead. If there was something more than dead, then that's what she is.*

Under other circumstances, Chase would have wrapped things up right here and driven back to Quantico or New York or wherever.

But she'd been here for less than a day.

And she still had four more to kill.

"Officer?"

He'd already started to make his way back to his car.

"Yeah?"

"Do you have the keys to Roger's house? And the electronic store?"

Instead of answering, he reached into his pocket and pulled out a chain with about a half-dozen keys on it. He handed them over.

"I brought 'em from the station just in case."

"Thanks."

"Just make sure we get 'em back before you leave."

"Not a problem."

The officer stayed a moment longer.

"Any idea how long you'll be in town for?"

It's none of your damn business.

Chase didn't even try to make her smile look genuine.

"Three days."

Even Floyd was surprised by the specificity of her answer.

But she wasn't.

I'm going to stay three days, even if I spend ninety percent of my time in a bar. And then I'm going back to Tennessee.

Chapter 21

"SEE?" CHASE SAID. "A HOUSE you can afford!"

In stark contrast to Henry Saburra's house, Roger Evans lived in what could only be described as a glorified trailer. It was also much further from the city center, and while not quite in the suburbs, it was teetering on the edge.

"But would I want to live here?" Floyd asked.

They strode up the walk, their shoes crunching loudly as if the ground beneath their feet were made of bubble wrap instead of gravel.

"See that?" she said, indicating the torn screen door.

"I see it. Not sure it's out of place, though. What exactly are you expecting to find here, Chase?"

"I'll know it when I see it."

Maybe. Or maybe I'm just killing time.

Out of habit, Chase knocked on the door. She didn't expect an answer—the file indicated that Roger lived alone—and didn't get one. The door was locked, so she started the annoying task of trying to find the correct key to the lock.

And, predictably, it was the last on the chain.

Chase pushed the door open and was struck by a smell. If it hadn't been for her most recent exposure, she would have thought Roger's home smelt vile. Now, it just smelled like a toilet hadn't been flushed in some time.

"What is it with this case and the fucking smells?" Floyd said under his breath.

Roger's house was more in a state of disarray than it was dirty. The counter wasn't covered in a layer of dust, there weren't dirty dishes piled in the sink. But there were magazines, posters, tchotchkes, ornamental spoons, and elaborate beer steins all over the place. It was not quite hoarder level, but if Roger had had a few more years on this earth, it may have transitioned. Of note were several envelopes that contained overdue bills. She showed them to Floyd, who was busy searching for the source of the smell.

They found it in the corner of the family room. In the corner stood a worn cat tree and at the bottom was a full litter box.

"Here, kitty, kitty," Floyd said. "Heeeere, kitty."

While Floyd attempted to find the cat, Chase continued her search of the trailer. The bathroom was relatively normal, and perhaps the least cluttered room in the house, but it was in the bedroom that she found something interesting.

Face down on the dresser was a frame with a photograph in it.

Chase held it up to the light.

It was taken outside, probably Henry Saburra's backyard, if she had to guess, and featured three people: a younger Henry Saburra, Roger Evans, and a girl who was about thirteen or fourteen years old.

They were all smiling.

"Looks like one happy family," Floyd said as he peered over her shoulder.

Chase was inclined to agree. It did indeed look like a family shot, which made her wonder if the relationship between Roger and Henry had been more than just business. But even though the girl was smiling, she looked sad.

"Who is that?" Chase asked, pointing at the girl.

Floyd shrugged.

"Don't know."

"Could she be their adopted daughter, maybe?" Chase asked. "Could this actually be a family?"

"I—" Floyd held his hands up. "The file said nothing about Roger having a daughter." He lowered one hand and reached into his pocket. "I'll put a call in to the Bureau, see if they can do some digging."

Chase placed her palm on his elbow.

"Good idea, but let's finish here first."

Floyd nodded in agreement.

Chase turned the frame over, undid the back, and removed the picture. Out of the frame, she got a better look at the girl.

"Does she look happy to you?" she asked.

"I guess. What do you think?"

I think this is a fake smile, Chase thought, *and I should know. I wore one for years.*

"I'm not sure." She chewed the inside of her cheek. "You visited Meredith, right? Wayne's wife?"

"Yeah."

"How was she? I mean, how did she behave?"

Floyd didn't even pause to take a breath.

"She was a bitch. Real bitch. Pissed off."

"And Julia? Wayne's mistress?"

"Very nice. Upset, though." Floyd's eyes drifted to the photograph. "Crying."

"And Henry? How was Henry?"

To Chase, Henry had seemed almost detached.

"No, I know what you're thinking," Floyd said. "Chase, I'm a rookie, but I know that people can behave all manner of ways when it comes to grief."

Chase pointed at Henry, the girl, then Roger.

"Yeah. Trust me, I know. And unlike Jessica and Meredith, Roger was Henry's business partner." She let this hang in the air. The seconds ticked by and after ten of them, Floyd suddenly pulled back.

"No—you think?" his eyes darted to the photograph and then to Chase. "Really?"

"You said it: one happy family. Imagine they were a family… now, what do you think of Henry's reaction when we visited him?"

Floyd sighed and massaged his forehead with one hand.

"Fuck, I don't know. If it were me…"

"Me, too." Chase folded the photo and put it in her pocket. Then she went back to the bathroom and started to rifle through the drawers.

"What are you looking for?" Floyd asked.

Chase found a pink brush tucked at the back of the cupboard under the sink.

"DNA," she said, holding it up. "If that girl in the morgue is the same as the one in the photo, then this is going to prove it."

It was just an off-hand idea when it had first crossed her mind, but now it seemed to have teeth. If it was true, however, then what was Henry's role in all of this?

"Yeah, I dunno," she said, mostly to herself.

"Me neither—we can always just ask Henry," Floyd suggested.

Chase thought about it.

"Not tonight. Let's just drop this off with the ME—I'm pretty sure I can get him to run a comparison—and then grab a bite and some rest."

Floyd yawned.

"Rest would be good. Can I ask you a favor, though?"

"What?"

"Can we get a place that looks more like Henry's than Roger's? And something that smells good. For the love of God, no more smells for today."

Chapter 22

AFTER DROPPING THE HAIRBRUSH THAT they'd procured from Roger Evans' place and strong-arming the ME into performing one more test—this time a DNA comparison with the decomposing corpse—they found a hotel. Chase tried her best to accommodate Floyd's requests and managed to pick a place that smelled clean. It was far from luxurious, however, she wanted something close to E-Tronics. They checked into separate rooms, with Floyd paying for his using Uncle Sam's money while Chase used cash.

Next door to their hotel they found a restaurant that had an identity crisis, falling somewhere between a diner and a sports bar. They were both so hungry that they didn't care.

They served food and beer.

Hard stop.

Floyd, who hadn't finished what he'd ordered in Columbus when Chase had come on the scene, got the same thing: a double cheeseburger with a side of fries and a vanilla milkshake. Not wanting to deviate from the norm, Chase copied her partner, swapping the milkshake for a beer, instead.

They decompressed in silence while they waited for their order, but once their food arrived and they started to fill their bellies, the conversation began to flow.

"How's Georgina? She goes to school, now?" Floyd asked.

"Yeah, she started shortly after I came back from New York City. You remember Louisa?"

Floyd took an impressive bite from his burger and then wiped the grease from his chin.

"Yeah."

"She has two boys—they're both a little older than Georgina—but they get along well. She goes to school with them."

"Is that where she's staying with now? Louisa and her kids?"

"Yep. They really look out for her."

"Sweet. When you called, though, you said something about being in Tennessee, right?"

And just like that, the mirage of two people, two colleagues, and friends talking about their lives outside of work evaporated.

Chase saw Brian, his grin, and even heard his voice.

I have my people, my wives, looking out for me, but who is looking out for you, Chase? Anyone? Anyone at all?

She grabbed her beer and took a long pull.

"I'm sorry, you don't have to answer if you don't want to."

Chase didn't want to lie so she flipped the script.

"How are things with you? You look good."

Floyd made a face and looked at his stomach. Then he squeezed his belly, but his fingers came up with very little substance.

"Getting fat. Tate likes fast food like you wouldn't believe. Doesn't work out, either, but somehow doesn't gain a pound."

Chase finished her beer and then signaled for another. She'd been hungry when they'd come in here, but she hadn't touched much of her food.

It was the drink that her body craved.

"Who is this guy, Tate, anyway? You two seem like a good fit."

Floyd chuckled.

"You know what, I think I'll have a beer, too." He ordered one and pushed his half-drunk milkshake aside. "Tate's—well, you met him. He's interesting."

"I'm sorry, you don't have to answer if you don't want to."

Floyd laughed and sipped his beer.

"Naw, he's great. Really. Hampton set me up with him after New York, and we haven't looked back. He's got a ton of experience and I'm learning a lot from him. Guess who his last partner was?"

Chase shrugged.

"No idea."

"Constantine Striker," Floyd said the name like it should mean something to Chase. He was quickly disappointed. "Seriously?"

"Seriously. Floyd, I don't know if you know this about me, but I'm not one for gossip. Neither was Stitts, my partner before you. And the one before that? Well, Martinez was a psycho, didn't say much about J. Edgar or whatever."

"Ah, so you know something about the FBI," Floyd joked.

Chase could tell that Floyd wanted to tell her about this Constantine fellow, so she indulged him.

"Go on, tell me about the revered Constantine Striker."

"I don't know about revered, but as I said, Constantine was Tate's partner before me. He was the one who brought down *The Sandman* — remember him?"

Now this, Chase did remember. Twenty years ago, a serial killer dubbed '*The Sandman*' terrorized Los Angeles. The press had given him the name based on evidence that the sick bastard had cuddled and slept with his victims post-mortem. The fact that there was never any evidence of sexual abuse somehow made *The Sandman's* crimes even more twisted.

"Constantine was the one who finally caught him."

Floyd nodded. He looked proud for some reason.

"But that's not the whole story. Constantine's twin sister? Well, she was one of his victims. But the kicker is, her body is the only one that has never been found. And…" Floyd suddenly went pale, and he stopped speaking. "I'm sorry, Chase. I didn't—"

"No, it's okay, Floyd. It's alright. I asked."

Floyd looked uncomfortable continuing, and it was obvious that he'd abbreviated the rest of the story.

"Anyway, Constantine's still with the Bureau, but he spends every spare minute researching the case, and putting in requests to visit *The Sandman* in prison. Requests that are always denied."

A man lost, trying to find his sister. That's something I can relate to.

"Tate told me all this stuff. He does this thing—Tate, I mean—where he can shift from one persona to another, from thug to professional in a split second."

Chase pictured the man with his mustache and suit. Thug, she wasn't so sure about. Then she was reminded of the note that he'd given her—*Fuck you, too.* That had been unexpected, and something that had put a grin on her face.

"He's like a chameleon. I don't know how he does it, but it's more than just becoming someone else. That part's easy. The hard part is knowing *what* to become. And he's damn good at it. He says that he learned this from Con and that Con is even better than he is. And, if you know Tate, that admission didn't come lightly."

Something else I can relate to, Chase thought.

Floyd sipped his beer and then changed the subject, eager to move on to something a little lighter.

"So, are you back, Chase? I mean, did Director Hampton approve you for full duty or what?"

It was Chase's turn to grow uncomfortable.

"No, just this case. I just... I needed something new, you know? Stuck in a house with a pre-teen... compared to that, this case is baby games."

Floyd laughed.

"I can't even imagine. But you sure know how to pick your cases, don't you?"

Chase glared over the top of her beer at Floyd.

"What do you mean?"

Floyd looked down.

"Nothing, sorry. It's the beer, I guess."

Chase wasn't buying it. The man hadn't had more than five sips.

"After all we've been through, you still can't speak frankly to me?"

Floyd looked up, the expression on his face reading 'challenge accepted'. This might not be speaking to a victim's parents, but it was a step in the right direction.

"I was just saying, the last case was about those girls who committed suicide. This one is about a murderer who kills herself afterward. And then there's your father's history and your own..."

Floyd was wrong. Chase hadn't selected this case based on anything—it was simply the case that Floyd was on when she needed to get away from Tennessee.

It was nothing more than a coincidence.

I wonder what Stitts would say about that?

"Chase?"

"I guess, I know how to pick them," Chase said absently. She shook her head. They had come full circle, back to the reason why she was here. "Speaking of this case, have you or Tate looked into any other cases like these two?"

Floyd raised an eyebrow.

"Vagrants who murder and then take their own lives." Chase considered this for a moment. "Murder weapon is probably a knife."

"Nothing in Charleston or Columbus."

"What about surrounding states?"

"To be honest, Chase, the only reason we're here is that Dr. Wayne Griffith III had some important friends. You should have seen it. We go to Columbus to investigate his death, and they send a lieutenant to chaperone us. Here? For Roger Evans who owns a little electronics store and lives in a trailer? They send us Mr. Bean in a uniform. Probably left us because he had to rush off to AA or something."

"It's not how you're killed, it's who you know." Chase finished her beer. "Floyd, when you call your FBI buddy back in Quantico to see if they can find out who the girl in the photo is, ask them to look into other cases like these ones in adjacent states."

"Do you think that these cases are related? Wayne and Roger?"

"Could be a coincidence."

And there it was again. *Coincidence.*

"Stitts—"

They both said the man's name at exactly the same time, which made them laugh. Then they thought about the four dead bodies and the laughter stopped.

Chapter 23

TATE ABERNATHY ANSWERED HIS CELL phone.

"Yes, daddy?" he said. "How's it going with mommy?"

There was an uncomfortable pause, followed by the sound of Floyd clearing his throat.

"Oh, I get it—Chase is with you. Okay, well, then, what can I do for you, Agent Montgomery?"

As he waited for Floyd to reply, he stared out the windshield. Meredith Griffith was unloading groceries from the back of her trunk and bringing them into her house.

"Think you can do me a favor? I tried calling Quantico, but they're giving me the runaround, saying they're busy with other cases. I thought maybe they'd listen to you."

"I live to serve," Tate said. "What do you need?"

Meredith was behaving incredibly normal for someone whose husband was just brutally murdered.

"I need you to do a deep dive into Henry and Roger, see if they had a child. A girl."

"*They?*"

"They."

Tate shrugged. That was something he hadn't expected.

"Will do. Anything else?"

"Yeah, Chase suggested that we look into similar crimes—women who kill and then commit suicide immediately afterward, especially with a knife—in surrounding states over the past three to four years."

"Oh, so now I'm taking orders from Chase, is that right?"

"Tate..."

"Kidding, kidding. I'll send in the request. Did you guys find something in beautiful West Virginia?"

Tate heard a muffled conversation between what he suspected was Floyd and Chase, and then his partner came back on the phone. Tate didn't mind sharing Floyd. It might be good for the man. He just wished that Floyd would take some initiative and he feared that he was just doing Chase's bidding. He'd seen flashes of Floyd's independence, something that was critical in this business. He'd seen it at Junkie Row, and he thought he'd seen it right here when Floyd had 'accidentally' called Meredith, Julia. But it wasn't enough.

"No concrete links. Just crossing our 'T's and dotting our 'I's."

"Uh-huh. And spending a couple of nights on the government's dime in West Virginia. Am I right?"

"Chase paid cash. Anyways, see if you can get either Patricks or Tompsen back in Quantico to run that for me, please."

Me, not us.

Interesting. Maybe Floyd is spreading his wings after all.

"No need," Tate said. He reached over and grabbed his laptop from the passenger seat. "I've got remote access right here. The perks of being in the business for longer than you've been alive."

"I'm only in my twenties, Tate."

"Funny guy. Aren't you going to ask me how my day is going? I feel like in this relationship all I do is give and all you do is take."

Floyd sighed and Tate wondered if he was laying it on too thick.

Probably not.

Floyd was wound tighter than a dreidel during Hanukkah.

"Ok, I'll bite, what are you up to?"

Meredith slammed the trunk and headed inside.

"I'm on a top-secret stakeout," Tate said. "*Very* secret."

"What?"

Tate picked up on something in Floyd's voice. Stress, perhaps. He dropped the act.

A little.

"I'm just sitting in this car that smells like Cheetos farts and keeping an eye on Meredith Griffith. I'm pretty sure she's due to receive a hefty insurance policy. She doesn't seem to do much other than yoga classes, which just happen to be run by a stallion named Juan. Between you and I, I think she should focus more on the exercises than Juan's abs."

"Anything out of the ordinary?"

"Now, that's the thing. Meredith is being completely and utterly normal. *Painfully* normal. But you know the stats. Anyway, Wayne's funeral is tomorrow. I hope something interesting happens, otherwise, I'm just wasting my time."

"Why don't you have a beer with Lieutenant Lehner and shoot the shit?" Floyd asked.

A smile crept onto Tate's face.

"I think I'll pass on that one. I'm not sure I want to spend my afternoon talking about the dangers of 5G towers or how the earth is flat."

"I doubt our friend Lieutenant Lehner would be discussing both those things," Floyd suggested.

"I wouldn't put it past the man."

"No, think about it. If the earth was flat, why would we need so many towers? Couldn't you just put one on either end?"

Tate nodded to himself.

"You're not just a pretty face, are you, Floyd? Oh, before I forget, I did some digging on our vagrant girl before starting to tail Meredith. Checked out two homeless shelters and another one of those Junkie Row places. Even used your time-honored technique of offering cash for tips—although, I was smart and doled out ones instead of fives. Nobody remembers seeing or smelling her. Either she laid low before she killed Wayne or — "

"Maybe she's from out of town?"

Tate licked his lips.

He was about to say maybe she laid low before she killed Wayne, or her condition worsened recently.

For some reason, he hadn't thought about what Floyd had just suggested, even though now that it was out there, it was painfully obvious.

"Tate?"

"Yeah, shit, that's a good idea. Did Chase suggest it?"

Silence.

"I'm kidding, Floyd. There's no way she drove, and flying would be impossible looking the way she did," Tate mused. "Bus. It had to be bus."

"That's what I would think."

"And if she took the bus, then someone would remember her. Impossible to forget that stench."

There was more of that muffled conversation.

"Gotta go, Tate. Please look into the girl and other similar crimes."

"Aye, aye, Tonto."

Tate hung up and unzipped his laptop bag. He was just opening it up when he spotted movement in the upstairs of the Griffith house.

Meredith was sweaty after her yoga workout. And what do you do to get rid of the sweat?

You shower, of course.

"Sorry, Floyd, but your little computer investigation is going to have to wait."

Chapter 24

"YEAH, I'M FINE. LISTEN, AFTER the debacle at County, I forgot to get the list of Brian Jalston's visitors," Chase said into her phone. "Think you could do me a favor and pick that up for me?"

Terrence didn't reply right away so Chase continued.

"I just want to know the names of his visitors, that's all."

Terrence sighed.

"Yeah, I can swing by and pick that up for you tomorrow — it's late and I'm beat."

Terrence didn't just sound beat, he sounded defeated. It was tough being Chase's colleague, even tougher being her friend.

If that's what they were.

"Thanks, Terrence, I really appreciate it."

Without waiting for a reply, she hung up just as Floyd emerged from the diner, holding his own cell phone.

"Tate's going to look at it for us. Was that Georgina?"

Chase tucked her phone away.

"Yeah."

"How's she doing?"

"Good. No, great," Chase lied. "She loves spending time with Louisa and the boys. It's getting late, Floyd. I think I'm going to wrap it up for the night. Maybe tomorrow we pay Henry another visit?"

Floyd looked at his watch.

"Yeah, okay."

They walked together to the hotel and then said good night at their adjacent rooms. Once inside, Chase pulled her cellphone out and stared at it. It wasn't that she felt guilty about lying to Floyd — correction, it wasn't *only* because she felt guilty to him — but also for not calling Georgina at all.

She started to dial Louisa's number then stopped.

"Damn it."

All she could think about was that bastard Brian. Leering, sneering, laughing.

Instead of calling her niece, Chase went to the mini bar. She grabbed a bottle of Johnny Walker and downed it. She debated having another, but instead just sat on the bed for ten minutes.

When she heard the shower come on next door, Chase silently left her room and made her way downstairs to the hotel bar.

Just one more drink. Something to help me sleep, that's all.

She took a seat by herself and ordered a scotch.

Most of the TVs were showing sports, but one was displaying a twenty-four-hour news channel. The *news du jour* was of a man in New York City. A business owner by the name of Kevin Park. He'd been accused and had confessed to murdering his partner. Police said they found the man sleeping on his work couch, covered in his partner's blood.

Authorities had yet to find the body.

"Yep," a voice said from her left, "and that's why I hate New York."

The man was young, maybe in his late twenties, and attractive. His blond hair was short on the sides, and longer and messy on top. He had a groomed beard and was wearing jeans and a T-shirt.

"It's not just New York," Chase remarked, her mind on her own case.

"True, true." The man drank some of his beer and then held out his hand. "My name's Casey," he said with a slight grin.

Chase just looked at the hand.

He pulled it back and held it up, his smile growing.

"Okay, stranger danger, I get it."

Chase chuckled. It wasn't that she found the joke amusing—in fact, if this Casey knew her profession, she doubted he would find it funny, either—but the implications were hilarious.

If one of them posed a danger to the other, it wasn't the cute frat boy.

"Chase," she said. "My name's Chase."

"Nice to meet you, Chase. I noticed you don't have an accent. What brings you to Charleston? Work?"

"You don't have an accent, either," Chase remarked. "In town for your next lay?"

The man full out laughed at that one.

"Spicy—I like it."

Chase was trying to put up a front, but it wasn't working. Whether it was the booze, or the stress she was under, it simply wasn't working.

It didn't help that the man before was attractive. And kind, at least on the surface. She could imagine them settling up the bill and heading next door to her room.

Shit, Chase wanted that. Needed it, even. It had been so long…

Her thoughts turned to Floyd next door to her, to Georgina, to Brian.

Chase finished her scotch.

"It's nice to meet you, Casey. I hope you find what you're looking for tonight."

The man nodded.

"I hope you find what you're searching for, too, Chase," he replied.

The kindness that this stranger expressed was so refreshing that when Chase rose, she nearly leaned in and kissed him. Not in a sexual way, but in a motherly way. But that would have led to something else, something more, and ended in regret.

"Take care."

Chase left the bar less than ten minutes after entering, which wasn't enough to cure her wandering mind. But instead of heading upstairs to her room, she went outside. Tucking her hands into her pockets, Chase started to walk.

In one pocket was her cell phone, in the other a set of keys she didn't recognize. Chase pulled them out.

They were Roger Evans' keys.

Chase glanced up. Everything looked the same here, but she thought she recognized the strip mall across the street.

E-Tronics.

With nothing better to do, Chase hurried across the street. It was *E-Tronics*, and she cupped her hands and peered through the glass. It was the same as earlier in the day.

Chase went to the door next and started the laborious task of selecting the correct key.

"Why couldn't someone label these things?"

Unlike at Roger's house, she found it earlier than the last key.

It was the second to last one.

God only knew what the others were for.

She entered and grimaced. It smelled like Roger's house.

Shaking her head, she spotted another one of those cat house things near the back and an unemptied litter box.

"What is with these people?"

E-Tronics' shelves were about half full. One section contained various connectors and cables, which were likely to be obsolete in a year or two. In another section, behind several locked cases, were the higher-priced items. There was even less stock of these, but it explained the keys.

Chase walked around the store, not sure what she was looking for. She kept tilting her head at odd angles, her eyes trained downward.

The cat. Your super-powered subconscious is making you look for a cat, Chase.

She rolled with it.

"Here, kitty."

If it was there, it was quiet. Or dead.

How long since you've been fed?

There were two bowls dangerously close to the full box of kitty litter, but both were empty.

Chase went to the counter in search of a bag of cat food, thinking that if the cat were just hiding, she had better feed it.

She couldn't find any.

Maybe in the back?

Chase did, however, notice that the garbage was half-full, and this reminded her of what Henry had said about Roger taking the garbage out front and then down the alley.

In the small office, she found two garbage bins. One was empty, while the other contained a banana peel, which wasn't helping the smell situation.

Okay, so he didn't take the garbage out — at least not all of it.

Curious now, she put herself in Roger's shoes, imagining the man's steps if he had taken the garbage out. In addition to the two in the office and one under the front cash, she found a third in the storage room in the back. This one was empty, and it was located right next to the rear exit. It was locked, and she turned the deadbolt and opened it.

Chase stared into the back alley. There was a dumpster right there, three feet to the left of the exit.

She massaged the back of her neck and was in the process of closing the door when a thought occurred to her.

Why would Roger take the garbage out front and down the side alley, a good, thirty to forty feet away when there was a bin right here? He would have to come back here anyway to lock this door, wouldn't he?

And yet, she was fairly certain that Henry had said, or at least agreed with her when she'd suggested that Roger would have taken the garbage out front.

For the second time, Chase started to close the door again only to stop.

She spotted a brief flash of white by the dumpster.

Chase's hand moved to her holster, and she stepped into the alley.

"Hey," she shouted. "Hey, who's there?"

Craning her neck, she looked around the front of the dumpster.

Her rational mind was telling her that it was just a piece of garbage floating in the breeze. But the irrational part wanted it to be a white dress.

Chase took another step around the dumpster when she heard a click from behind her. She looked over her shoulder and saw that the door had closed.

Then she heard a growl. Not behind her, but in front of her, tucked in the shadow of the dumpster. And then the creature lunged, driving something hard and sharp into her neck just above her collarbone.

Chapter 25

FLOYD WAS ABOUT TO HOP in the shower and scrape the filth of the day off of him, and perhaps even work on getting rid of the stench, when he heard the door to the room next door open and close.

"Just shower," he told himself. Just shower and get some sleep.

He was exhausted. Even though Chase had done all the talking at Henry's house, his anxiety had still peaked. And he was now dealing with the fallout from the adrenaline rush.

Floyd knew that he had to somehow get over this fear of his. If he didn't, he was destined to play backseat to all the Chases and Tates of the world. This wasn't the worst thing for him, after all, for every alpha there was at least one beta, but in the FBI, it was move up or move out.

And he didn't want to move out.

Floyd shut off the water. The shower would have to wait.

Sleep, too.

He was still subordinate, and although it wasn't under his purview to make sure that Chase was safe at all hours of the day, he felt it was his duty as her friend.

She wasn't right. Even for her, Chase was acting odd. And she was lying. He knew this, although Floyd couldn't identify the exact reasons underlying his confidence. But there had been a look... when Floyd had first asked about Georgina, something crossed over Chase's features.

And despite his best efforts, Floyd couldn't suppress the images that flashed in his mind. There had been another time when he'd that darkness on her face. Not long thereafter, they'd found Chase in a gravel pit, her body covered in scratches, her heart barely beating.

So, Floyd followed her. He watched Chase interact with a man at the bar and silently wished that he took her home, or vice-versa. At least that would keep her off the streets where the real danger lay.

But she didn't.

And when he saw his partner stop outside of *E-Tronics*, he grinned. This was a good sign. Chase, throwing herself into a case that, truthfully, neither of them believed was actually a case.

Another indication that she was going to stay out of trouble.

Floyd shook his head admonishingly.

She's not a child, Floyd. Even if she were, it's not like you're qualified to give her advice. Ye, who cannot even speak to a grieving individual without breaking down.

Floyd, feeling as if he'd done a good deed, turned, intending to head back to the hotel and get that well-deserved shower and rest.

But something caught his eye. Whether it was Chase's story about seeing the woman in the white dress that had primed his mind, or just simply the fact that Chase and alleys generally didn't mix, Floyd could have sworn he saw a flicker of white near the dumpster.

He started in that direction, head down, hands in pockets. When he reached the dumpster, Floyd's eyes were drawn to the stain on the ground. It took him a few seconds to avert his gaze. As a final act of due diligence, Floyd glanced all around the dumpster.

There was nothing there and what had, moments ago, felt like a good deed now just felt dirty and intrusive.

Head hanging even lower now, Floyd stuck to the shadows as he started back to the street. He'd taken a dozen steps before he heard the scream.

It was Chase.

Floyd broke into a run, shouting her name as he rounded the back of the building. The first thing he noticed, however, wasn't his partner. It was another stain. A stain uncannily like the first—even its proximity to the dumpster was similar.

The only notable difference was that this one was still wet.

"Chase!"

Floyd rounded the dumpster and what he saw made him stop in his tracks. Chase was lying on her back, eyes open but blank. Blood seeped from a wound on her neck, soaking the collar and front of her shirt.

Floyd dropped to his knees and pressed his hands against her neck. Her blood was still pumping, but weakly so.

"Oh, God, Chase," he whispered, struggling to stem the bleeding while also dialing 911. "I need help! Please!"

He relayed the address and then hung up, needing both hands to try and save Chase's life.

A gurgling sound came from her throat and Floyd whined, thinking that this was a death rattle.

It wasn't.

It was Chase trying to say something.

"Shh, quiet… save your strength," Floyd begged. "Just… quiet."

But in true Chase Adams fashion, she refused to be told what to do. Even in her final moments.

"Save her," Chase whispered. "Save *her*."

"Her? Who?"

Chase's eyes rolled to her left and Floyd looked in that direction.

A woman in a white dress—mostly red now—lay slumped against the wall, bleeding to death. There was a hunting knife with a brown handle lying beside her right hand.

"Please, save her," Chase whispered again. She said something else, too, but her words were silenced by the scream of a siren that filled the night air.

Chapter 26

TATE FOUND HIMSELF BACK IN the stinky loaner but today he wasn't spying on Meredith Griffith's house. He *was* spying on her, but not at home — at Morris Cemetery.

From where he was parked, Tate had a clear view of Dr. Wayne Griffith III's funeral. It was fairly standard, and without anything interesting of note, he decided to multi-task. With his laptop open on his lap, Tate searched for any record that Roger Evans or Henry Saburra had a child. So far as he could tell, they did not — at least, not according to any official state registry. Neither man was very active on social media, either, and Tate could find no evidence of a child there. The only photo that was telling at all was one of the two men holding each other, red-faced from alcohol and looking happier than pigs in shit.

Next, Tate looked into crimes that matched the two that they were currently investigating. He found two that were of interest. Upon digging deeper, one of them turned out to be a simple robbery that transitioned into murder. The other had merit. It took place nine months ago about two hours south of Columbus in a city called Portsmouth. The details were sketchy, but it appeared as if a local drug dealer had been murdered in his car. The killer was in the backseat — a filthy woman who was also dead. The reason why this case didn't immediately pop up, was because there were so many question marks on the file. Whoever had been in charge had done the bare minimum amount of work.

It was the nature of the wounds and the murder weapon that tipped Tate off. Although the drug dealer had several punctures in his arms and chest, he died from a lacerated throat. The vagrant had died in a similar fashion and a generic hunting knife had been found on the floor of the backseat.

Tate looked up when he heard a shout.

"Oh shit!"

He tossed his laptop onto the passenger seat and got out of the car. Wayne had a large funeral, full of fancy, important people, who were carbon copies of each other: custom suits, monogrammed shirts, white hair, and clean-shaven faces. They were politicians, they were bankers, they were businessmen.

The commotion hadn't been started by any of them, but by two women.

Two women whom Tate recognized: Meredith Griffith and Julia Dreger.

They were standing near the grave site, and Meredith was wagging a finger in Julia's general direction. Tate couldn't imagine anything more uncomfortable than this scene: the dead man's mistress and wife fighting at his funeral.

No one seemed to know what to do. Half the people were ignoring the altercation while the other half were staring in disbelief. A young man stepped forward and said something, clearly meant to diffuse the situation. When Meredith shot him a look, he crawled back into his shell.

"What's the problem?" Tate said as he strode toward the crowd. "What's going on here?"

He knew that in situations such as this one, the general public liked to defer to the authorities. This had been a Constantine Striker specialty, and Tate liked to think of himself as a worthy apprentice.

"This bitch has the nerve to come here," Meredith spat, still sticking her finger in Julia's face. "This *whore*."

"I just wanted to say goodbye," Julia said, her voice soft. "I don't want any trouble. I'll leave."

"Oh, you don't want any trouble, do you?" Meredith shot back. She was dangerously close to pushing Julie onto the casket, which was lowered halfway into the ground by a mechanical winch.

Wouldn't that be ironic? Julia lies on top of Wayne in death while Meredith condemns her for lying on top of him in life.

He shook his head, trying to clear himself of the bizarre thought.

"Everyone needs to calm down," Tate offered, slowly wedging himself between the two women.

"She shouldn't be here!" Meredith shouted.

Tate addressed Julia.

"This is a private gathering, Julia."

"*Julia?* You're on a first name basis with this *whore?*"

Tate held his hand up, silencing Meredith. He wasn't sure if she recognized him, but he hoped she did—he didn't want to have to pull his FBI badge out here.

"I was just leaving," Julia said, lowering her head.

"Yeah, you were."

"Quiet," Tate hissed.

Meredith looked appalled at being spoken to this way, but she didn't open her mouth again.

"I'm—I'm sorry. I didn't mean to cause any problems. I just wanted to say bye to Wayne."

Meredith sucked her teeth at the mention of her husband's name but remained silent.

"I understand." He gestured for Julia to move away from the crowd. "Let me walk you to your car." Then to the rest of the funeral, Tate said, "I'm sorry for the interruption. And my condolences to the friends and family."

Chapter 27

FLOYD TAPPED HIS FOOT INCESSANTLY as he watched Chase's chest rise up and down. The sound of loose change in his pocket combined with the beeping of the machines that were hooked up to his partner made for an interesting symphony.

He still couldn't comprehend what had happened. And what *might've* happened had he not followed Chase last night.

The woman who had attacked Chase was a carbon copy of Wayne and Roger's murderers. Reeking, filthy, and with no apparent concern for their own body. Not only that, but the MO was the same. Knife to the throat, knife to the throat. Thankfully, Chase's attacker had been less efficient.

What it all meant, Floyd had no idea. But one thing was for certain: this was no coincidence. It also suggested that all of these crimes were indeed connected.

But why Chase? Was she specifically —

"Is she alive?"

Floyd was startled and stopped moving his leg.

"Chase, shit, you scared me."

Chase grimaced and tried to sit up, but only made it halfway. Floyd propped some pillows behind her back.

"Is she alive?" Chase repeated.

No thank you for saving my life, no I'm so glad you were there, Floyd.

But that was Chase for you.

"You need to focus on yourself, for now. The knife nearly severed your carotid artery, Chase. A half-inch to the left and you wouldn't have even made it to the hospital."

Chase winced and adjusted her position.

"Please, just take it easy."

"Floyd," she said hoarsely. "I need to know if she's alive."

Floyd looked at his partner. He knew that if he didn't tell her, she'd probably drag her ass out of bed and go searching the hospital for herself.

"She's alive," he said glumly. "But she's in worse shape than you are—in the ICU. Doc says it's fifty-fifty for her to p-pull through."

"Damn it."

Floyd's upper lip curled. He was too exhausted to remain congenial.

"R-r-really? You're pissed at me because I saved *your* li-life? Because I saved you over her? A girl who tried to k-k-k-ill you?"

"What were you doing there?" Chase demanded. "Floyd, what were you doing at the electronics store?"

Floyd instinctively looked away, then immediately glanced back at Chase.

"Why was I there? These are n-not the q-questions you should be asking, Chase."

Chase just stared at him, unblinking, and Floyd sighed.

"I was following you, all right?" he said defensively. "I was f-f-f-following you because I was w-w-worried about you."

Chase continued to stare at him, her expression still hard, then she broke.

"Thank you," she said softly. "Floyd, thank you."

Another sigh from Floyd, this one accompanied by a substantial shudder.

When he managed to get a hold of himself, he said, "What happened?"

"I just went for a walk, ended up at the Roger and Henry's store. The garbage... the garbage was bothering me."

"G-garbage? What do you mean?"

Chase bit her bottom lip.

"Henry Saburra... he told us that Roger would have walked the garbage out the front and then to the dumpster in the side alley. But that doesn't make sense. Nobody would do it that way. They would use the dumpster out back — it's literally right beside the rear exit."

Floyd squinted.

"I meant what happened to you, Chase. What the h-hell happened to you?"

Chase appeared momentarily confused.

"I was attacked," she said slowly. "The girl in the ICU tried to kill me then cut herself."

"Yeah, but why —"

Floyd's phone started to ring, and he looked at it. It was Tate and he ignored it.

"Is that Tate? Answer it," Chase encouraged.

Floyd didn't want to answer his phone. He just wanted to stay here until Chase got better.

But she insisted.

"Tate? I'm at —"

"Guess what I just did."

"I don't —"

"Oh, just broke up a fight between Julia and Meredith. Can you imagine? Your girlfriend and your wife nearly duke it out at your funeral?"

Floyd looked at Chase.

"Tate, I'm in the hospital."

Tate suddenly became serious.

"What happened? Floyd, are you all right?"

"I'm fine, but Chase isn't. She was attacked. Stabbed in the neck."

"*What?*"

"Yeah, she was stabbed, and the woman who tried to kill her put the knife to her own throat. She's in the ICU now. Not sure if she's going to survive. Tate, whatever we thought about this c-c-case before, it's all changed now. They're all connected and it's on us to figure out how."

Chapter 28

TATE'S EYES WENT WIDE.

"Jesus? Is Chase okay?"

"She's gonna be okay. Lost a lot of blood, but she's gonna p-pull through."

Tate looked through the windshield and wipers that were moving at full blast as he parked outside the bus station. The rain was coming down in sheets.

"You want me to come to you?"

"No, I don't think so. We'll be fine here."

"What about the person who attacked her? Really tried to kill herself afterward?"

"Yeah. I managed to keep her from bleeding out, but she's in an induced coma now. Received six units of blood."

Tate shut off his car and stepped out into the rain.

"Fuck," he said as he started to sprint. "Tell her—" Tate hesitated. He'd gotten a pretty good read on Chase from their first meeting and based on what Floyd had told him about his ex-partner. But now he wasn't sure what to say, what would serve her best in this instance. He settled on something genuine. "Tell her I'm glad she's okay."

"Will do. Is it—is it raining there?"

"Oh, it's just fucking beautiful here. Love Columbus. Just gorgeous this time of year."

Floyd offered a strangled chuckle, an abbreviated *ha*.

Fucking guy—he can't catch a break, Tate thought. He moved quickly through the main foyer of the bus station and up to the ticket booth.

"Where you headed?" a woman with light blue eyeshadow asked from behind a glass partition.

Tate didn't answer. He just pulled out his badge and slapped it on the table.

"Listen, Floyd, I looked into Roger and Henry—no kid that I can see. Pretty sure they were more than just business partners, though. If that means anything." Tate placed the phone against his chest while he produced a photograph of Wayne's murderer. "Have you ever seen this girl before?"

The woman's pudgy fingers extended through the slot in the glass, and she sucked onto her side. As she inspected the photo, Tate got back on the phone.

"I also found a similar case—drug dealer killed in his car two hours south of here. Similar MO."

The woman behind the glass looked at Tate when he said this, and he just nodded at her.

"Want me to head there?" Floyd was just being polite, and they both knew it.

"Hell, no." Tate lowered his voice. "I gotta get out of this place, man."

"Okay, let me know if you find anything else."

"Be good. And give my best to Chase."

Tate hung up.

"Well, have you seen her before?" he asked.

The woman raspberried.

"Naw, I don't think so." She slid the photo back under the glass. "Sorry."

Tate wondered if the woman's memory might improve with a little cash, but he was strapped.

"You sure? She smelled *real* bad. Like the worst thing you've ever smelled before. We're talking, rotting—"

"Sewage?"

Tate turned. A man in a blue uniform was standing behind him, a newspaper tucked underneath his arm. He was balding, and like the woman behind the glass was also on the heavier side.

"I was gonna say baby diapers — that's a favorite of mine — but sewage works."

"Can I see the photograph?" the bus driver asked.

Tate nodded and handed it over. The man only needed one glance to confirm.

"Yep, yep, I recognize her — that's her. Had to get my bus fumigated after she got off. To be honest, I'm not even sure why I let her on the bus. Maybe 'cuz it was nearly empty, and I thought I'd — " he shook his head. " — I dunno. I guess I felt bad for her."

That's our girl. Just an unfortunate... murderer.

"Fingers crossed, she used a name?"

The man shook his head.

"Nope. Didn't say a single word. When she was getting off, I asked her if she had a place to stay or if she wanted to know where the local homeless shelter was. She just stared at me, then walked off."

Tate wasn't surprised. Disappointed, but not surprised.

He rubbed his mustache.

"And where were you coming from, kind sir?"

This answer, like the previous, wasn't a surprise either.

"Charleston," the bus driver informed him. "Charleston, West Virginia."

Chapter 29

TATE WAS A GOOD MAN. IF there had been any question of this before their conversation on the phone, they were dashed now. Any number of other partners that Floyd could have been teamed up would have seen their communication go very differently. More than likely, they would have told him to fuck off, that they weren't going to take orders from someone who was their junior.

But not Tate Abernathy.

Tate was accommodating, Tate was caring, Tate was very different from Chase, and he was exactly what Floyd needed.

"What was that about?"

Floyd tapped the back of his cell phone before putting it in his pocket. Then he looked at Chase and relayed what Tate had told him. At the last second, he decided to hold back the information about the drug dealer. She needed to focus on her health, on getting better. The rest was just a distraction.

"Anything else?" Chase asked.

Floyd wasn't sure how to answer, wasn't sure how much Chase had heard when he'd been on the phone. In the end, he was saved by a nurse who entered the room. She was pretty, with dark hair pulled back into a ponytail and high cheekbones. Floyd put her somewhere in her mid-twenties until she looked at him disapprovingly.

Then she appeared much older.

"Mrs. Adams, my name's Audrey. I'll be your nurse for tonight." She removed the pillow from behind Chase's back. "You need to get some rest. Have you spoken to the doctor yet?"

Chase shook her head.

"Well, I'm sure he'll be in later to talk to you. You were very lucky." Audrey touched the side of her neck on the left side, just above her collarbone. Chase and Floyd looked at the bandage covering her wound. "The blunt side of the knife actually struck your carotid artery—bruised it fairly badly. You really need to rest. Any strain on the artery could spell disaster."

The idea of sitting still—*resting*—was like a death sentence to Chase, Floyd knew, and she made no effort to hide her displeasure.

"How long?"

"How long, what?" Audrey asked.

Chase appeared visibly annoyed.

"How long until I get out of here?"

The nurse frowned.

"Three days, maybe more. It depends."

"Yeah, that's not happening."

Audrey sighed and checked one of the monitors. It was clear that she'd dealt with stubborn patients like Chase before.

Or at least she thought she had. Except there was no one like Chase.

"If you push yourself, that weakened carotid artery can develop an aneurysm. That is life-threatening. Not to mention all the vessels that were severed. You lost a lot of blood—a *lot*."

Having read the room the way only a nurse knew how, Audrey looked at Floyd for support.

Floyd mobilized immediately.

"Chase, she's right. What happened... you need to rest. This case will be—"

"I am the case," Chase snapped.

If anybody else had uttered those words, Floyd would've thought them the most egotistical things ever spoken.

But given the circumstances, he had a time arguing with her on this point. She was the case because she was almost the third victim.

Then Floyd remembered what Tate said.

Third or fourth.

"Just rest, please."

For a moment it looked as if Chase was going to complain, perhaps even get out of bed, but she grimaced and slumped.

She was weaker than Floyd had thought.

"Who's the girl? The one who attacked me?"

The question was posed to the ether, and Audrey took it upon herself to answer.

"She had no ID on her when she was admitted. But a police officer is staying outside her room." The nurse looked at Floyd. "He might have a better idea of who she is."

Floyd shook his head.

"Already spoke to him — he doesn't. No one knows who she is or where she came from."

"Alright, well I think that's enough excitement for now," Audrey suggested. She gave Floyd that look again.

"Try the homeless shelter," Chase said, completely ignoring the nurse. "Floyd, go to a couple of the nearest homeless shelters and see if they have any record of the girl in the ICU or the one who killed Roger. It's a long shot, but you never know."

Floyd nodded.

It was a good idea. Homeless shelters and Charleston's version of Junkie Row. Maybe someone had seen one of them or, better yet, maybe someone *knew* them.

"I'll do that," he said softly. "Get some rest, Chase."

Floyd was at the door when the nurse addressed him directly.

"Before you go, I don't seem to have any sort of insurance on file for Mrs. Adams. Do you—"

"Cash," Chase said quickly from her bed. "I'll pay cash."

"No, that's alright," Floyd said, confused by her outburst. "I'll call Director Hampton and he'll set things up."

"No, please," Chase insisted. "There should be a credit card in my wallet. I want to pay out of pocket."

Floyd would've pushed back harder, but Chase was looking pale, and the nurse was gesturing toward the door. He gave it one last attempt.

"Chase, it's going to be—"

"It doesn't matter. I'll pay cash."

Floyd shrugged, said goodbye once more, and then stepped into the hallway, scratching his head in confusion.

There was only one reason he could think of for someone to want to pay cash, especially when they had insurance.

They wanted no record of where they'd been.

Chapter 30

CHASE SLEPT FOR A GRAND total of ten minutes.

Then she opened her eyes and looked around.

She was aware of just how close she'd come to death, but it didn't frighten her. Chase had been closer.

Still, she would be more of a burden than anything else if she didn't get some rest. But there was one thing she had to do first.

Chase took the lead off her finger and then slowly peeled back the sheets. It wasn't until she'd swung her legs over the side of the bed that she felt weak. The dizziness, however, didn't appear until after she stood. While Chase waited for this to pass—both hands, palms flat on the handrail—Chase tried to understand why she was targeted.

Was I getting close to something? Was I a threat? If so, to what? To whom?

It didn't make sense. At least, not yet.

Moving slowly, trying not to shock her system any further, Chase grabbed her FBI badge and dragged herself and her IV bag out of the room.

She looked around, feeling more than a little like a criminal executing a poorly planned prison escape. But this was fleeting, and when Audrey or any of her minions failed to intercede, Chase followed the overhead signs to the ICU. Even if the area hadn't been clearly indicated, the uniformed officer sitting outside the door was a dead giveaway.

"Can I help you?" the man asked in a gruff voice.

Chase held up her badge.

"Chase Adams, FBI."

This officer wasn't impressed by her credentials. Truthfully, Chase doubted she would have been either. A woman in a hospital gown, pale, frail, dragging an IV cart, flashing a badge, FBI or not, didn't instill anything but confusion.

Chase had met many young and impressionable police officers who grew up watching shows about the FBI and had become enamored with the idea.

Not this man.

He was neither young nor impressionable.

"I want to go see her," Chase said bluntly.

The man shook his head.

"I'm sorry, Agent Adams, no one is allowed in."

Chase pulled down the front of her gown, revealing the bandage above her collarbone.

"She did this to me and I want to see her. I need to speak to her."

The officer's eyes never left hers.

"All the more reason for you not to see her. Besides, she isn't awake yet."

Yet—that was an upgrade from what Floyd had told her about the would-be killer's chance of survival being no more than a coin flip.

"If she's not awake, then what's the big deal?" Chase indicated her weakened body. "I just want to talk to her."

The cop was unmoved—literally.

"Strict orders not to let anybody see *or* speak to her. Not until the doc gives it the okay. She can't even see her lawyer or guardian."

This last part surprised Chase.

"Guardian?"

The cop shrugged.

"Not sure if she's underage or not. I'm sorry, but you're not going to be able to go in there tonight."

Chase grimaced.

"Please, I—" a strong dizzy spell came over her and Chase closed her eyes. Unlike the one back in her room, this took a good ten seconds or more to pass.

"Agent Adams?"

"Fine," Chase said through gritted teeth. "I'm fine. Let me see her, please."

There was sympathy in the man's eyes, but not enough.

"If you want to see her so bad, you can look through the door. That's as close as you're going to get, I'm afraid."

Chase gave up and shuffled to the door as the cop leaned away to allow her access. She approached the door as if she were going to peer through the window, but at the last moment grabbed the door, opened it, and slid inside.

"Hey!" the cop hissed. "Goddamn it."

There was only one patient in the ICU. Either it was a slow night or Charleston PD had cleared everyone out.

The woman who had tried to kill Chase was inside a protective bubble. Someone, probably the nursing staff, had tried to clean her up. But her hair was still grimy and the pillow on which her head lay was streaked with stains. Her skin was the color Chase had only known previously on corpses and if it weren't for the heart rate monitor that pinged with every labored beat, Chase would have thought her dead.

"I told you can't be in here," the cop warned.

Chase ignored him. What was he going to do? Tackle her? What about a bear hug from behind? Would he risk reopening her wounds? Why? Because she snuck into the ICU to get a better look at someone who was unconscious?

Chase didn't think so. But he would do something, eventually.

She walked right up to the bubble and peered down at the sleeping woman.

"Why did you do it?" she whispered. "Why did you try to kill me and then try to kill yourself?"

"Agent Adams, you can't—"

"Why?"

The officer thought this was a question for him.

"Because she's unconscious, for Christ's sake! You can't interview an unconscious person!"

But Chase wasn't interested in interviews. Even the fact that she was unconscious was of no consequence to her. If the woman couldn't speak, there was still one way that Chase could learn something from her.

She shuddered when she recalled what had happened back in the morgue.

The reek of death and the oppressive darkness.

But Chase couldn't get into the hermetically sealed box. There were no holes for gloved hands, no hidden slots. It seemed impossible—*How can the doctors treat her?*—but it bested Chase.

"Agent Adams!" The officer was directly behind her now.

Chase cursed under her breath and looked around. There was a table off to one side and on it, she spotted several extra-large evidence bags.

She stepped away from the bubble.

"Are those her things?"

The cop didn't answer so Chase tried to go look for herself.

Only, she couldn't.

Her IV was stuck.

The cop had finally figured out how to stop her — hold the IV trolley.

"I just want to know if she was wearing a white dress."

"You need to leave," the cop ordered. "Now."

They got into a mini tug-of-war with neither participant willing to apply more than a small percentage of their strength to the liquid-filled tube that ran into the back of Chase's hand.

"Listen, just tell me if the dress is white and I'll leave. I swear."

Now it was the police officer's turn to curse. He reluctantly let go of the IV and walked over to the table. He rifled through the bags before picking one of them up.

"This is what she was wearing," he said, jabbing the bag angrily.

"Is it white?" Chase asked.

The officer looked at it.

"It's red. It's covered in her blood."

And some of mine, too, I bet.

"But is it white? Is the dress white?"

The cop pointed at a small patch that hadn't been soaked.

"Yeah, I think it was white. You happy now?"

No, I'm not happy. I'm fucking pissed.

"Yeah, you're welcome!" the man shouted as Chase left the ICU without a word. "Entitled asshole."

As Chase retired to her room, she wondered if they would be better off if she'd been wrong. If the whole white dress thing had just been in her head.

Because now things were complicated.

Three days? They want me to stay here for three days?

Chase lay her head on the pillow.

That's not happening. I have a date in four, and I need to get ready.

Surprisingly, it wasn't Brian Jalston who flooded her dreams that night. It wasn't anything.

For Chase Adams, there was nothing but darkness.

Chapter 31

FLOYD STRUCK OUT AT CHARLESTON'S version of Junkie's Row. No amount of money he shelled out brought him any closer to the woman who had tried to kill Chase.

With his wallet a little lighter, he decided to check out the homeless shelters next. Floyd thought he might have more luck there, given their strict rules about alcohol and drug use, and considering that none of their killers had anything in their systems.

The largest homeless shelter was the most promising—there was a security guard out front, and they tended to be a little more reliable than the patrons.

"Floyd Montgomery, FBI," he said sternly. "I have a few questions for you."

"Yeah, fine," the guard said. "But not here. Not where people can see us."

Floyd agreed and followed the guard into the shelter. A dozen or so people were waiting in line for food even though it didn't appear as if the cooks were ready to serve. The guard led them to an adjacent office, and he knocked on the door before opening it. A woman with square glasses on a beaded chain looked up from behind a desk. She smiled when she saw both of them and gestured for them to enter.

"This is Margaret Stacy, she's the director here," the guard said as way of introduction. "And this is agent..."

Floyd showed the director his badge.

"Agent Montgomery of the FBI."

The woman looked down her nose and above her glasses.

"Not too often we get FBI agents in here. What can I do for you, Agent Montgomery?"

"Just Floyd, please."

"Okay, Floyd, what can I do for you?"

Floyd looked at Margaret, then the guard, and wondered what Tate's approach would be here. What would make these two comfortable? What would make them open up?

He had no idea. And the more he thought about becoming someone else, the more Floyd got confused. And when he got confused and nervous, his stutter came back with a vengeance.

"Floyd?" Margaret asked.

He shook his head and took a deep breath.

Tate could do his chameleon act, but he couldn't.

"I-I was ju-just wondering if either of you has seen this girl before?"

Floyd showed the photo of the woman who had attacked Chase to the security guard first. He looked it over and shook his head before passing it on to Margaret.

Glasses up this time, she observed it closely.

"I don't think so. I'm usually on the administrative sides of things, however, so I can't say that she wasn't here."

"And I've been off for the past week," the guard offered.

Shit.

Floyd had been hopeful.

"Is there anybody else I can ask? Somebody who's maybe a little closer to the... *uh...* guests here?"

So far, Floyd's approach had worked. But now, it was falling short.

"Why? Is she in trouble?"

It wasn't that Margaret didn't want to help, she just cared for these people and wasn't keen on contributing to their problems.

"She's in the hospital."

Floyd was tempted to add more information but held back. Sometimes, less was more. And he thought, in his limited experience, that this was one of those cases.

"Is it serious?" Margaret asked. "We don't allow drugs or alcohol inside the building. But outside..."

"It's serious, but not drug or alcohol-related so far as we can tell. I'm trying to reach this girl's friends or family or someone who knows her."

Margaret looked at the guard.

"Steve, why don't you take Floyd to see Martin. If she was here, he'd have seen her. He sees everyone."

The guard nodded at the director.

"Martin?" Floyd asked.

"Head cook. If people come in here, they're usually hungry. C'mon."

"Thank you, Margaret."

They left the office and entered the cafeteria. There were more people in line now and it looked like it was time to eat. A portly man sporting a white apron stood behind a massive metal pot of simmering soup. Having not eaten since his burger the night prior, Floyd's stomach started to grumble.

"Stevie, you hungry?" the cook, presumably Martin, asked.

The man had tight, dark curls on his head and a scorpion or spider tattoo was creeping up his neck from beneath the apron.

"Not right now, smells good, though, Martin," Steve replied. He indicated Floyd. "This man's from the FBI. He wants to know if you've seen someone."

Martin smiled, revealing a large space between his two front teeth.

"If they've eaten here, I've seen 'em. You got a photo?"

Floyd showed the photo to the man behind the vat of soup.

"My eyes ain't that good. Can I...?"

Floyd leaned across the soup and Martin reached for the photo. Before he came even close, his other hand came up and shoved the massive metal vat in Floyd's direction.

Floyd cried out and jumped back, but while he avoided most of the scalding liquid, a fair amount splashed the thighs of his jeans.

"Fuck!"

Thinking that it was an accident, Floyd instinctively put his arm to protect the security guard from the soup that still sloshed from the overturned cauldron.

"He's running!" Steve shouted.

Floyd looked up. Martin was sprinting toward the rear exit.

He cursed again and tried to go after the cook, but he slipped on the broth and dropped to one knee. His burnt thighs cried out in protest.

"Go after him!" Floyd yelled. "Get him!"

Steve the security guard looked at him as if he had three heads and didn't move.

"Go after him!" Floyd screamed. "Go get him! *Now!*"

Chapter 32

"HIDEY-HO, I'M SPECIAL AGENT Tate Abernathy, I'm looking for Officer Dwight Connors?"

"I'm Officer Connors," a thin man with large brown eyes and a narrow face replied.

Tate let the station door close behind him.

"We spoke on the phone. I have a couple of questions about the Owen Allman Case… drug dealer who was killed in his car just under a year ago."

A grin suddenly formed on Conners' face.

"What's so funny?" Tate asked.

"Come wit' me. I wanna show you something."

They walked past an oversized whiteboard with officer names and associated cases—as well as a running closing percentage—toward another board, this one of the cork variety.

On it, were various newspaper articles. Officer Dwight Connors pointed at a specific article near the top.

Local dealer rips off drugstore for thousands worth of anti-herpes medication.

The photograph beneath this creative headline showed a man leaping over a typical pharmacy counter.

"Anti-herpes medication?" he asked.

Connors chuckled.

"Yeah, you wanted to know what was so funny? Well, this asshole, Owen Allman, apparently doesn't know how to read. Broke into the pharmacy and instead of stealing Vicodin he grabbed —" Connors leaned close to the article and squinted, "—Valacyclovir. Drug for herpes."

"You can't be serious," Tate said.

"That's what we figure. Don't know for sure, 'cause," Connors dragged a finger across his throat, "he gone."

"You mind?" Tate asked, indicating the article.

"Be my guest."

There wasn't much more to glean from the article, other than what Connors had already told him. And while Tate was no doctor, he was fairly certain that unless this Owen Allman had an uncontrollable outbreak, then his dash and grab of the anti-herpes medication was a mistake.

"He's a bit of a legend here," Connors said with a hint of pride. "America's stupidest criminal."

Tate pulled back from the board and looked at the officer.

"What happened to him?" Now, Tate replicated Connors' throat slash. "I mean… *that*, but…?"

"I guess I lied to you, Owen is the *second* dumbest criminal in America. He robbed the store, then someone tried to rob him." Connors started wagging his head and Tate knew why: the man was remembering the smell. "Some crazy junkie. They fought, and both ended up dead."

So cavalier, Tate thought.

"Yeah, I have some questions about what happened in that car."

Connors shrugged.

"Pretty much already told you everything."

"I know, I know. Just need some clarification."

This time Connors did nothing but stare. Tate continued.

"Is it possible that the vagrant killed Owen, then herself?"

"Why would she do that?"

"I'm only asking if it's possible."

Over the phone, Tate had made it seem like he was interested in Owen Allman because of a related unsolved drug case. Now that it was clear that his motivation was different, Connors wasn't so keen on lending a hand. Nobody liked other dogs shitting in your backyard.

"I suppose it's possible," Connors said flatly. "But unlikely. After all, who lies in the backseat to kill a drug dealer only to off yourself afterward? Don't make sense to me."

Tate shrugged.

It didn't make much sense to him either, but nor did killing a doctor on the street, or a man after he took out his work garbage, and then committing suicide.

"Why's the FBI interested in this case, anyway?" Connors asked.

Tate completely ignored the question.

"Just going out on a limb here—the homeless chick in the backseat... she smelled, didn't she?"

"Did she ever. Jesus, she fucking reeked. We were going to auction off Owen's car but even after leaving it out for weeks, hiring anybody who would dare try to clean it, we couldn't get the smell out. Had to burn the fucking thing."

"Did anyone claim her body? Friends? Family?"

Connors shook his head.

"Nope. Still a Jane Doe."

"You go to the homeless shelters? Ask about her?"

This came off as more of an accusation than a question, and Tate cleared his throat.

"Just want to be thorough, is all."

Connors' large eyes narrowed.

"She's a Jane Doe."

The response signified an end to their discussion.

"All right, thanks for your help."

"You could've just done this over the phone," Connors grumbled as Tate made his way to the front of the station.

"Eh, not really a fan of phones," Tate said. Truthfully, his special skills worked much better in person. "Just one last question and then I'll be gone for good."

Connors crossed his arms over his chest and frowned.

"Did you find the herpes drugs? The Val-whatever it's called?"

Connors slowly shook his head.

"Nope, never found it."

Tate tapped his chin and said, "All right, thanks."

He didn't understand a drug dealer not being able to read. He didn't understand a vagrant killing the dealer and then herself. And he *definitely* didn't understand who came later and stole a truckload of anti-herpes medication.

Chapter 33

CHASE AWOKE TO THE SOUND of a beeping coming from her right.

"How are you feeling today?"

The nurse from yesterday was checking her IV fluids.

"Fine." Chase's voice was dry.

"Compared to yesterday?" Audrey asked. She switched out one bag of clear fluid for another. And then she started to change the dressing on Chase's throat wound.

"A little better." She was going to say that no matter what but was surprised to find that it was true. "How long was I out?"

Chase winced and Audrey leaned back.

"All night."

This was surprising. She remembered her little visit to the ICU but not much else after that.

Audrey sighed and lowered the iodine that she was in the process of cleaning Chase with.

"I know that you're itching to get out of here, but I have to, seriously, recommend against it. If you weren't in such good shape, Agent Adams, you'd be dead right now."

"I've heard that before."

The problem with Audrey's warning was that, over the years, nobody had tried to kill Chase harder and with more vigor than herself. And if she had been unsuccessful, what were the chances that someone else would get so damn lucky?

Audrey finished dressing Chase's wounds.

"What's going on with our friend in the ICU?"

"I heard about that, too," Audrey muttered under her breath. "She's awake."

Chase shifted to a seated position without much effort.

"Seriously?"

"Yes, woke up three hours ago."

"I need to speak to her." Chase pulled her gown up and put her feet on the floor. The nurse eyed her disapprovingly but made no attempt to stop her.

"I don't know if they're gonna let you," Audrey said. "And I don't think you should be out of bed."

Chase only heard the second half of her sentence.

"Old curmudgeonly police officer by the door?"

"He was swapped out for someone more junior."

That's good, Chase thought. *That's really good.*

Chase slowly stood, holding on to the bed in anticipation of a dizzy spell that never came.

"I don't think you should—"

Chase looked at Audrey sternly.

"I get that you're just doing your job, and I appreciate your concern. But I have work to do and there's nothing you can do to stop me."

Audrey looked as if she'd been physically slapped.

"I know I can't stop you," the nurse said, sounding frightened. Her tone made Chase immediately regret what she'd said and how she'd said it. "I just want to make sure you're okay."

"I'll be fine," Chase said. "And I do appreciate it—what you're doing. But I have to speak to her."

"Your room will be here when you get back since you paid cash."

That last part gave Chase pause, but it didn't slow her down. The IV trolley tried—its wheels were stickier than last night—but she overcame this minor obstacle.

The next would be more formidable.

Worst case scenario, Chase simply did the same as last night. She just hoped it didn't come down to that.

"FBI Agent Chase Adams," she barked, flashing her badge. The police officer who looked as if he was working on his GED while at the same time finishing police academy, appeared startled.

Good start.

"I need to speak to the suspect."

The officer started to stand, but Chase stayed him with her palm.

"I've been told that—"

"Do you know who I am?"

"I—I think—"

"I'm with the FBI. *F. B. I.* I need to speak to the suspect. Now."

The officer started to slide his chair out of the way and Chase thought to herself, *this is working out better than I could have hoped.*

Until it wasn't.

A doctor stepped to her side.

"Who are you?" he asked. The man was in his mid-fifties with a manicured white beard and spectacles.

"I'm—"

"Mrs. Adams, I see that now. You shouldn't be here. You need to get your rest." There was a familiarity to his voice and Chase concluded that he was the one who had operated on her.

She should thank him for saving her life, but there would be another time for that. It wasn't a priority.

Speaking to the girl who tried to kill her was. But tact was required here. This doctor was neither young nor impressed by the letters F B and I.

"I hear that she's up and talking."

The doctor licked his lower lip as a way to bide his time.

"She's awake, but not up. Very weak—deficiencies across the board." The doctor glanced at her throat. "To be honest, I'm surprised she had the energy to attack you."

"I guess I'm lucky she was too weak to finish the job, then," Chase said. "I just need to have a few words with her, doctor…"

"Heinlin. Dr. Greg Heinlin." Another lower lip lick. "If it's okay with the officer, I think you can have a minute or two."

Chase lowered her eyes at the still seated police officer.

"Yeah, s-sure. Fine by me."

Dr. Heinlin opened the door to the ICU and held it for Chase.

"I'm guessing not, but you find any drugs in her system?"

"Nothing."

Chase approached the bubble. It was still closed, but the girl's eyes were open. And her chest slowly rose and fell.

Dr. Heinlin touched her arm gently.

"Just a few minutes. In her present state, getting her agitated might make things worse."

Chase nodded.

"What's your name?" she asked the girl in the bubble.

Nothing. The girl didn't even turn in Chase's direction.

"Can she speak?" Chase asked the doctor.

"We ran multiple scans—CAT, MRI—her brain is dehydrated, and she shows decreased volume in the anterior insular cortex but other than that—"

"Can she speak, doc?"

Dr. Heinlin nodded.

"She should be able to."

Chase turned back to the bubble.

"Hi—can you speak?"

Not so much as a blink.

"Can you hear me? Hello? What's your name? You can tell me that, can't you?" Chase could feel her temper beginning to simmer. She pulled down the front of her gown. "You tried to kill me, and I want to know why."

And now the woman did turn, not her head, but her eyes. They appeared to scan Chase's face before returning to neutral.

Fuck. I risked my life telling Floyd to save you because I thought you'd be able to help. Speak to me. God damn it, speak to me.

"I *deserve* to know why."

"Please don't upset her," Dr. Heinlin said softly in her ear.

Don't upset her? Chase thought miserably. *I'm the one who she tried to kill!*

"Why were you wearing a white dress? Who told you to wear it? Brian? Did he have something to do with this?" When there was no response, Chase placed her hands on the bubble. "Why were you wearing the dress?" she demanded.

"It's time to leave," Dr. Heinlin stated.

Chase glared at the doctor.

"I need to know. I *need —* "

A scratching sound drew her attention back to the bubble.

"No!" Dr. Heinlin shoved her aside and raced to his patient.

The woman had removed the plastic end to the IV port from the back of her hand and was using it to claw at the stitches on her throat.

The doctor was trying to save her, but he was having the same problem Chase had last night: he couldn't get into the plastic bubble.

"Go get someone!" he yelled. "Now!"

It took Chase a few moments to realize the man was speaking to her.

"Go get someone before she kills herself!"

Chapter 34

EVENTUALLY, STEVE THE SECURITY GUARD started after Martin, but the man was already out the door.

Floyd wanted to follow, but his legs and his right hand, still clutching the photograph like a prized possession, were burning.

"Where's the sink?" he asked.

Those who had been waiting for their meal had gathered around him, and one of them pointed to the corner of the room. Floyd hurried to the large metal basin and turned on the cold water. He removed everything from his pockets and set the items on the ledge and then splashed his burnt hand with the water.

What the hell happened? he thought, angry with himself. *How did I let my guard down?*

Floyd glanced behind him and saw a particularly savage-looking man with tattoos on his face eyeing him up and down.

In a place like this, Floyd? Really? While investigating a murder/suicide? When your partner is in the hospital after nearly being killed?

The cool water did its work and Floyd noted that his hand was more scalded than actually burnt. He turned his attention to his legs next, and although he wasn't in a position to remove his pants, he grabbed a roll of industrial paper towels and started to soak up as much soup from his jeans as best he could.

"What happened?" Margaret asked. "Are you okay?"

Margaret reached for the paper towel, but Floyd said, "I'll be fine, thanks. Your cook—Martin—tried to burn me alive and then he ran."

Margaret looked genuinely surprised. She pulled her glasses from her face and let them hang around her neck.

"I'm so sorry, Floyd. I didn't—why did he do that?"

"I don't know, but Steve is—damn."

Steve reappeared near the back door, out of breath and empty-handed.

"I'm sorry," he said, breathing deep. "Too many cigarettes— I'm sorry. Martin got away."

Floyd was incredulous. Smoker or not, Martin was four-foot-three in all directions.

How the fuck did he get away?

"Steve, what happened?"

Floyd wondered if she was in shock, having asked the same question a moment ago.

"He—Floyd was showin' him the photo and the soup spilled."

"Could it have been an accident?"

Now Floyd was the one who was in shock.

"Accident? That was no accident. You don't run from an accident."

"We've never had a problem with Martin before. He's been here for years."

"Well, it looks like you don't know everything about Martin."

Margaret looked offended by this, and Floyd swiped at his jeans angrily.

"Sorry—I'm sorry. I guess in this place, everyone has secrets they want to keep from the FBI."

And you should've known better, Floyd. This is why you don't like to do things alone.

"I'll get you something for your arm," Margaret said. "I have a first aid kit in my office."

Floyd waved her off.

"I'm fine, seriously. But I will need Martin's address."

"That's easy. He lives here."

"What?"

Margaret nodded.

"Volunteers can stay over if they want — and they always get a bunk. Martin spends most of his time here."

Margaret thought she was being helpful, but this was bad news for Floyd. There was no way Martin was coming back.

"Hey, who's that?" Steve asked. He was pointing at the pile of stuff that Floyd had pulled out of his pocket.

"What?"

"That photograph — " Steve began but Margaret interrupted him.

"Is that Henry?" she asked.

Floyd grabbed the photo. It was the one that Chase had taken from the frame at Roger's house. He must have grabbed them from her at the hospital, even though he didn't remember doing so.

"You know this guy?"

"Of course," Margaret said. "I know them both — Roger and Henry." She squinted and leaned closer. "You know what? I think I know her, too."

Floyd was flabbergasted.

He'd come here looking for someone who knew the woman who had attacked Chase, not the girl in Roger's and Henry's photo.

"Sure, Henry and Roger volunteer here, and I'm pretty sure — yeah, she was here, too."

Floyd rubbed his brow.

"What do you mean by here? She was also a volunteer?"

"No, she was a guest."

Guest.

It took Floyd a second to understand; the girl in the photo was using the shelter.

"Wait—both Henry and Roger volunteer here?"

"Yeah. Mostly Henry because Roger is looking after the store."

"The electronics store?" Floyd asked.

"Mmm-hmm."

"Any idea why they would be in a photo together? Were they friends, or...?"

"No clue," Steve replied, and Floyd looked to Margaret.

"I don't know. Like I said before, I'm usually in the office most days. Oh, but because they volunteer, I have their addresses if you want to go talk to them."

Floyd made a face.

"Except one is—" he stopped cold. She didn't know. Neither Steve nor Margaret knew that Roger was dead.

"Hmm?" Margaret asked.

"N-n-nothing." Floyd was suddenly having difficulty swallowing. "I c-c-c-can f-find their addresses. Th-thanks."

Margaret stepped toward him and once again touched his arm.

"Floyd, let me look at your arm in the office. Just to make sure."

Floyd pulled his arm free.

What would Tate do? Tate would double down. He wouldn't let this bother him. Most of all, he'd do his fucking job.

"I said, I'm fine. If M-Martin stays here, does he have any be-belongings?"

"I'll go get them," Steve offered.

Margaret and Floyd waited silently for Steve to return. He felt bad for her—she seemed like a nice woman who wanted to help—but Floyd was concerned that if he said anything not directly related to the case, he would break down again.

Steve came shambling back with a garbage bag in one hand.

No wonder Martin got away. The man has two left feet and emphysema.

"This is—"

Floyd grabbed the bag and immediately dumped the contents right there on the ground. There was an opened pack of cigarettes, a toothbrush, a novel—*Tell Me Where She's Buried*—a few articles of dirty clothes, and a bottle of pills.

No hunting knife. No photos.

Floyd picked up the bottle of pills.

"Valacyclovir?" he read out loud.

"That's herpes meds," Steve blurted and then he started to blush. "I-I get cold sores."

That sounded like a lie.

Floyd wasn't sure why, but he had an inkling to keep the pills.

"I'm going to hold on to these." In case Margaret had a mind to complain, he added, "If Martin comes looking for them, just let me know."

"I would but I need your number."

Floyd passed her one of his business cards.

"If Martin comes back, please call me. And th-thank you."

He was surprised to discover that his hand wasn't shaking. That all changed when he got back to his car.

Chapter 35

"WHERE ARE YOU GOING?"

Chase, who was in the process of slipping on her jacket, turned around. She was surprised, and a little annoyed, to see Floyd standing in the doorway of her hospital room.

"I'm—" she noticed two large stains, one on either thigh. "What happened to you?"

"Long story, which I thought I'd have time to tell you because you're supposed to be here for another three days."

Chase grimaced.

"I'm not sticking around here."

"Chase, you can't—"

"I swear, if one more person tells me what I can or cannot do, I'm going to blow a fucking gasket."

Chase took one step then winced and grabbed her collarbone.

Floyd reached for her, but she waved him away.

"I'm fine."

Floyd looked as if he was going to argue, but then he shook his head.

"I heard," he sighed deeply, "I heard she woke up."

Chase nodded.

"She woke up all right. She woke up and then tried to kill herself again."

"You can't be serious."

"You know me, always with the jokes."

Chase zipped her coat and searched the room to make sure she had all of her belongings.

"You said tried? Is she still—"

The door behind Floyd opened. Chase expected either Audrey or Dr. Heinlin, but it was neither.

"Tate?" Floyd said.

Special Agent Tate Abernathy looked at Chase, then Floyd, and then back at Chase.

"What in the fuck is goin' on here?" he asked. And now Chase and Floyd were exchanging glances. "Lucy, you've got some 'splaining to do!"

Neither Chase nor Floyd so much as smiled and Tate dropped the accent.

"Let's go have a drink," he suggested.

Floyd scoffed and Chase knew what her partner was thinking: that it was a ludicrous idea given what she'd been through. But Chase thought differently.

She thought it was a splendid idea.

"Sounds good. Let's just get the hell out of here."

***

It took three pints and forty minutes for Floyd and Chase to share their stories. For the most part, Tate remained silent, only interjecting on a handful of occasions. When it became his turn to speak, Tate took a long haul of his beer and licked the foam from his mustache.

"Well, well, well... I wish my tale was half as exciting as yours, but it ain't. I did get to break up a fight at a funeral, spoke to a public servant who spent hours cleaning the smell out of their bus, which, by the way, carried Dr. Griffith's murderer from Charleston to Columbus. Then I — "

"Wait, the girl who killed Dr. Griffith came from here?" Chase cut in. "From Charleston?"

"That is correct," Tate confirmed. "But wait, I'm not done yet." He drank some more beer before continuing. "I drove to Portsmouth and met an officer there who told me about a case.

A case involving a dumbass drug dealer and a particularly odoriferous woman who killed him and then killed herself. *Maybe.*"

"Drug dealer?" Chase asked, trying to understand how this was relevant to their current investigation.

"Yeah, illiterate drug dealer. Tried to steal Vicodin and got Valacyclovir—herpes meds—instead."

Floyd suddenly sat bolt upright. His knee jostled the table and Chase's beer wobbled.

"Sorry—what did he steal?"

"Val-acy-clo-vir," Tate said, pronouncing every syllable.

Floyd reached into his pocket and pulled out a prescription bottle and placed it on the table.

"Coincidence?"

Chase leaned forward and read the label.

"Where did you get this from?" she asked.

"The cook who burned my legs and ran away as soon as he saw the picture of the girl who had attacked you, Chase. This was in his belongings."

"Well, I'm not much for coincidences," Tate offered. "But if this—" he indicated the pill bottle, "—is connected, I would like to know how."

"Henry Saburra," Chase said without hesitation. "That's the connection."

"What do you mean?" Floyd asked.

"Henry worked at the homeless shelter, his partner was murdered, and I was attacked outside his store. And I wouldn't be surprised if the DNA comes back, and we find out the girl in the picture with Roger and Henry is the same one in the morgue."

As this comment hung in the air, they all sipped their respective drinks.

"Why were you attacked, Chase?" Tate asked. "What makes you so special?"

"Just lucky, I guess."

Despite her reply, Tate had raised a good point. Chase's attack didn't jive with the Henry connection, aside from the location. A more glaring inconsistency, however, was the white dress and its link to Brian Jalston.

Chase elected to keep this last part to herself. Once she figured out how that all fit in with things, then she would share.

Maybe.

"Speaking of lucky," Tate began, "my old partner Con told me once that when people were being killed all around you, it didn't make you lucky. It made you—"

"The culprit," Chase finished for him.

Tate grinned.

"You got it. So, let's finish our beers and visit the culprit, then, shall we?"

Chapter 36

"**YOU WANT TO DO THE** talking?" Tate asked as the three of them stood in front of Henry Saburra's home.

"Yeah, I'll do the talking."

Chase glanced at Floyd who appeared nervous but was keeping it together. She gave him an encouraging nod before knocking on the door. When she heard nothing from inside, she tried the bell.

"Maybe he's at *E-Tronics?*" Floyd offered.

The mention of the electronics store made Chase frown.

"When's Roger's funeral?"

"Two days," Tate said.

"Well, if we can't find Henry before that, I'm sure—"

Chase was cut off by the sound of her phone buzzing. She took it out of her pocket, looked at it, and then held up a finger.

"I'll be right back. Tate, try the bell again."

Chase walked halfway to her car and answered the call.

"Terrence? Do you have the list of Brian's visitors?" she asked, keeping her voice low.

"Yeah," Terrence replied.

"And? Can you send it?"

"I'll send it," he said after clearing his throat. "But that's not why I called."

Chase's eyes narrowed.

"He didn't get out early, did he? That bastard—"

"No, he's not out. But…"

Chase didn't have the patience nor the time for this.

"But what, Terrence? Please, I'm busy."

"But you're going to get a subpoena."

"A subpoena? For what? For what happened in the visitor room? I barely—"

"For Georgina," Terrence said.

What?

Chase could feel an uncomfortable throbbing in her neck in the area where she'd been stabbed.

"What do you mean, Georgina?" she demanded, fighting a sudden dizzy spell. Chase wasn't sure if this was a result of her injuries or if it was all in her head.

"Chase, I'm sorry, but Brian is seeking custody of Georgina."

Chase's vision went dark. She stumbled and was about to go down when Floyd caught her.

"Chase, what's happening? You okay?"

Chase shook free of Floyd and forced her body straight, grinding her jaw to keep the darkness at bay.

"Chase?" It was Terrence calling her name this time.

"I'm here," she whispered, gesturing for Floyd to leave her alone. "I'm here."

"Right, and did you hear what I said? A friend in family court gave me the head's up that Brian is seeking full custody of your niece."

Chase couldn't believe what she was hearing.

"This is a joke, right?"

"No, it's not a joke."

"How is this possible?" Chase snapped. *"How is this fucking possible?* Brian kidnapped and raped my sister. And now he wants the baby?"

"Chase, take it easy," Floyd said, trying to comfort her. She shot him a look and he backed off.

"I'm just the messenger, Chase."

"He's in prison for raping and kidnapping those women!" Her voice faltered. "Don't tell me he has a shot at this. Terrence, don't tell me that there's any chance Brian can get my Georgina!"

There was a short pause before Terrence said, "I'm no law-yer, Chase—I don't know what kind of chance he's got. But he is the biological father, and even though he did kidnap those girls and probably raped them, that's not what he was in prison for."

Chase threw her head skyward as she remembered what Terrence had said in Tennessee. About Brian's plea deal, about how none of the women would testify against him. And about how they continued to visit him in prison.

Chase's frantic mind then settled on another idea. The no-tion that if she hadn't gone to see Brian, none of this would have happened. That her visiting him, using her sister and niece's name, had inspired the man to go after Georgina.

"Fuck," she said.

Tears threatened to spill over, but she forced them away with a hard swallow and a severe blink.

"I'll send you the list of visitors, Chase. I feel like I keep say-ing this, but I'm sorry."

"I'm sorry, too," she said and then hung up the phone. "I'm sorry I didn't fucking kill the bastard when I had the chance."

Chase closed her eyes and tried to stretch her neck. Not only was her wound throbbing but it was cramping up, as well.

She opened her eyes and discovered that her two colleagues were staring at her.

If either Floyd or Tate had spoken at that moment, Chase might have lost it. It wouldn't matter if they said something like, *what happened* or *are you okay*, if they'd said anything at all, she would have either collapsed into a puddle or become vio-lent. Either option was equally as likely.

But they didn't.

They just stared and Chase stared back.

Until the phone in her hand rang again.

She quickly answered it.

"Terrence?"

"I'm sorry, is this Agent Adams?"

It wasn't Terrence, it was a voice she didn't recognize.

"Who is this?" Her first thought was that it was a lawyer, trying to get a hold of her to tell her that her niece, the one whom she'd legally adopted, was about to be reclaimed by her serial rapist and pedophile father.

"It's Dr. Woodley."

"Who?" Chase thought she'd misheard. "Dr. Heinlin?"

"No," the man on the other end of the line said hesitantly. "Dr. Woodley. The Medical Examiner. You came in a few days ago with the... vagrant?"

Chase understood now.

"Did the DNA results come back?"

"That's what I'm calling you about. The results came back, but no match. Whoever the person who donated the hairbrush is, it's not the same one as the girl in the morgue."

"Shit." There goes that theory. "What about toxicology?"

"That came back, too."

"And?"

"I doubt this is relevant, but—"

"But what? What did you find?"

Dr. Woodley cleared his throat.

"Very high levels of acyclovir and L-valine. Abnormally high."

"Did you say, *valacyclovir?*"

"No—*acyclovir*. It's the active metabolite of valacyclovir. So is L-valine. It's used to treat herpes, but I see no evidence of an outbreak."

Chase scratched the back of her neck, and this time her eyes met Tate's.

"Thanks."

"Wait, one more thing," Dr. Woodley said quickly.

"What?"

"The Horvath clock test results also came in."

"The what?"

"The methylation of the DNA… to determine her age?"

Chase closed her eyes.

"How old is she?"

Chase cringed in anticipation of the answer.

"Between fifteen and eight years of age."

Fuck.

"Okay. Thanks again."

She hung up.

"That was the ME," Chase said. "Our murderer had high levels of the herpes drug in her system when she died. And she was a teenager."

Tate opened his mouth, then closed it again without speaking. Chase was certain that he wanted to ask about the first call but was either dissuaded by her stern expression or frightened by it.

Floyd spoke up instead.

"Another connection," he said absently. "But what does it mean? Please, can *anyone* tell this ju-ju-junior agent what any of this shit means?"

Chapter 37

TATE HUNG UP THE PHONE and looked at Chase.

"Confirmed. The murderer in Columbus also had valacyclovir metabolites in her system."

Chase wasn't surprised.

"What about the girl who killed the drug dealer?"

Tate made a face.

"I don't know, and I doubt that Officer Connors in Portsmouth would be willing to pay for toxicology."

Based on Tate's tone, Chase got the impression that Officer Connors, whoever that was, would be unwilling to speak to Tate again, as well, but it didn't matter.

"First order of business, find Henry. We can't wait two days for the funeral."

I *can't wait.*

"I can go back to the electronics store, see if he's working," Floyd suggested.

Chase didn't like the idea of leaving Floyd alone, especially to go searching for a man who just lost his partner, but they had to divide and conquer. The only other option was—

"The shelter," Tate said. "I'll go slink around there to see if that Martin guy returns." He looked at Floyd. "He'll recognize you, but I'll blend right in."

I *bet you will.*

"And I'll go back to the hospital, talk to Dr. Heinlin about the woman who attacked me. Maybe even try to talk to her again."

They parted then, Tate going with Floyd, while she got into her rental alone. She was pulling out of Henry's driveway when she got a text. It was the visitor log.

As if caused by this message, Chase felt a pain in her neck. She made sure that Tate had since driven away before inspecting her bandage. It was dark red and soaked through.

Shit, you need to take it easy, she told herself.

But Chase didn't know how to take it easy. She only knew one speed: maximum. It was how she lived her life ever since she'd been grabbed by Tim and Brian all those years ago.

And now that her niece had been threatened, she had no time to slow down. Chase would find out why she'd been attacked, who was behind Roger's and Wayne's murders, if it was someone different than the girls in the morgue, and then be waiting for Brian when he was released.

The list only contained four names, one of which—Horatio Barnes—sounded like a lawyer. The other three, Chase recognized.

Sue-Ellen, Portia, and Melissa Jalston.

The fact that these women used the names that Brian and Tim had forced on them angered Chase even further. For the past two years, they had visited every Monday, Wednesday, and Friday, respectively.

Chase shook her head in disgust. It sickened her that these three women continued to dote on Brian even after he was behind bars. It was a twisted addiction, and she knew firsthand how hard it was for humans to break their patterns.

Especially longstanding ones.

To break the pattern would mean admitting to oneself that they'd wasted a huge portion of their lives. Sometimes, it was easier to continue to live a lie than it was to admit the truth.

There was, of course, a fifth name on the list.

Her name. Or, more specifically, her sister's name.

Why did I go? Why couldn't I just stay away?

Shaking her head, Chase was about to toss her phone on the passenger seat when she spotted an additional entry near the bottom — after her sister's name.

Melissa Jalston.

According to the list, Melissa came on Fridays, but this was a Tuesday. And the time listed was a mere two hours after Chase had left.

Did he call her? Tell her to visit? Why? Did he have some pent-up anger from Chase's visit? Did he need someone to slap around a little?

That didn't jive with the calmness, the serenity, that she'd felt when touching Brian's hands. But how much could she rely on her 'voodoo'?

If it wasn't broken, it was bent. It hadn't worked in the morgue, and it hadn't worked with Brian. Something had happened with Father David, or so she thought, but who's to say that wasn't just Cerebrum working its way through her system.

Why did she visit?

Chase closed her eyes for a moment and took a deep breath. A white dress appeared in her mind.

First Tennessee, then the alleyway, then right before the attack.

Stitts was right, this was no coincidence.

A stab of pain in her throat forced her eyes open.

"You're just wasting time," she told herself. "And you only have two more days."

Chase started her rental and drove back to the hospital. On the way, she dialed Louisa's number. She'd previously avoided speaking to Georgina for fear of reminding her of Brian, but that cat was already out of the bag.

"Hey, what's up, Chase? How's work?"

"Fine, it's going fine," Chase lied. It was anything but fine. This whole thing had been a clusterfuck from the moment she'd stepped into the prison, intending to see Brian Jalston.

"Yeah, you're lying. But that's alright. Anything I can do to help?"

"I just need to speak to her," Chase said softly. She parked in the hospital lot and got out of her car.

"Georgina? Chase, she's in school right now." Louisa grew serious. "It's the middle of the afternoon. Everything okay with you?"

Chase grunted and looked down. There was blood on her shirt now.

"Just fucking peachy. Listen, Louisa, I need you to keep Georgina home. Like, home for school for the next few days. Think you can do that for me?"

There was a pause.

"Okay. Yeah, I can do that."

Bless you, Louisa, for not asking questions.

"Thanks. I'll be home as soon as I can. A couple of days."

But in her heart, Chase knew that this was also a lie. In two days, she would be in Franklin, Tennessee. In three, she had no idea.

"Mrs. Adams? Mrs. Adams, you're bleeding."

Chase looked up and was surprised to see Audrey standing in front of her, a startled expression on her face. She followed the nurse's gaze to her own chest.

The blood on her shirt, what had been a small dot moments ago, was now the size of her fist.

And growing.

"I am," Chase said. Her voice sounded faint. Faint and thin. "I am bleeding."

And then she toppled, falling into Audrey's waiting arms.

Chapter 38

"IS CHASE... SINGLE?" TATE ASKED as they drove toward *E-Tronics*.

Floyd looked at the man, blinked once, twice, and then shook his head.

"She's not?" Tate said, sounding disappointed.

"Single or not, that's..." Floyd collected his thoughts. "I'm not sure that's something you want to get involved with."

Floyd loved Chase. He loved Chase for what she'd done for him, who she was, and what she'd overcome.

And he liked Tate.

But the idea of Tate becoming romantically involved with Chase was incomprehensible.

"Why not? She's hot. Nice set of —"

"Trust me, Chase's complicated."

Tate shrugged.

"I can do complicated."

Floyd knew the man was referring to his previous partner, Constantine Striker, and agreed. But Con was one thing, Chase was another. Come to think of it, the two might be perfect for each other.

But not for Tate.

"Not this kinda complicated," Floyd said, becoming serious.

"Meh, maybe."

Tate pulled into the parking lot. The lights were off and the sign on the door was still turned to 'CLOSED'.

"You have the keys?" Tate asked.

Like the photograph of Henry, Roger, and the random girl, Floyd had gotten the keys from Chase after she'd been attacked.

"Doesn't look like anyone's here," Floyd said in the hopes that Tate would suggest that they go straight to the homeless shelter together.

"Someone has been here, though," Tate said absently.

Floyd peered through the shop's windows.

"What makes you say that?"

"The lights are off."

"So?"

"So? So, is Chase so concerned with the environment that she wandered back inside, bleeding to death, shut the lights off, and then collapsed in the alley? That make sense to you?"

Floyd, still looking at *E-Tronics*, said, "Maybe she didn't turn them on. Or maybe the cops shut them off after they arrived on the scene."

When Tate didn't respond, Floyd looked at him. He had a strange expression on his face.

"What?"

"Have you... have you spoken to the cops?"

"Yeah," Floyd said hesitantly. "Gave them a statement after Chase was admitted. Why?" Once again, Tate didn't answer right away. He had a far-off look in his eyes, and Floyd could almost hear the gears inside his head turning. "What are you thinking, Tate?"

"I'm thinking that when I was at the hospital, I didn't see a lot of police presence. No detectives, no Lieutenant Lehner-types. That's a bit weird, *innit*? An FBI agent is nearly killed... you'd think there would be some sort of investigation, right?"

Floyd mulled this over.

"They already have the person responsible," he said with a shrug.

It was a weak response and they both knew it. Tate was right, the lack of overt investigation into Chase's attack was strange. But so was everything else about this… these… cases.

"Maybe." Tate leveled his eyes at Floyd. "Go take a look in the store. See if there are other… pictures, anything. If Roger or Henry have paperwork, see if there's a mention of Martin anywhere. Or the herpes drug."

"Like a calendar? A big red circle around a date with the words 'OUTBREAK'? What am I really doing here, Tate?"

"Becoming a big boy. Go on, I'll come grab you in less than an hour."

Floyd tried to think back to a time when Tate might have been alone with Chase. He didn't think there had been. But this felt like a setup.

"I—"

"Just fucking go."

Floyd shook his head and got out of the car.

"If you need anything, give me a call," Tate said out the window as he sped off.

The instant he was alone, Floyd felt a familiar tightness in his chest. The simple act of walking toward the store suddenly felt difficult as if the air had been replaced by something thicker.

Come on, Floyd! For fuck's sake, there's no one here.

But no amount of admonishment would make his legs move any more fluidly. He imagined what someone would think if they observed him walking in this way.

They'd probably assume he was recovering from a spinal injury, relearning how to walk.

It wasn't funny.

It was embarrassing.

Floyd's breathing had become labored as well, but this was mostly because of anger. Anger at himself for being such a coward.

Chase had told him to find what works for him.

But how the hell was he supposed to do that?

His hand was shaking so badly that the set of keys sounded like a maraca as he tried to find the correct one to slip into the lock. It took him five minutes to get the door open.

There's no one here… there's no one here.

The mantra was moderately reassuring. And it proved correct.

There was a smell, though. Not quite as pungent as a corpse, but not even remotely pleasant, either.

Floyd flicked on the lights and spotted the source: a litter box. He thought about the cat that Henry had been holding when they'd visited him and the similarly full litter box at Roger's place.

He was considering what this might have to do with their case if anything when he heard movement from the back of the store.

"Hello?"

This time, unlike at the shelter, his hand immediately went to his gun.

"Hello?"

Floyd listened as he slowly moved toward the storeroom. There was a sudden flurry of movement, and he heard the rear exit open.

"Hey!" he yelled and broke into a run. "Stop!"

Floyd's foot struck the litterbox and he nearly fell.

"Fuck!"

By the time he collected himself and burst into the alley, the woman was fifty yards ahead. Floyd raised his gun, took aim, then lowered it.

What the fuck are you thinking?

"Hey!"

The woman, who was wearing some sort of gray suit, didn't slow. Floyd couldn't make out any of her features either, other than the fact that she had straight brown hair. And that this woman was no corpse.

The door clicked closed behind him and Floyd looked at it.

There was a key still in the lock, and it was hanging from a keyring. Squinting, Floyd removed the key and then held it up to the yellow light above the door.

He pulled his keys out, the ones from Chase, and compared them to this set.

They were identical.

Floyd looked down the alley, but the woman was gone. Whoever she was, she wasn't a run-of-the-mill burglar.

She'd come here with a purpose.

She'd come here looking for something specific.

And Floyd sincerely doubted that it was a new iPad.

PART III – Control

Chapter 39

"You must be Margaret Stacy," Tate said with a small smile.

The woman behind the desk smiled back, and Tate instantly knew how to talk to her.

"That's me."

"And I'm FBI Agent Tate Abernathy," he said, extending his hand.

Margaret shook it.

"Martin hasn't come back. How is your friend doing... the other agent? Agent Montgomery?"

Tate dropped the smile for a concerned expression.

"He'll be fine, sore for a while, but it's nothing serious."

"That's good. It's not like Martin to do anything like this... he's been working here for a long time, and like I told your partner, he's one of the most reliable volunteers we have."

Tate considered this for a moment before asking, "Henry and Roger were volunteers, too, weren't they? Did they know Martin?"

Margaret nodded and she adjusted her glasses.

"Definitely. We're not a very large group here." She gestured to her office. "Lots of space, not so many volunteers."

"Tough to find good help."

"Speaking of which, how are Roger and Henry? I haven't seen either in more than a week. Maybe even two."

Tate had to invoke all of his willpower to suppress the cringe that threatened to break his façade of the caring individual, the gentle agent. He should have known that Floyd would have avoided discussing Roger's death at all costs.

Tate bowed his head slightly and grasped one wrist in front of his waist.

"I'm very sorry to tell you this, Margaret, but Roger passed a few days ago."

Margaret's mouth fell open.

"What? What happened?"

Tate politely averted his gaze and noticed a cross hanging on the wall.

"I don't want to shock you, but Roger was murdered. I can't discuss any of the details because it's an ongoing case, but rest assured that he is in a better place with our Lord."

Tate thought that maybe he laid it on a little thick, but Margaret seemed appreciative.

"That's... that's terrible."

Tate nodded.

"It is indeed a terrible shame. I'm very sorry to break the news to you this way, but that's kind of why we're here. Like I said, we can't reveal too much information about what happened, but we're trying very hard to figure things out."

"I—" Margaret swallowed hard and adjusted her glasses again. "If there's any way that I can help... you don't—you don't think that Martin had anything to do with this? Do you?"

Tate shook his head.

"I don't think so. Right now, we're just trying to learn more about Roger. My partner... he showed you a photo, right? Of Henry and Roger and a girl?"

Margaret nodded.

"Yeah. I thought I recognized the girl, so after your partner left, I looked around a little. Hold on a second."

She reached into the desk drawer, sifted through its contents for a moment, and then produced a photo of her own.

"I knew I recognized her, but I didn't realize that the girl in your partner's photo was the same person as this. Here."

Not the same person?

Tate accepted the photo with a nod and instantly understood.

He spotted Roger and Henry instantly. In the background was a rotund man in an apron, presumably the cook, Martin. Then there was the girl. She appeared to be in mid-conversation with Henry. She was… grimy, to say the least. But Tate did see similarities between this girl and the girl from Floyd's photograph. It was like looking at a photo before and after heavy use of social media filters.

Tate tapped the photo.

"Her name is Rebecca," Margaret said. "At least, I'm pretty sure her name was Rebecca, but she insisted on being called Becca."

"Did you—"

Tate stopped when Margaret began to smile. Regular people, people not involved in law enforcement, loved to play detective. And he loved to let them.

"Yep, I asked around. Apparently, Henry and Roger took Becca under their wing. Helped her get cleaned up, turn her life around. They got pretty close."

Tate recalled Floyd's picture. They did indeed look like one happy family.

"How old would you say Becca is?"

Margaret thought about it.

"Seventeen?"

Tate looked at the photo.

"Do you know when this was taken?"

"A year ago? I'm not sure. We don't take many photos around here... try to protect our guests' anonymity."

Tate couldn't find a date on the photo, but he thought it was older than a year. Henry looked three years younger. And that would make Becca twenty-*ish* today. Tate recalled what Chase had said about Roger's killer. She was in her late teens. DNA had proven that they weren't the same person, but the girl in the photo was filthy just like the cadaver. Not quite as bad, but...

"Can I keep this?" he asked.

Margaret shrugged.

"Sure."

Tate slipped it into his pocket.

"Just one last thing," he said. "When's the last time you saw Becca?"

"Oh, gosh, a year?" she pointed to Tate's pocket. "I can't remember seeing her after that photo was taken, actually."

And you also can't remember when it was taken.

Civilians loved to play detective, but they just weren't very good at it.

"Well, thank you, Margaret. You've really been a great help. You have my partner's card, right?"

"Yes," she found it on her desk and held it up with a smile. "I have it right here."

"Well, if you think of anything else, or if Martin shows up, please give Floyd a call." Tate smiled. "You know what?" he continued, handing over his own business card. "You can call me, too, if you want."

Chapter 40

"MAYBE THIS TIME YOU'LL THINK better of leaving early," the nurse said, the moment Chase opened her eyes.

Normally she would have been offended by this, maybe even get angry. But she hadn't the strength, and Audrey looked, and sounded, legitimately worried about her. She didn't appear to have a mean bone in her body, either.

"Maybe," Chase said in a dry voice.

Then she spent the next thirty seconds to a minute feeling about her body and taking in her surroundings. It was like Groundhog Day.

There was a monitor on her finger, and an IV in the back of her opposite hand. She winced when her fingers prodded the wound by her throat. The bandages were fresh, and if the sensitivity was any indication, the stitches beneath were also new.

Chase sucked in a harsh breath. It burned.

"Mrs. Adams, you need to rest."

Yep, Groundhog Day.

Audrey sighed. The woman knew that she was wasting her words.

"Thank you," Chase said hoarsely. Then, when it looked as if the nurse was about to leave, Chase called her back. "I need to speak to Dr. Heinlin about the girl who tried to kill me. I need—"

Chase suddenly started to cough, and she felt severe pain spreading from her wound to the entire circumference of her throat. Audrey stepped forward to help her, but Chase refused. She wiped the back of her mouth with her hand after the coughing fit passed.

"Sorry, I'm sorry. Dr. Heinlin—" The door behind Audrey opened and a doctor entered, his head down, his eyes on a clipboard. "Okay, well, he's here."

"How are the stitches healing, Mrs.—" the doctors' eyes shot up, "—Agent Adams."

Chase did her best to sit up and managed a half-decent job.

"I'll leave you two alone," Audrey said. "Dr. Heinlin, please try to convince her to stick around this time?"

Dr. Heinlin made a face similar to the one that Audrey had made earlier. He set the clipboard down and then looked Chase in the eyes.

"Have you ever heard of Cotard's syndrome?" he asked.

Chase frowned.

"If this is about me—"

"No, it's not about you, Agent Adams. This is about the person who tried to kill you. I assume that's why you came back, right?" he pointed at her throat. "And not for a regular check-up, am I right?"

Chase said nothing.

"Yeah. I think that the person who is attacking you is suffering from Cotard's Syndrome."

"Never heard of it."

The doctor licked his lips, his expression severe.

"It's rare. Very rare. It's a condition that has various symptoms, some of which can be quite—"

Chase cleared her throat. This was normally the time where she would interject, where she would say something along the lines of, *get to the point and stop mansplaining*, but Dr. Heinlin, experienced as he was, held his hand up.

"As I was saying, a person with severe Cotard's can experience various symptoms but—" he held up a finger, once again preemptively cutting her off, "—*but* the most alarming is that they believe that they are dead."

Chase expected Dr. Heinlin to expound on this but when he didn't, she repeated what he'd just said.

The words sounded strange coming out of her mouth.

"A person with Cotard's—am I saying that right, Cotard's—believes that they are dead? Like, dead, dead?"

Chase was familiar with psychopathy and sociopathy in which the sufferers place no value on others' lives, but this?

"Are they suicidal?" she asked.

The motion that Dr. Heinlin made was neither a nod nor a shake—it was somewhere in between.

"Not classically so. They make no conscious effort to end their lives. They don't actively self-harm either. They actually believe they're dead. And because of that, they stop bathing, cleaning, eating, taking care of themselves. Some can suffer from delusions, think that they're ghosts, think that everyone else is a ghost... the list of potential symptoms is vast, but the theme remains the same: they do not think they are alive."

Chase's eyes widened, as did her nostrils as she was transported back to the alley behind *E-Tronics*. She smelled the girl, saw the glint of the knife, felt it pierce her flesh.

"Jesus," Chase whispered. "We were saying it all along... they looked like they were already dead. They smelled like they were dead... but we didn't once consider that they *thought* they were dead."

The doctor frowned.

"They?"

Chase nodded.

"Yeah, *they*."

"But—"

Chase, fearing that the doctor was going to start mansplaining again, raised her voice.

"You're sure that the girl who attacked me suffers from Cotard's?"

"Sure? No. Fairly confident, however. It was a differential for the decreased anterior insular cortex volume and given her physical condition... yeah, confident. I believe that the person who attacked you thought—thinks—that they're actually dead."

Chase took a deep breath. More burning.

"Are people with Cotard's prone to violence? Murder?"

Dr. Heinlin cocked his head.

"No. Not traditionally. Typically, the damage they do is restricted to their person."

The doctor fell silent.

"This doesn't make sense," Chase grumbled. She shook her head, only to immediately regret it. It felt as if porcupine quills were lodged in her throat. "Why the fuck did she attack me? And why the white dress?"

"The white...?"

"Never mind. I'm just trying to understand. This—" Chase pointed at her bandage, "—this was no accident, doc. She stabbed me, tried to kill me, and then tried to kill herself. Why would she try to kill me?"

This time, when Chase cleared her throat, it was to encourage speech, instead of discouraging it.

Dr. Heinlin sighed heavily.

"I'm no expert in Cotard's syndrome, and a psychiatrist would—"

"Just tell me, *please*. Enough of this song and dance already. I get it, it's not your specialty. You're not an expert. Fine, but I'm a fucking pin cushion and I'm trying to figure out why."

The doctor stiffened.

"My best guess?"

"Yeah, your best—"

"Someone told her to. Somebody told that girl in the ICU to kill you, Agent Adams. That's my best guess."

Chapter 41

FLOYD STEPPED BACK INTO *E-TRONICS* and put his hands on his hips. The key rings, one looped through each thumb, jangled loudly.

"What were you looking for?" he mumbled out loud as his eyes scanned the shelves.

If only I'd been here two minutes earlier... if only I hadn't hesitated at the door, he scolded himself, *I could have just asked her why she was here.*

The more he thought about it, the more Floyd was convinced that this was no ordinary robbery. The woman, whoever she was, likely entered from the rear, then moved to the front to lock the door and turn off the light just in case someone passed by. Next, she began searching for something until Floyd interrupted her by fumbling with the lock. And that said nothing of the fact she had a set of keys. Where the hell did she get those from?

"And what were you looking for?" Floyd repeated.

The only thing he was sure of, was that it wasn't a phone charger.

Instead of wasting his time with the generic items on the shelves, Floyd returned to the entrance and approached the cash register. It was locked, but the key was on the ring—both rings—and he opened it. He estimated that there were close to two-hundred dollars in there, but when he lifted the tray, he found nothing of interest.

Frustrated, Floyd placed both hands on the glass counter and peered around the shop.

He was starting to get that feeling again, the feeling of being totally and utterly useless.

It was something he was unfortunately familiar with. It started back in New York City with the suicide girls: while Chase and Detective Dunbar were running around town, making progress, Floyd was either moping in his car or trembling on someone's doorstep. He'd been so debilitated that he'd nearly been late to the church, to Blessed Sacrament, and Father David…

He shuddered at what could have happened to Chase and millions more.

But now, in Charleston, West Virginia, far from the bustle of New York City, the feeling was even worse. It was worse because he'd been so close.

Martin.

Martin with his filthy apron and his fucking soup.

Floyd could have grabbed him. But instead, he'd not only let him get away, but he'd spooked him. It would have been better if he'd never even showed up at the homeless shelter, in the first place.

Shaking his head in condemnation, Floyd moved from the front of the store to the employee's lounge. It was a tiny room, with just enough space for a table, a couple of chairs, and a small fridge.

Running out of ideas, Floyd opened the fridge. Inside, he found a can of Fresca and two bottles of Sinai hot sauces. He swore, then flicked the small flap that separated the freezer from the fridge.

It lifted for a second, then snapped back into place.

"Well, I'll be damned." A smile crept onto his lips as he lifted the flap and held it open while taking his cell phone out of his pocket at the same time.

His first inclination was to call Chase, but he quickly quashed that idea. She'd been through enough. If it were up to him, Chase would still be lying in a hospital bed resting.

Truthfully, he was a little surprised that Director Hampton had let her on this case, given what had happened in New York... and Albuquerque... and Washington... and... and...

Floyd called Tate instead and he answered on the first ring.

"What's up, my man?"

"We should meet up. I think I've found something," Floyd said, his eyes still locked on the items in the freezer.

"I knew you could do it, Kemosabe. Look at that, all by your lonesome, too!"

"Ha, ha, funny guy."

Tate's voice grew serious.

"I've got something to show you, as well."

"It's probably too small to see, but okay."

"Oh, now who's the funny guy?"

"Anyway, I'm thinking that we need to pay Henry another visit," Floyd said. He reached into the freezer and pulled out the large plastic bag.

"That's the first good idea you've had all week," Tate said. "I'll pick you up in ten."

Chapter 42

"YOU HAVE TO UNDERSTAND, AGENT Adams, Cotard's sufferers can be very, very impressionable."

Chase was still finding it difficult to wrap her mind around this strange condition.

"The dead can be influenced?"

The doctor made a face, clearly not impressed by her attempt at humor. The issue was that Chase wasn't trying to be funny. She was just trying to understand why she'd been attacked.

"They're not actually dead." Dr. Heinlin paused to scratch his chin. "In all my years in medicine, I've only come across one patient with Cotard's, and that was years ago when I was a resident. A patient was admitted into the psych ward and the consensus was that she was suffering from some sort of drug-induced psychosis. She refused to eat or drink, and she was filthy. Emaciated, on the verge of multiple organ failure from years of neglecting her nutrition. Just waiting to die. I spoke to her, tried to understand. She told me that she was a spirit amongst the living. I asked her how she'd died, and she didn't know. Didn't know anything except that she was dead. A few days after she was admitted, one of the nurses got fed up with her smell—she would just defecate and urinate on the spot—and lost her cool. Literally screamed at the patient to clean herself up. And she did. It was eerie the way the woman listened."

Kill.

The word comes from nowhere and everywhere and it fills every putrid pore and every fetid cavity.

Kill.

Chase squeezed her eyes together tightly.

"So, you think that this girl was told to kill me?"

When there was no answer, she opened her eyes. The doctor was again moving his head in a noncommittal circular gesture.

"I... it's nearly impossible to perform a psych eval at this point, but if she has Cotard's, then maybe. Someone in her state... she would have no intrinsic motivation. None. That being said, if her hallucinations and delusions are powerful enough, then there is another option."

"Which is?"

"She might have thought you a demon."

Chase scoffed then winced at the pain in her throat.

"She's not wrong."

Kill.

But the white dress had Chase leaning toward the first option.

"There are many things about Cotard's that aren't known, considering how rare it is and the diversity of symptoms."

"Wait a second. If she was told to kill me, then —" Chase stopped and raised her hand to her throat.

Dr. Heinlin frowned.

"If we are proceeding with that assumption, then, yes, she was likely instructed to kill herself, as well. Luckily, she wasn't good at either."

This case had gone from bizarre and now verged on the supernatural.

Her thoughts suddenly went not to the girl in the alley who had attacked her, but to the vagrant who had killed Roger.

And the moment her skin had touched the corpse in the morgue.

Chase had been instantly overwhelmed by the void, the darkness. The complete and utter emptiness of it all.

Cerebrum had done nothing to change her opinion on religion, or life and death, for that matter.

Why hadn't I seen it sooner?

The woman's unspoken expression of death was fairly close to Chase's expectations.

Darkness.

No, not darkness. The notion of darkness suggests the presence of light.

There is no light.

There is nothing.

At the time, Chase had thought that her voodoo was broken. Now, she wasn't so sure.

Could it be that her subconscious had picked up on something? The idea that the girl—based on her appearance and smell, prior to her death—thought she was dead?

Chase shook her head slowly from side to side, which ignited the pain in her throat. But rather than distract her, this focused her thoughts and rooted her in the present.

Dr. Matteo would be so fucking proud.

"Doc, you said that this was a rare disease. Exactly how rare is it?"

Dr. Heinlin blew air.

"*Extremely.* It's more common in younger people, women, primarily, who have a history of depression, anxiety, substance abuse, that sort of thing. There's also..." he trailed off as if not comfortable discussing this anymore.

"What?"

"Chase, much of what I've told you so far is just general medical knowledge. And doctor-patient confidentiality..."

Chase glared at the man. She couldn't believe that he was pulling this card now.

"Okay, okay, I guess because she doesn't actually have herpes..." it was as if the doctor was trying to convince himself to continue speaking. He did a decent job of it, too. "We found metabolites of a popular herpes medication in the woman's blood."

Chase's jaw fell open.

"Like I said," Dr. Heinlin continued slowly, "she doesn't have herpes. I did a quick literature review and discovered that there are reports of a rare, but real, side effect of valacyclovir treatment."

It suddenly clicked.

"Cotard's syndrome," Chase whispered.

"Yeah, rare, but..."

Chase stopped listening.

"My phone! I need my phone!"

"It's—"

Chase reached for the side table and pushed her badge and wallet aside, the former of which fell to the floor. Her fingers found her phone and she immediately brought it to her ear.

"Floyd? Floyd!"

Chapter 43

"GET IN."

Tate leaned over and opened the passenger door.

Floyd jumped into the car and then held up the bag from the *E-Tronics* freezer.

Tate looked at it, then at Floyd.

"Had an outbreak, did you?"

Floyd chuckled despite himself. Then he glanced at the bag. It contained more than forty cardboard boxes with 'Valacyclovir Tablets, USP, 1 gram' written on them.

"Something like that."

Tate pulled away from the curb so violently that Floyd was thrust back into his seat.

"In a rush?"

"Meh, haven't slept in a while."

Once they were on the road, Floyd told Tate about the woman who had broken into *E-Tronics* and ran. He showed his partner the two key rings and the process by which he'd come to find the drugs. He also explained that he was sure the woman was there looking for them.

"Was she a zombie?" Tate asked.

"What? Oh, no, she seemed normal."

"Huh," Tate said to himself.

"What did you—"

"Check this out." Tate tossed a photograph in Floyd's direction.

He looked at it.

"Hey, that—hold on."

Floyd got out the photo that Chase had taken from Roger's trailer. He compared the faces of the two women.

"They're the same."

"Yep. Margaret said that this girl, the one in the photo, whose name happens to be Becca, was basically adopted by Henry and Roger. She said they took her in, cleaned her up, all that kinda shit."

Floyd wasn't surprised that the head of the homeless shelter had shared so much more information with Tate than him. After all, that was the man's specialty. Still, it was a little annoying.

Floyd brought the photo that Tate had given him close to his face. The girl had dirt smeared on her cheeks and her hair appeared greasy. Her eyes—it was tough to tell from the image—but to Floyd, they looked vacant.

"And we're sure she that this Becca isn't the one who killed Roger? I mean, it wouldn't be the first time—"

"According to Chase, DNA has ruled that out."

Neither man spoke for a good three minutes until Tate said, "What do you think is going on here, Floyd?"

His partner's voice was strange, prompting Floyd to look over at him. Tate was staring straight ahead, tiny wrinkles forming around his eyes as he squinted.

"I don't—" Floyd stopped himself. This wasn't an inquisition; this wasn't even Tate playing a role. This was his partner asking for an opinion. "You said that they adopted her?"

Tate shrugged and he rubbed the corners of his mustache.

"Unofficially."

"All right," Floyd took a deep breath. "Roger and Henry run a successful electronics store and spend their free time volunteering at the shelter. They meet a young girl, a young sick and disturbed girl, and they help her get cleaned up. Bring her into their home. But then something happens. Roger and Henry's fairytale relationship hits a bump—they have a big fight, and separate. Henry gets all the cash, while Roger gets relegated to the trailer. Then… Roger is murdered."

Tate dramatically raised one eyebrow and then popped his tongue into his cheek.

"Ninety percent of what you just told me isn't theory. It's fact."

Floyd couldn't argue.

"Okay, smart guy, what do you think happened?"

Tate's eyes drifted back to the road.

"I buy everything you said, District Attorney Montgomery, but I would like to add to your theory. Let me pose a question? What was the fight about? The one that sent Henry and Roger to different ends of the socioeconomic spectrum? Money troubles? Not for Henry, anyway. So, what—"

"The girl," Floyd blurted. "Becca ran away. The adopted child runs away, and—"

Tate was shaking his head.

"—what?"

"No, not ran away," Tate countered. "Remember, they unofficially adopted her. I don't think her running away would be a big enough event for them to separate so dramatically. I think Becca died."

Floyd slumped back in his seat.

"You can't assume—"

"Sure, I can—Becca died. She died and then the two men separated. For some reason, maybe Henry has the bigger cock, he got the house while Roger got the fucking shanty. And— here's the kicker, Floyd—to add insult to injury, Henry has Roger killed."

Floyd said nothing for a good ten seconds.

"I retell facts and you just completely make shit up? Is this how it works? Okay, I'll play along. Let's, for a moment, ignore the most bizarre facts of this case—that a corpse killed Roger and then offed herself—why would Henry want to kill Roger? Wouldn't it be more logical the other way around? Given their relative financial situations?"

Tate had no answer for this. Either that, or he just wanted his theory to fester. And it did. Floyd found himself seeking an answer to the question that he'd formulated.

Nothing came to mind until they pulled into Henry's driveway and the rental's headlights illuminated the front door.

"The cat," Floyd whispered.

"What's that now?"

"The cat," Floyd repeated.

"Yeah, the cat, sure."

Tate started to open his door, but Floyd grabbed his arm. He didn't know why this idea had stuck in his brain, but it wasn't ready to work its way out just yet.

"You—" he shook his head. "No, I asked why Henry would kill Roger. In the store, there was a litter box—full. Same thing in Roger's trailer. And remember when we came here to—"

"You mean a cat burglar?" Tate said, freeing himself from Floyd's grasp and exiting the car.

"No, what the fuck's wrong with you? Not a cat burglar, but an actual cat. You know, *meow, meow?*"

Tate raised a finger and pointed towards the side of Henry's house.

"That's a cat burglar trying to break into Henry's house. You know, like, *meow, meow,* only bigger and more human."

Floyd leaped from the car and then immediately broke into a run.

"It's Martin," he yelled over his shoulder. "It's the fucking cook!"

Chapter 44

CHASE CURSED AS SHE HUNG up her phone, wondering why the hell Floyd wasn't answering. It was late, but it wasn't *that* late. He hadn't checked up on her at all—they had parted hours ago, and he hadn't so much as texted.

He didn't know about her collapse, about the new sutures. And he definitely didn't know about the link between her would-be murderer and the drug that seemed to be popping up everywhere.

Chase tried her partner one more time and when he still didn't answer, she changed her mind. She didn't need to talk to Floyd.

"I need to talk to *her*," Chase said almost absently. Dr. Heinlin, who had since started reviewing her vitals when it was clear that their conversation had been cut short, now looked at her.

"You talking to me?"

"Yeah, I need to speak with the girl who stabbed me."

"She's stable and improving, so I don't mind. But it's not really up to me, anymore."

"What do you mean?" Chase asked.

"The police," he said simply, and Chase understood.

She couldn't imagine that the girl had lawyered up, but it was unlikely that the cops were taking any chances given her precarious mental state.

"I also think that you should—" Dr. Heinlin threw his hands up. "Fuck it."

"Yeah, fuck it," Chase said with a grin. Audrey and Dr. Heinlin were evidently quick character studies.

Save your breath, people.

"Just take it easy, I can only stitch you up so many times."

The pain was such that Chase stopped smiling as she got out of bed. She was surprised to see that Audrey, or maybe it had been Dr. Heinlin, had changed her out of her street clothes. All she was wearing now was her bra and underwear and another ill-fitting hospital gown.

Her shirt and pants were draped over the back of a chair, and she picked them up. The pants were fine, but the shirt was a mess. Blood covered it from collar to nipple on the left side.

"Fuck it," she said, electing to remain dressed in her current outfit. "Is the girl still in the ICU?"

Dr. Heinlin shook his head.

"She's been downgraded—she's at the end of the hall. You can't miss her because of Charleston's finest sitting outside the door."

Chase peeked into the hall and while she could see the cop, his back was to her.

"Young or old?"

"Young guy."

"Good. All right, wish me luck."

"I wish you'd stay in bed," Dr. Heinlin remarked, but she was already out of the room and walking toward the police officer.

When she neared, the cop, the same as the other night, straightened, and, for a moment, Chase thought he was going to salute her.

She suppressed a smirk.

"I need to speak to her."

The officer gave her the up-down.

"Wh-what happened to you?"

"You know what happened to me."

"Yes, uhh, sorry."

"Can I speak to her?"

The cop squinted one eye.

"We've read her rights and she's refused a lawyer."

Chase said nothing.

"Right, you're FBI, you know all this." His eye opened all the way. "I don't see a problem with it. She's also restrained."

The cop scuttled out of the way and Chase peered through the glass. She had to get on her tiptoes to see.

The bubble was gone and the girl was now sitting on the side of her bed. Her right wrist was handcuffed to the frame. She was staring blankly ahead.

Even after Chase entered the room and closed the door behind her, the girl didn't acknowledge her presence. But it was perhaps this fact that confirmed to her that a mistake hadn't been made. Because the person in this room was very different from the girl in the bubble.

For one, she wasn't dirty. The thick layers of grime and dirt were gone from her skin. Her hair appeared damp, but it had recently been combed. Like Chase, she was wearing a fresh hospital gown.

Chase continued to observe the woman—girl, she was a teenager—as she approached.

While Chase had deduced that her attacker had been Caucasian based on her features, for some reason, she didn't expect for her to be this pale. And petite.

Chase herself was a small woman, but the girl on the bed made her look like a linebacker.

Never one for niceties and formalities, Chase wasn't about to start now.

"Who told you to kill me?"

The girl shuddered slightly, or perhaps this was just an unrelated tremor, but didn't answer. She still wouldn't look up, either. Her eyes were strangely locked on the metal cuff on her wrist.

"I asked you a question," Chase said, taking a step forward. She felt the aggressive movement in her throat. "Two nights ago, you tried to kill me. I want to know why."

Still nothing.

Chase took another step forward. She was within touching distance now and reached to do just that. A second before she made contact, however, the girl raised her eyes and Chase stopped.

Despite her bony features, she was pretty. Chase thought that if she was at a healthier weight, she'd be knocking on the door of beautiful. It was just her eyes that held her back. They were a dull brown. Chase wasn't the type of person to believe in romantic notions such as a twinkle in one's eye, but there was a flatness that she'd seen in many of the people whom she'd put away over the years that couldn't be ignored.

And most recently in that asshole Brian Jalston's eyes.

Chase was so taken aback by this asepticism, that she momentarily forgot that she was interrogating this girl.

"Why did you try to kill me? Why did you try to kill yourself?"

"I don't know," the girl said in such a soft voice that Chase wasn't sure if she'd heard correctly.

"Excuse me?"

The girl blinked once, twice, and then her chest rose and fell. It was strangely like watching a newborn trapped in an adult body learn how to blink, breathe, and speak.

"I don't know," she said again. "I don't know who you are. I don't... I don't know who *I* am."

Kill.

Chase instinctively looked down at herself, at the wound on her neck. It wasn't bleeding through, but it felt as if it should be.

Kill.

The lightheaded feeling that she'd thought was behind her, returned. Chase reached out, but not to touch the girl.

To grab the bed and steady herself.

Kill.

"But you were…" Chase took a deep breath. "But you were told to kill me, weren't you?"

Kill.

For a long moment, the girl said nothing and Chase thought that she'd gone back to her catatonic state. But then she did that two-blink and a breath thing and, in an eerie, chilling voice, said, "Yes, someone told me to kill you."

And all of a sudden, Chase was back in the void.

"I do not eat, for I am dead. I do not sleep, for I am dead. I do not bathe, for I am dead."

Her liver is decomposed, her brain encephalitic. Her lungs, fibrotic. Her skin, ulcerative.

"Kill."

Chapter 45

WITH HIS THIGHS AND HAND burning from Matzo ball soup or whatever the hell it was, Floyd had no chance of catching Martin.

But now? Outside on a temperate night feeling refreshed? Floyd had no issue catching Martin even though the man had a good twenty-yard head start.

It didn't hurt that Martin was pushing three hundred pounds.

"Stop!" he shouted. "Stop!"

This was mostly for ceremony. He didn't expect Martin to stop, and unlike the altercation in the alley behind *E-Tronics*, or maybe because of it, Floyd had no intention of pulling his gun.

He just kept running, pumping his arms and legs and within twenty strides, he caught Martin the homeless shelter cook. The first option he considered was tripping Martin. Just throwing his right toe out and connecting with Martin's right heel, sending it careening into his opposite leg. But that would feel wholly unsatisfying given what he'd been through, and the layers of skin that he'd lost.

Instead, Floyd did something he'd always wanted to try but, until now, never had the opportunity.

He dove headlong into the man, driving his shoulder into Martin's lower back, while at the same time wrapping his arms around him. A perfect tackle.

The landing was surprisingly cushioned, at least for Floyd.

Martin, on the other hand, had a less than graceful fall. The man's giant gut struck the patio stones just at the rear of Henry's house. He released a guttural cry as his momentum carried him forward, but his belly was glued to the concrete. Floyd nearly flew over the top of him but held on for dear life.

He might have also helped Martin's forehead smack off the grass when the whip became lashed.

Floyd, surprised that he was completely uninjured and strangely invigorated, sat up and tried to spin Martin around.

That was a no-go.

The man was simply too heavy.

"Need a hand there, John Cena?" Tate asked, gracing them both with his presence. He didn't seem out of breath, so Floyd assumed he'd just walked from the car. He didn't get the reference, either.

"Yeah, let's roll him over."

It took both of their collective efforts and even then, it was difficult. Martin grunted, and his belly sloshed back and forth like a liquid ballast. The front of his shirt was dotted with blood from the chest down and Floyd winced, thinking about the road rash beneath the man's flimsy T.

"Hey, Martin, fancy meeting you here. Have any soup?" Tate asked.

Martin moaned.

"Never mind."

"Get up," Floyd instructed. Rolling the man was one thing, picking him up was out of the question. "Get the fuck up."

Martin licked his lips, groaned, and then started the rather laborious process of pulling his girth off the ground. Twice, he wobbled, but like one of those punching bags that always returns to center, didn't fall.

"Why did you run back at the shelter?" Floyd demanded.

Martin's eyes rolled back, and he put one hand on his forehead.

Tate slapped him.

This, like Floyd's tackle, was something that he'd never witnessed in real life.

It was more a medieval challenge slap than an attempt to injure, but it did the trick. Lucidity returned to Martin's eyes.

"Martin, my man. Why'd you run?" Tate asked this time.

"I—what? I—"

Tate threatened with an open palm.

"The picture..." Martin stammered.

Now that he seemed willing to talk, Tate no longer appeared interested. Floyd watched his partner look around and then point at the side entrance to Henry's house.

"You know what? I feel kinda tired from all that running you guys did. And you look like you could use a chair. What do you say we head inside and get more comfortable?"

The question had been posed to the fat man in the Disney T-shirt but had been intended for Floyd.

Floyd looked at the side door.

"This is your house, isn't it, Martin?" Tate said.

"It's—"

Floyd cuffed the man on the back of the head. It was another thing he'd never done before, and it felt good.

"He said let's talk inside. And I'm just going to assume that this is your house, given that you were trying to get in."

Once more, Martin looked as if he was about to speak but was dissuaded by some unforeseen force. Or maybe it was Floyd's cupped hand and Tate's open one.

"Okay, okay. I'm going. The door's unlocked."

Floyd deemed this speech acceptable and didn't lash out.

"Isn't that convenient," Tate said. Then he gestured with his slapping hand. "Why don't you lead the way? Oh, and it would be wonderful if you invited us inside, Martin. And while I'm not particularly hungry, if you have any soup simmering on the stove, I'm sure my partner, Floyd, would love a little taste."

Chapter 46

SHE WASN'T LYING. CHASE KNEW from the moment she started to talk to the girl that everything she said was the truth. She wondered briefly if this was another symptom of Cotard's syndrome and considered that perhaps it was.

But that didn't matter.

Chase knew that she was telling the truth because those strange flat eyes told her so.

It seemed inconceivable that the person before her was the same one who had tried to kill her, a filthy vagrant with no regard for human life including her own.

"The person who told you to kill me… do you know what they look like? Were they a man or a woman?"

The bridge of the girl's nose crinkled. She was still confused and frustrated with her inability to recall.

"I don't remember."

Chase was equally as frustrated, but the anger she'd felt moments ago was gone. Being furious at this girl would be tantamount to admonishing a hammer that fell on your toe.

"I saw a picture of you, and I was told to kill you. Then I was told to kill myself."

There was something incredibly off-putting about her cavalier nature. Chase had come across some of the most savage killers that the world had ever seen, but this level of insouciance was unparalleled.

"A picture…" Chase tongued the inside of her cheek as she thought about this. "A picture of me?"

The girl nodded. This must have been the way that Dr. Griffith and Roger had also been targeted.

And the message was likely the same: kill the person in the picture, then kill yourself.

"What about before?" Chase asked. "Do you remember anything about before you got sick?"

"I—" The girl blinked slowly, and Chase thought she might have triggered something in her. She hadn't. "I don't know."

"Are you sure? Can you remember where you came from? Who your parents are, siblings, anything like that? What about your name? Do you know your name?"

The girl shook her head. She was beginning to look overwhelmed.

"Can you remember anything before you saw my picture?"

"No—sorry. Everything was just... *dark.*"

Darkness.

No, not darkness. The notion of darkness suggests the presence of light.

There is no light.

There is nothing.

Chase ground her teeth.

"You can't remember *anything* from when you were a kid?"

Despite her firsthand experience with traumatic experiences reshaping her mind and memories, Chase was having a hard time keeping herself from becoming annoyed.

How could you forget *everything*?

"I'm sorry. I really don't remember anything."

The girl looked down at her hands then and Chase saw that they were trembling.

"I just don't—I don't remember."

The door behind them opened and Chase expected it to be the police officer saying he changed his mind or that his shift was done and that the new officer said she had to leave. But it wasn't a cop. It was the doctor.

"She needs to rest," Dr. Heinlin said, placing a hand on Chase's shoulder. Chase instinctively pulled away.

"She doesn't remember anything. How can that be? Co-tard's... when do you usually get sick?"

The doctor looked at the girl then at Chase.

"Not sure. Usually teens, though."

"And is she going to remember anything? She's clearly get-ting better."

Once more, Dr. Heinlin glanced at the patient.

"Can we discuss—"

"I need to know. Will she—"

This time when the doctor grabbed her arm and guided her toward the door, there was no shaking him off.

"Probably. That's the best I can do, Agent Adams. Now, she needs her rest and so do you."

Chase left the room and acknowledged the officer with a nod. Then she looked back through the glass insert in the door.

The girl was once again staring down at her cuffed wrist as if confused by how it got there. Chase felt a strange kinship with this girl, a bizarre Stockholm syndrome where kidnapping had been usurped for attempted murder.

She also felt bad for her.

Because Chase knew what it was like to feel lost and con-fused, to be so completely alone in this world that it felt as if you were alone on an island.

"You should rest," the doctor advised for a second time. His eyes drifted to her chest, and Chase followed his gaze.

She was bleeding again.

"Yeah," she whispered. "I think I will rest, if only for a short while."

Chapter 47

FLOYD GRABBED THE FIRST CHAIR he saw, an old wooden one, and spun it around. Then he shoved Martin into it. The man collapsed hard and leaned forward at the last second to avoid toppling.

"Should we cuff him?" Floyd asked, his eyes never leaving Martin's shirt, which was smeared with blood and reeked of soup.

Tate shook his head.

"He's not going anywhere, are you, Martin?"

A wide-eyed Martin shook his head.

"Good." To Floyd's surprise, he felt embarrassed by what happened back at the soup kitchen, about how he'd been bested by this slob. "Now, Martin, you're going to tell me why you ran."

Martin's expression suddenly went hard.

"I don't have to tell you nothin'. And this ain't—"

Floyd placed his hands on the chair's armrests and leaned in close to Martin's doughy face.

"You're right, Martin, you don't have to. But you will. You will, because if you fucking don't, then I'll—"

A strong hand came down on his shoulder and Floyd, fists balled, turned around.

"Allow me, Floyd," Tate said. Floyd was surprised at himself and how close he'd come to actually striking the man. Cuffing him in the back of the head was one thing. Bare-knuckle pummeling him was another. And he'd been on the verge. "Please, allow me."

Scowling, Floyd forced his fingers straight and then backed away, palms up. He wasn't sure if they were doing the classic 'good cop, bad cop' routine or if Tate was just saving him from a broken knuckle or two.

"Martin, we haven't met yet. My name is Tate, and I'm with the FBI. My partner, Floyd, you've already met. He's the one you threw hot soup on. Now, I know —"

"That was an accident," Martin pleaded. "The soup just spilled."

"Yeah, fucking right. There's —"

Tate hushed him.

"An accident, sure, whatever. To be honest, I don't give a shit about that." Floyd wanted to complain, to insist that he really did give a shit about that, but he bit his tongue. Tate was working now, and it was in his best interest to observe and learn. "Really, I don't. And I think my partner can get over it, too. The only thing I care about," Tate snapped his fingers behind his back. It took Floyd a good ten seconds to realize what his partner wanted. Floyd quickly pulled the photograph out of his pocket and handed it over. Tate proceeded to remove a second photograph from his jeans and held them both in front of Martin's face. "Is this girl. Who is she, Martin?"

Martin looked at the two photos, then quickly glanced at his shoes.

He's afraid, Floyd realized. *Martin's afraid of something.*

But what?

"I don't know," he said.

Tate just held the photos out until Martin was compelled to look at them again. Then he said, "Martin, you *know*. Why you're trying to play me like a fool is beyond me, but you know." Tate sighed and tucked both photos back into his pocket. "I'll admit it, Martin. You're in control here. Look, if I'm honest? We're probably going to book you. But any lawyer worth his salt, and that includes state-appointed ones, will get you to plead no contest to the soup spilling incident. We might get the DA to bite on a resisting charge because you ran, but what's that going to amount to? Six months' probation, if that? What you think, Floyd?"

Tate looked back at Floyd expectantly. Floyd wasn't happy about this development, but he had a role to play. And Tate was probably speaking the truth.

Depending on history, Martin might get six months in county and not probation, but that was a big if.

Floyd nodded.

"So, you're the one in control, Martin. You can tell us who this girl is and why we found you here at Henry Saburra's house, and we can talk about it. It's up to you."

Neither of the three men said anything, and Floyd thought that Tate's empowerment tactic would fail.

But then Martin's fat lips started to tremble, and he looked down. When he started talking, his voice was so low that Floyd had to lean in close to listen.

"I don't know who the girl is. I mean, I heard about her, but I never seen her."

"What did you hear about her?" Tate prompted in an equally soft tone.

Martin's bulbous shoulders lifted, then fell.

"I heard that she was like a kid to them, Henry and Roger, I mean. She was all fucked up, when she came in, dirty n' shit. Then they gave her a place to stay… you know."

Martin shrugged again.

"Any idea where she is now?" Tate asked.

"Naw. No idea."

Tate was satisfied with this answer, and he pulled out a third photograph. Even from behind, Floyd could see that this was of the girl who had killed Roger. Floyd's heart did a little flutter when he thought about whether or not Martin knew that Roger was dead. His anxiety started rising, even though he knew that this was irrational—*more* irrational than usual. Not only was the relationship between the deceased and the cook unknown, but the latter had literally spilled soup on Floyd and run away.

Twice.

"What about this girl?" Tate asked.

Instead of a shrug this time, Martin swallowed really hard. The man's trembling lips were now moving like swollen, plucked violin strings.

"Martin, now's your chance."

Martin sucked air through his teeth.

"I didn't do nothin'," he whispered. "I don't know what they was up to, but I didn't do nothin'."

Floyd knew they were close now. *'I didn't do nothin''* was the universal precursor to a confession. It was like when someone leads with a compliment that ends in 'but'. None of the words before the 'but' mattered.

Martin sighed heavily and a drop of drool formed on his bottom lip and hung precariously.

"Roger just asked me to tell him if, like, a girl came in, you know?"

Floyd didn't know, but he nodded, nonetheless.

"What did Roger want with these girls?" Tate asked.

"Roger *and* Henry—I dunno. He was helping them, I guess. I know what you're thinking, but he wasn't fuckin' 'em. Man's queer as they come. Roger just said if a girl comes in, real dirty-like, stinkin' like shit, confused, but not an addict, to call him. That's what I did. I seen what he did wit' the other girl," Martin nodded in the direction of Tate's pocketed photographs. "Helped her out. Got her fixed up. So, what the fuck? Every time someone like that came in, I called him, and he gave me a couple bucks, man. That's all."

Something wasn't making sense.

"So, let me get this straight," Tate said. "Roger and Henry ask you to recruit underage girls —"

"Wha —? No — Underage?"

"Okay, fine, of age girls, who aren't addicts but who are dirty. That about right?"

Martin's upper lip curled.

"Okay, I'm guessing that's about right," Tate concluded. "Why does he — why do *they* want the girls?"

"I dunno."

"C'mon, Martin," Tate pleaded.

"I said, I dunno."

"Martin, Martin, Martin," Tate stood up tall and stretched his lower back. "You gotta give me something."

Martin shook his head and Tate turned to Floyd.

"Should we tell him?"

"Tell me what?" Martin asked, his voice increasing an octave.

Floyd, not sure what Tate was referring to, just went with it. "Tell him."

"Okay," Tate looked at Martin. "Roger's dead."

Floyd watched Martin's reaction closely. His pupils dilated. "What?"

Tate nodded.

"Yep. Roger's dead — he was murdered."

Martin's eyelids pulled back now, and he had the appearance of a drunken doe.

"You think that's a surprise?"

Floyd felt his neck muscles tighten.

"Get this," Tate continued. "He was murdered by..." Tate pulled out the photo of the girl from the morgue again. "Tada! This girl! The one you recruited."

Martin was flabbergasted.

"This—what? No. No, can't be, bro. They fuckin' try to help and she kills Roger? What about Henry?"

"Henry's fine... well, I think he's fine. But here's the thing— you know how I said you'd get probation for Soupgate?"

Martin did something that might be construed as a nod.

"Well, this here," he tapped the photo of the dead girl, "is murder and that makes you—"

"An accomplice," Floyd blurted.

Martin looked at him and his chin rose rapidly as if he were struggling to swallow a bolus of food.

"No."

"Yes," Tate countered.

"Man—I don't fucking know... I just... I was trying to help?"

"You can still help," Tate said. "By telling us what you're holding back."

"I don't know anything, man! What happened to Roger is fucked up. But I didn't have nothin' to do with that! What's it gonna take for—"

"Valacyclovir," Floyd said suddenly.

Tate and Martin both looked at him.

"The herpes drug," he said, recalling the bottle he'd found among Martin's possessions.

Martin threw his head back as if remembering some long-lost secret.

"Oh. Yeah, I gave the girls the pills, man. Roger said—naw, Henry, it was Henry—he said, in case they had STDs, you know? Help get 'em on their way to be cleaned up. It wasn't nothin'. I even Googled it, man, just to make sure it wasn't poison or something."

"Ah, there you go," Tate said. "One more thing, Martin."

"What?"

"Why are you here?"

"What do you mean?"

Tate waved his hands about.

"In Henry's house. Why are you here?"

"Because you—"

"No, because you were already breaking in when we arrived."

Martin frowned.

"When I saw you," he indicated Floyd, "with the picture, I knew something was up."

"But you didn't know that Roger was dead, right?"

Martin puffed his cheeks.

"Naw, I didn't but, look, a cop, or a fed, comes in and starts waving pictures around? Only means one thing. I told you everything, man, for real."

Maybe it was his anxiety, but Floyd couldn't tell whether Martin was telling the truth or not. Tate seemed on the fence, too, because he didn't say anything for some time.

Floyd used this opportunity to look around a little. The first thing that struck him was that, unlike Roger's place, this was clean. Nothing else was of note, except for a photo on the fridge.

It was the same one that Chase had taken from Roger's house.

"Okay, Martin. I believe you. Just a tip: you should stick around town for a while, in case we have more questions for you."

Tate grabbed Floyd by the arm and led him outside.

"Tate, what the hell? We can't—"

"Leave him," Tate said. "He doesn't know anything else."

"But he—"

"Yeah, he spilled some soup on you. Get over it. We have more important shit to figure out. Like where the fuck Henry Saburra is. And how many other girls he's trying to 'help'."

Chapter 48

SOMETIME IN THE MIDDLE OF the night, there was a knock at Chase's door. She startled awake and watched Dr. Heinlin enter.

"I'm sorry to wake you, Agent Adams."

"Call me Chase. None of this 'Agent Adams' bullshit."

Dr. Heinlin looked exhausted, and Chase wondered how many hours of sleep the man was currently working on. Every time she turned around, he seemed to be there.

"Okay, Chase. I know that I told you to sleep, but Jane Doe is asking for you. She's... agitated and I'm worried that in her current state she might harm herself. I can't sedate her—her kidneys are overtaxed as it is from the valacyclovir. Do you think you could...?"

"I'll talk to her," Chase agreed. She pushed herself to a seated position and then the doctor helped her off the bed. The pain that had once been isolated to her throat had spread downward and she saw bruising that covered nearly all of her left breast.

"I changed the dressing while you were asleep," Dr. Heinlin remarked, noticing her gaze. "No signs of infection."

Chase nodded.

She wasn't in any shape to argue or strong-arm a police officer, even one straight out of the academy, but she didn't have to: the cop stationed at the door was fast asleep.

"Please," Dr. Heinlin said softly so as to not wake the officer. "I just need her to relax, preferably to get some sleep."

Again, Chase nodded.

Something in the man's face suggested that he was already regretting this decision, but it was too late to turn back now.

Chase opened the door and stepped inside.

Jane Doe immediately looked up, her eyes wild and face animated.

"Agent—Agent—FBI—I—"

"Chase, my name is Chase."

"Oh, okay, Chase, I-I-I-"

There was color on the girl's face, but it wasn't good color. It was almost glowing red.

"Calm down," Chase urged. "Take a deep breath."

"But I—"

Chase held her hand up.

"I'm not going anywhere. Just take a deep breath and try to relax."

The girl did the best she could. She shuddered on the exhale, but the color in her cheeks became less intense.

"Okay, good, that's good. Now, what do you want to tell me?"

"I remember," the girl said absently. "I remember who told me to kill you."

Chase shivered.

"It was Henry, wasn't it?"

The girl's eyes widened.

"I-I don't know who that is."

Now, Chase told herself to calm down.

Just let her speak.

"I'm sorry, go ahead." Behind her, Chase felt Dr. Heinlin's presence as he silently entered the room. "Don't worry about him, just tell me what you remember."

The girl's breathing picked up, and her eyes couldn't stay focused on either one of them for very long.

"Everything's still... I remember it being dark. But not like outside," Jane's eyes flicked to the window.

Darkness.

No, not darkness. The notion of darkness suggests the presence of light.

There is no light.

There is nothing.

"It kinda pushed against me, you know? The darkness," the girl continued. "It feels like your ears are plugged and it's hard to breathe. Like you want to fill your lungs with air, but you can't. They don't inflate because there is nothing to inflate. You're just—you're just not there. I don't—I can't explain it. But you don't exist."

Chase was reminded of the similarities between this strange rhetoric and what she'd felt at the morgue.

The girl took a deep breath—no shudder this time—before continuing.

"But then, just when you think you're all alone, someone talks to you. Not—not talks, no, that's not it. It's more like it's in your head. The voice is coming from nowhere and every-where... I-I can't—"

"It's fine," Chase soothed. "I get it."

And she did. It wasn't just her experience in the morgue, ei-ther. What the girl was describing was a dissociative experience that all junkies strive for, whether they know it or not.

The girl nodded.

"You have to listen. *I* have to listen. Because... because there's nothing else. Do you understand? You don't exist. And it doesn't matter. Nothing matters. You just... you just do what-ever the voice tells you to do. I-I didn't—I—"

Dr. Heinlin started forward, but Chase beat him to the bed.

The girl sniffed and wiped tears from her face.

"I'm okay, I'm okay," the woman said, holding up her hand. "It's just—none of it matters because you're not even alive. You're dead. You've always been dead, and you always will be." The girl was suddenly not okay. She broke down and began to sob, her body quivering violently. "I didn't want to hurt anyone, I didn't want to kill anyone."

Chase moved on instinct. She reached out and hugged the mess of a girl in front of her. Her body was tiny, and she could feel her ribs and spine jutting through her flesh. Chase held her until the girl's breathing began to regulate.

"I'm sorry," Jane Doe said, dabbing her nose and mouth with her hospital gown.

She looked so young and lost that Chase couldn't help but be reminded of her own life when she'd been that age. A Narc who was lured into a trap house that had taken her decades to crawl out of.

"Don't be sorry. This isn't your fault."

"But I tried to—" the girl's voice hitched.

"It's okay," Chase repeated. And she meant it—she wasn't going to hold what happened against her. "Just tell me what you remember. Who told you to kill me?"

"It wasn't Henry or whatever you said his name was. Everything is still foggy, but it couldn't have been Henry."

"Why not?" Chase asked.

"Because it was a woman."

Chase stiffened.

She had not been expecting this.

"She was tall, brown hair, I think."

Chase was trying to stay cool, but when she spoke next, her voice was tight.

"Do you remember her name?"

To her dismay, the girl shook her head.

"I don't remember her name, but I remember mine... at least, I think I do." The next word that came out of the girl's mouth made Chase freeze completely. "Riley. I think my name is Riley."

This can't be, Chase thought. *It* can't *be.*

"I wish I could remember her name, but I can't. But that's my name... Riley."

As Chase tried to wrap her mind around what was happening, the girl dropped another bomb.

"She was... she was wearing a white dress. A long, white dress. And she told me that I had to wear it when I tried to kill you, Chase."

Chapter 49

"YOU'RE SERIOUSLY LETTING HIM GO?" Floyd said as they got into the car. He thought that this was another of Tate's tactics to gain more information, one he'd never seen him utilize yet, but that didn't seem to be the case.

"Where's he gonna go?"

"I don't know. *Away*. He attacked me and set up those girls."

"I know what he did," Tate replied as he started to drive. "I also know what he *didn't* do. Trust me on this one. He's not the mastermind here."

"Then who is?"

"Henry, I think."

Floyd watched Henry's house fade in the distance.

"The fuck is going on here, Tate? Why is he giving them herpes meds? You think he's... sleeping with them? Auctioning them off? I-I don't know."

Tate shook his head.

"I'm not sure, either. Let's think about it over a drink."

"I'm tired," Floyd said, sinking into his seat. "Really tired."

"Sleep when you're dead," Tate blurted and then immediately took back his words. "Sheesh, sorry, slipped out. Call the local PD and get an APB out on Henry's car. We need to talk to that man."

Floyd did as he was asked, which required fewer hoops to jump through than he expected. He also noted that he had several missed calls from Chase, but no messages. When he was off the phone, he was calmer than before.

"Back there, at Henry's house, how did you know that strong-arming Martin wouldn't work?"

Tate kept his eyes on the road when he answered.

"I don't want to come off as sounding condescending, but when I was a younger agent, Constantine gave me the best piece of advice I ever received."

"Shoot."

"Don't be what people *expect* you to be, be what they *want* you to be—what they *need*." Floyd made a face and Tate laughed. "Okay, yeah, I know, it sounds like some mumbo-jumbo. But hear me out. Men like Martin expect to be pushed around, to be bullied. He's been 'strong-armed', as you put it, his whole life. You push, and he just curls into a ball, goes to his happy place, and won't reveal a thing." Tate paused, allowing time for Floyd to let this sink in. "Instead, he wants to be em-powered. You give him the power, something Martin has never had in his whole life, and not only will he answer your ques-tions, he'll also tell you shit you didn't even know to ask for."

Floyd felt himself nodding.

"But how did you know? How did you know what Martin wanted you to be? You didn't even hesitate."

"Experience," Tate replied.

This, Floyd knew was something he could push back on, and did.

"Bullshit."

Tate offered him his patented half-smirk.

"Some of us have been on this job for more than six minutes, Kemosabe."

"Any practical tips for a beginner?"

"Sure... Martin's job, for one. He's serving food to people, giving him a level of power over them, even though they all sleep at the shelter."

"Yeah, but lots of—"

"Eager! I love eager learners. But why don't you just shut the fuck up so I can speak?" Tate teased.

"Go ahead, Richard Feynman, do continue."

Tate chuckled.

"Love the reference, but I'm no master storyteller or teacher. Anyways, not only was it Martin's job that gave it away, but also the fact that he smelled like soup. He spilled that soup yesterday and hadn't changed yet. This indicates one of two things: either he has no other clothes to change into or has very little regard for himself. I would lean towards the latter, especially given his size. But in this case, both are probably true. And speaking of his size... morbidly obese people often eat as a coping mechanism, a way of exacting some control when everything else seems outside of it. I noticed other things, too, but they're more difficult to explain."

Floyd was impressed and he was suddenly reminded of Chase. They had a lot in common, his current partners. And what Tate was describing wasn't that different from what Chase did. Only, his was a more conscious effort, whereas hers was more... esoteric.

"So, maybe not Feynman level, but how'd I do? Am I a good teacher?"

"Surely, you're joking." Floyd laughed. "Naw, that was pretty good."

"You sure you don't want a drink? You owe me a round, after all."

"For what?"

They neared the hotel and Tate moved as if to pull into the lot. But at the last second, he pumped the accelerator and headed toward a new destination. A place called Harper's Roost, and while neither of them had ever heard of it, it was obvious that it was a bar based on the crowd outside and the lighting. If they'd had the window down, they would have recognized the smell as well.

"For the lesson, Floyd." Tate held up two fingers. "You buy me two rounds, and I'll teach you something else."

Floyd, whose phone was still in his lap, said, "Should we invite Chase?" When Tate didn't say anything, he shook his head. "Naw, better she rests."

Tate clapped him on the back.

"See? You're a quick study—be what Chase needs, not what she expects. Now, let's have a drink."

Chapter 50

A WOMAN IN A LONG WHITE dress...

Everything about this case was wrong. Chase had known it when she first touched the corpse in the morgue.

But this... this was different. Sure, the MO was the same. But the name Riley? The dress? That was Brian Jalston's doing.

Chase didn't know how he was involved in this, but he was.

The Franklin County Jail visitor log had revealed that Melissa Jalston had visited Brian after she'd left.

Did she follow me? Did Brian tell Melissa to follow me?

That didn't just sound reasonable, but plausible. How Melissa had then come in contact with 'Riley' was something she couldn't grasp.

Who is looking out for you, Chase? Anyone? Anyone at all?

The girl on the bed—whose name definitely wasn't Riley—had since laid herself down, but she wasn't sleeping. Her eyes were open, and she was staring blankly at the ceiling.

How many days and nights have I lost over the years? How many times did I get so high that I can't remember if it was Tuesday or Sunday?

Chase felt a strange kinship with the woman, as twisted as that was.

"What's going to happen to her?" she asked.

Dr. Heinlin peered over her shoulder and through the glass.

"Nothing for right now—she's still unfit to do anything."

Yesterday, the girl had been a corpse. Today, something more animated.

"How long until she gets better?"

The doctor was noncommittal.

"Not sure. These things can take time."

"And what about after she's more 'fit'? What happens then?"

"She'll undergo a series of psychiatric assessments. Then it's up to you and—" Dr. Heinlin pointed at the still sleeping officer. "—the police, I suppose."

Chase kicked the officer's foot. He woke and then sat up straight.

"Agent Adams?" his glassy eyes drifted to the doctor. "Is she—"

"She's fine. Ri—" the doctor glanced at Chase, and she corrected himself. "—Jane Doe is getting better."

"Then—"

She cut him off again.

"I want to know every person who comes to visit her," Chase said, her voice flat.

"I don't think she's seeing visitors. You're the only one who has stepped through that door."

"No, you don't get it. I want a list of every person who enters the room. Nurse, doctor, maid, you name it."

Chase had zero authority here—Floyd and Tate had been called in to help with Dr. Wayne Griffith III's murder, which was two cases removed—but she'd learned long ago that when authority was lacking, the need to assert it was even greater.

The officer appeared confused.

"Every single person!" Chase snapped.

"Yes—yes, Agent Adams."

"Good."

Chase ground her teeth against the pain in her chest as she walked away. She made it around the corner before needing to brace herself against the wall.

"Agent Adams, can I ask you something?" Dr. Heinlin said as he waited for her to catch her breath.

"What?" Chase was wheezing a little now.

"Why did you look like you'd seen a ghost when the girl said her name was Riley?"

Because I did, that's why, Chase thought. *I saw a dead girl who became a ghost and adopted the name of my sister. That's why. A name that only one person called Georgina, that's why. And that person just happens to be a pedophile and a rapist, a man who is about to get out of prison in two days. That's why. A man who is trying to steal my niece.* That's fucking why.

"Nothing, just the—" she tapped her chest. "—the pain."

The doctor wasn't buying it, so she gave the man a little of his own medicine.

"I already have a shrink, doc. What I need now is to—" get well enough to be there when Brian gets out, "—sleep."

Unsure if the doctor was following her, Chase shuffled back to her room and collapsed on her bed.

She closed her eyes and visions immediately swirled behind her lids. Visions of her sister, dying in her arms, looking up at her with her bright green eyes. And then everything went black. But this wasn't something to be confused with sleep. This was something different.

This was something that pushed against you, made your ears feel plugged, and made you shiver.

Chase opened her eyes again.

Dr. Heinlin was in the room with her.

"I'm tired, doc. I need to sleep."

An understanding look crossed the doctor's face.

"Any allergies? History with narcotics?"

History? No, of course not. I'm an FBI agent, for crying out loud.

"No. But you might want to make it a double-dose—bad dreams, you know?"

The doctor reattached her IV and then left the room. When he returned, he had a syringe in his hand.

"This should help you sleep."

Dr. Heinlin injected the drug into the port on the IV bag.

There was no instant rush like Chase was used to. No flood of endorphins. This was more muted, and she hoped that the doctor had given her a strong enough dose.

She wasn't a regular patient.

"This isn't something that you want to make a habit of, Agent Adams," the doctor said softly as Chase closed her eyes again. "If these 'bad dreams' as you put it, continue, you really should seek some help."

"Thanks, doc," Chase muttered. "But, as I said, I already have a shrink."

She turned on her side and after a while, she heard the doctor leave.

Sometime after that, sleep did come. But it didn't come alone.

Chapter 51

"**Wakey-wakey, eggs, murder, and** bakey."

Floyd wasn't sure if it was the distasteful rhyme or the hard knock on the door that roused him from his slumber. Either way, he was up in a heartbeat and pulling on his slacks. He didn't have a hangover *per se*, but his throat was parched, and he felt the beginnings of a headache.

"Let's go, Floyd," Tate hollered from behind the door.

"I'm coming, gimme a second."

With the knocks continuing with increased fervor, Floyd opted to pop a piece of gum instead of brushing his teeth. He was still tucking in his shirt when he opened the door.

Tate, looking as fresh as he had the night before, his hair neatly combed, his five o'clock shadow, not a minute past, stood in the doorway, a serious expression on his face.

"What's going on?"

"Come on, let's go," Tate said. He moved quickly and Floyd struggled to keep up.

"Where we going?"

Tate said nothing, he just drove away from the hotel. At first, Floyd thought that they were heading back to Henry's house, that perhaps in addition to an APB the local cops had set up surveillance and the man had come home. But then they turned north, in the direction of *E-Tronics* and the homeless shelter. Floyd could just make out the electronics store when he saw the first cop car.

"What's going on, Tate?"

"It's better if you see for yourself," he said simply.

Floyd was beyond frustrated now, and his headache had bloomed.

"I'm not in the mood for games, Tate. I get that you're trying to teach me something, but for once can you just tell me what the fuck is going on?"

"Oh, a bad word."

"I'm serious, Tate. Tell me—"

Tate pulled over and pointed out his open window.

Two cop cars were parked in front of the alley beside *E-Tron-ics*, a poor attempt at blocking the scene. If this had been a more affluent neighborhood, they probably would have already set up tents by now.

But not here.

Not when the victim was Martin the homeless shelter cook.

The fat man was slumped against the wall, his T-shirt stained with blood as well as soup. There was a wide gash in his neck, one that was nearly hidden by the folds of fat.

Floyd exhaled loudly.

"I told you," Tate said. "Sometimes seeing is believing."

In this case, Floyd tended to agree.

But what he didn't see, at least not until a few moments later, was a second body, on account of Martin's vast belly blocking his view.

But Floyd knew that she would be there. Both men got out of the car and made their way over to the scene.

Tate waved at the first officer they saw.

"Officer Maguire," Tate said with an air of familiarity. "Still no hits on Henry's car?"

The officer shook his head.

"No, sir. Still looking."

"Get your men to check the traffic cameras, see if they can get a hit on his license plate," Tate ordered. "Is there still a car parked outside his house?"

"Discrete, just like you asked," the officer replied. Then he relayed the order to another officer.

Floyd scratched the back of his head. He was still in shock over the fact that Martin had been killed — murdered — but that was only the first of several surprises. Last night, he and Tate had shared several drinks at the bar, talking about benign things to take their minds off the case. It was late when they finally went back to their rooms, and Floyd had passed out immediately.

It appeared as if Tate had continued to work.

Another lesson learned, Floyd thought. *And putting a car outside Henry's house? I should have done that.*

As the officer and Tate continued to discuss their plan to catch Henry, Floyd slipped by the two, and approached a crime scene technician who was hunched over Martin's corpse. When he came near, the tech looked up at him.

"Cause of death is exsanguination," the tech said, pointing at Martin's throat with a gloved finger. "The ME will be able to tell us more, but it looks like it's the same manner of death for... well, for *her*."

The man leaned back, offering a clear view of the murderer: a filthy girl with greasy hair dressed in rags.

The blood that had soaked, and since dried, on her outfit was nearly indistinguishable from the dirt.

Something in Floyd snapped. He spun and hurried back to Tate who was still speaking to the policeman.

"You knew," Floyd said as he grabbed Tate by the collar. Tate was a much larger man than he, and even though Floyd had youth on his side, he wasn't one for fighting. Still, whether it was a surprise or Tate allowing him to be manhandled, the two of them backed all the way up to the police car. "You fucking knew."

Tate's eyes remained even.

"You said last night that he didn't know anything else, that he wasn't going anywhere," Floyd hissed through clenched teeth. "Buy you knew, didn't you? You knew this was going to happen."

Tate remained silent, holding Floyd's gaze.

He wasn't defending himself, he wasn't denying the allegations, and he wasn't doing anything.

He was just staring.

With a final thrust, Floyd let go of his partner and stepped back. His fury had failed to illicit a response and it started to fade.

This wasn't him. Floyd wasn't the aggressive type. He was the type who broke down when confronted with the mere possibility of having to reveal bad news to a grieving friend or relative.

Floyd was the type who cried in his car, sobbed like a baby who didn't have his pacifier.

"The real question," Tate said, "is why you didn't, Floyd."

This was not the response Floyd expected, but it was the one he needed.

Now, he felt embarrassed, for both his actions and his lack of foresight.

"Looks like you owe me another drink," Tate said under his breath.

He was sporting that half-smirk again, and Floyd growled.

I should have known. I should have known that Martin would be next.

"Why didn't you tell me?" he asked.

Tate shrugged.

"Seeing is believing."

"And when did you know?

"I knew that this was a possibility as soon as we caught him at Henry's house."

Floyd's head was pounding too hard for him to shake it, but he felt the urge.

It made sense, of course. They'd come a long way from thinking that these murders weren't connected. And when they'd conceded that the cases were linked, then whoever was behind it—*Henry?*—was intent on covering their tracks.

After all, these murders—five of them now, if you included the drug dealer in Portsmouth and the attempt on Chase's life—were carried out by the perfect weapon: one who immediately self-destructed. No links back to whoever ordered the hit. And once they'd zeroed in on Martin, well, that was another loose end that needed to be dealt with.

"There's no such thing as a perfect murder," Tate said absently. "But this comes close."

Floyd was inclined to agree. Even if they found Henry, which seemed unlikely at this point, what could they charge him with? Helping sick women at a homeless shelter? How would this even look? A man whose partner was savagely murdered, and the only connection was because he volunteered to help the less fortunate? And motive? What in the world could possibly be the man's motive?

Yeah, the DA was going to have fits with this one.

"All of them are dead… except one."

"What's that?" Tate asked.

Floyd, who had been absently staring at Martin, suddenly shook his head. He'd forgotten about his headache, and this motion exacerbated it.

"I said," he sucked in a sharp breath, "that everyone's dead. Except for one."

Despite everything, Floyd had a surge of pride when he realized that Tate still hadn't caught on. Instead of enlightening the man, he pulled out a cell phone and began to dial a number.

"Who are you calling?" Tate asked.

"What's that?"

"I asked who you were calling," Tate repeated harshly.

"Oh, just wait, seeing is believing."

Chapter 52

"FLOYD? IS EVERYTHING ALL RIGHT?" Chase asked. She was already starting to get dressed even though Floyd had said nothing more than hello. She could tell something was wrong in his voice, even after a single word.

"We've got another death," Floyd said.

Chase stopped putting her foot into her pant leg.

"What? What do you mean, another death? Who?"

"Martin. He was killed just like the others. Stabbed and then the girl committed suicide."

Chase finished putting on her pants.

"Who's Martin?"

"The man from the soup kitchen. We—" Floyd paused, and Chase realized that they had a lot to catch up on. "Can you get down here? We're outside *E-Tronics*. You'll see the lights."

"I'll be there in ten. Any news on Henry?"

"No, but Tate has every cop in the city looking for him. We scoped out his house and..." Another curious pause. "He wasn't there. There's a car outside waiting for him to come back."

He's not coming back, Chase thought suddenly. Then her mind turned to the girl at the end of the hall. *Or maybe he is.*

"Floyd, can you give Quantico a ring?"

"Sure. What do you need?"

"Get one of the techs to look into Henry's past. I want to know if he's lived anywhere other than here, than Charleston."

"You think you might be holed up somewhere? Keeping the girls out of the city?"

Chase hesitated.

"Yeah, but I want to know if he has ever lived in Tennessee."

"Tennessee?"

"Tennessee," Chase confirmed. "Anywhere in or around the state."

Chase heard talking in the background and thought she picked up Tate's voice.

"Maybe keep this between us, as well."

"Chase, I don't think—"

"You still gonna be there in an hour?" she interrupted.

"Yeah, we can be. But I thought you said ten—"

"There's something I need to do first."

Chase hung up before Floyd could protest further. She picked up her shirt and frowned. It was caked with dried blood. Folded on the chair was a pale gray sweatshirt.

Audrey must have left this for me, she thought as she put it on. It was a bit large, but not ridiculously so.

"Leaving again?" Dr. Heinlin asked. There was no surprise or disdain in his voice. The man, who had come into the room as Chase was dressing, was only stating a fact.

As such, Chase felt no need to reply.

"You want me to bill the—"

"No," Chase said quickly. "You guys have my credit card on file. Use that."

Dr. Heinlin nodded.

"How's the pain?" he asked, lowering his gaze to her chest.

"Fine."

In truth, she was still quite sore. Chase could only raise her left arm a little over shoulder height before the pain was too great and she was forced to stop. The fact that Audrey's sweatshirt was too big made things a little easier for her.

"You're not fine," the doctor noted. He got his pad out and started to scribble something down. "I'll give you a script for—"

"I'm fine," Chase repeated.

The doctor tore the page off the pad and crumpled it.

"How's *she* doing this morning?"

"I don't know," Dr. Heinlin replied. "I just got in, went home for a few hours of sleep. I came to see you first."

Chase thanked the man and collected her belongings. Then she left her room for what she hoped would be the last time and made the familiar walk down the hallway toward Jane Doe's room—she refused to even consider the possibility that her name was Riley.

At first, Chase thought she'd somehow made a wrong turn somewhere. There was no police officer, asleep or awake, in a chair.

There wasn't even a chair.

Feeling her heart rate increase, Chase peered through the door. The bed was unmade, but there was no one lying on it.

What the hell?

Chase opened the door and rushed inside.

"It's beautiful, isn't it?" Jane Doe was standing by the window, her skin bathed in sunlight. "The sun, I mean?"

It looked like a normal day to Chase, but she didn't ruin the moment. She was pleased to see that the girl was no longer cuffed. It felt wrong to keep this victim in handcuffs.

"I suppose it is."

The girl slowly turned to look at her, and Chase was pleased to see that her skin had acquired a normal hue.

"She came last night, she came to visit me."

At first, the woman's airy voice was reminiscent of an epiphany. It reminded Chase of Father David after he'd consumed dozens of Cerebrum pills.

Chase didn't hold it against her.

Perhaps noticing the confusion on her face, Jane Doe clarified, "The woman in the white dress. Only she wasn't wearing a white dress this time, but a gray suit."

The inner corners of Chase's eyebrows lifted, and she took a step back.

"What do you mean? Someone came to visit you? Here?"

Now it was Jane's turn to step back, and she appeared frightened.

"No, I'm sorry, I didn't mean to scare you," Chase said calmly. "But you had a visitor?"

Jane licked her lips.

"Yes. The same woman... the one in the dress. Only she wasn't wearing a dress this time, and she... and she..."

Her fright transitioned to confusion. She was better today, but she still wasn't good.

"Take your time," Chase pleaded. "Please, just take your time. Tell me who visited you."

Jane Doe tried to catch her breath, but she was having some difficulty. Chase reached out for her, but she pulled back. Jane wasn't ready to be touched. Yesterday's embrace was a one-off, it seemed.

"Don't think about the past, just take a deep breath and center yourself in the moment. Think about now," Chase waved a hand across the large windows in front of them. "Think about how beautiful the sunshine is."

That seemed to do the trick. After a few moments, Jane Doe regained her composure.

"I'm sorry, I'm still confused. I just remember the woman. This time," Jane closed her eyes and shook her head. "This time, she said she was my lawyer. That I shouldn't speak to anyone." Jane opened her eyes and looked at Chase. They were still dull, but no longer flat. "Including you."

Chase pressed her lips together.

"What else did she say?"

"Only that she would come back and tell me what to do next." Jane paused and a shudder racked her tiny frame. "I thought… I thought she was going to tell me to… y-you know."

It took Chase several seconds to figure out what the girl was talking about.

Kill.

Loose ends. Melissa had come back to try and clean up the loose ends. And that included Jane.

But at whose behest? Surely not Melissa's own.

Bryan's or Henry's?

"She said to take this."

Chase cleared her head and looked at Jane. She was holding a small pill in her hand. Even though she couldn't see the markings, Chase knew exactly what it was.

Valacyclovir.

"Don't—don't take that," Chase said dryly.

Jane closed her hand around the pill.

"I won't."

But the girl didn't throw it out.

Chase had been there. She'd held on to baggies of smack for weeks, convincing herself that she'd get rid of it later.

That she wouldn't use it.

It never worked.

Lies slowly wormed their way in, making tacks in her brain. Lies telling her that she could control it. That she could do a little and then stop.

"Give it to me," Chase insisted.

"I'll throw it out."

This might not be heroin, and it wouldn't even get you high. But it was a crutch, it was the only thing Jane Doe knew.

"Hand it over," Chase said firmly. "*Now.*"

In addition to the drug, there was one other thing that was familiar to Jane: obedience. Chase felt bad for putting her back in that place, that den of oppressive darkness, but she had no choice.

The girl's fingers unfurled, and Chase took the pill and slipped it into her pocket.

Melissa had given Jane the drug and promised to return. Jane was right to be afraid because there was no question in Chase's mind what Melissa would instruct her to do.

Kill.

"Thank you."

Chase made her way to the door.

"One more thing," Jane said quietly.

"Yes?"

"The woman... she said *her* name was Riley, not mine. I must've gotten it wrong yesterday."

Chase scowled.

Still playing games, Brian?

She pulled the door open but didn't leave the room just yet.

"What did... what did she call you?" Chase asked without turning.

When there was no answer, she glanced over her shoulder.

The girl was sobbing.

"Bridget," the girl said. "She called me Bridget."

Chapter 53

"SHE'S NOT COMING," FLOYD SAID as he hung up the phone. Tate looked at him.

"What do you mean, she's not coming?"

Floyd raised one shoulder and let it drop.

"Chase said she's not coming."

"Yeah, I understand that, but *why* isn't she coming?"

"Didn't say."

Unaccustomed to the way that Chase's brain worked, Tate huffed.

"Where is she?" Floyd opened his mouth to issue an identical answer when Tate added, "Never mind."

Floyd was struck by just how similar Chase and Tate acted sometimes.

"We're pretty much done here, Agent Abernathy. The ME wants to take the bodies away if that's all right...?"

Tate waved the police officer away.

"Fine. There's nothing else we can do here."

Tate's phone started to ring, and he answered it. As his partner turned his back, Floyd took out his own phone. He didn't dial Chase's number, however, as much as he wanted to speak to her again. She had made it abundantly clear that there was something that she needed to do on her own. And as dangerous a proposition as that was, Floyd knew firsthand that there was no stopping her.

There's an old proverb in which a toad and a scorpion are stranded on one side of a stream. The water is rising, and the scorpion is going to drown. He asks the toad for a lift and the toad hesitates but eventually agrees. Halfway across the stream, the scorpion stings the frog. Before they both sink to their deaths, the frog looks at the scorpion and asks, "Why did you do that? Now we're both going to die."

The scorpion replies, "Because I'm a scorpion and that's what I do."

Chase was Chase, and Chase would do what Chase did, no matter the consequences.

Maybe it was because she had been electroshocked as a child and then addicted to heroin. Or maybe it was because that's who she was born to be. She would do what she thought was right, and if anybody got in her way, so help them.

Floyd dialed Quantico, instead.

"Agent Summers, any update on that search I asked for?"

"Floyd, I was just about to call you. Your guy, Henry Saburra? No other properties in West Virginia. Still running searches in other states, but I'm going to need more time. Hampton has us working on some other shit. He's all twisted about something."

Floyd grimaced. When Director Hampton was in a mood, it was best to just stay the hell out of his way.

"What about Tennessee?"

Floyd listened to the keystrokes.

"Yeah, looks like Henry went to school out there, Belmont University, in Nashville. This was twenty, twenty-five years ago. What's this about? If Hampton asks—"

"Tell him we're working the Columbus case, the murdered doctor. I owe you one, Summers. If you can, keep searching for properties owned by Henry out-of-state. Thanks."

Floyd saw that Tate was no longer on the phone, either. The man was just staring blankly at the ground.

"Tate, what is it? What's wrong?"

Floyd's thoughts instantly went to a dark place, thinking that something had happened to Chase. But that didn't make sense — he would've gotten the call, not Tate. Wouldn't he?

"That was Margaret," Tate answered. The man looked shell-shocked, which was something that Floyd had never seen in him before. Tate could transform into whatever you needed him to be, a true chameleon in human skin, but this was something new. Surprised? No, Tate was never surprised.

"Who's Margaret?" Floyd asked.

"The woman who runs the homeless shelter."

"Shit, she heard about Martin already?" Floyd was suddenly parched. He'd given his card to the woman with the glasses, as well. What if she'd called him instead of Tate? What if he had to break the news that her cook was dead? That he'd been murdered?

"No," Tate said.

Floyd's eyes, which had drifted to the back of the black coroner van where three techs were trying to hoist Martin's large body inside, flicked to his partner.

"What? Did you tell her? What did she want?"

"I didn't tell her," Tate said, shaking his head. "She called for something else... Margaret said that after my visit, she started to dig through some old documents and came across something. When the girl first came in, she had some sort of head injury and they needed to get her treated by a doctor. And that time, she had ID on her."

Floyd was confused.

"Wait, slow down, which girl?"

Tate blinked.

"The girl in the photograph, the one with Henry and Roger."

Thinking that this wasn't enough, Tate removed the photo from his pocket and showed it to Floyd.

"Yeah, I get it... wh-what's her name?"

Another blink from Tate, only this one wasn't on account of Floyd being slow on the uptake but a result of sheer disbelief.

"Rebecca Anne Griffith," Tate said softly. "It appears as if the girl in the photograph is Dr. Wayne Griffith III's daughter."

Chapter 54

"**Is this about the cuffs?** Because she's not going anywhere, I just thought—"

"No, it's not about the cuffs," Chase said. The young police officer's shirt was untucked. He'd been in the bathroom when she'd first arrived. "It's about you not doing your fucking job."

The cop blubbered.

"M-my—my job?"

"Yes, your job! I told you to write down the name of every person who comes into this room!"

"I did!" the man shot back, fumbling with a piece of paper he pulled out of his pocket. It was worn and creased.

Chase grabbed it, opened it, and scanned the names. There was no Melissa on it, there was no Riley, there was no mention of any lawyer.

"Where's the lawyer?"

"The—the what?"

Chase shook the piece of paper.

"The lawyer that visited her yesterday! Where's her name on this list?" When the man started blubbering again, Chase thrust the paper against his chest. "Doesn't matter. I want Jane—Bridget, I want Bridget moved."

"Excuse me?"

At the end of her wits now, Chase took an aggressive step forward, ignoring the pain in her throat and chest.

"That girl in there, her name is Bridget. And I want her moved," Chase said, raising her voice.

Down the hallway, she saw Dr. Heinlin step out of one of the patient rooms and glance in her direction.

Good, Chase thought, *because I'm going to need his cooperation, as well.*

"I was told..." The officer made a face and rubbed his triceps with his opposite hand. "I was told that she has to stay here."

"But I'm telling you, as a Special Agent in the Federal Bureau of Investigation that she needs to be moved."

The cop's eyes darted.

"Still..."

"Still, *what*? I'm not asking for you to relocate Bridget to a different goddamn jurisdiction. I just want her on another floor."

In addition to the triceps massage and darting eyes, the officer now started to bounce up and down on his toes.

"I wanna help, I really do, but I gotta call my boss. It'll take, like, two minutes. It's not really a big—"

"What's going on here?" Dr. Heinlin demanded.

"Agent... the FBI Agent," the officer began, clearly unable to remember her name, "she wants to move the prisoner."

When Dr. Heinlin glanced over at her, Chase gave him a subtle nod. The doctor looked back at the cop and said, "Yes, and what's the problem?"

"The problem?"

"What's the problem, officer?"

"Well, n-not a problem, really, but I gotta call my boss."

"You do what you have to do, officer. But I don't really care what you, your boss, or the FBI says. The girl in there? She isn't a prisoner. She's a patient. And *I* want her moved." This straightened the cop up. "If you want to go with her..."

"I think that's a great idea," Chase confirmed. "Make sure she doesn't wander off."

The cop broke.

"If it's doctor's orders, then..."

"It is," Dr. Heinlin said sternly.

"One more thing," Chase added. "If the good doctor deems that she is fit to stand trial and if charges are laid—"

"If charges are—"

Chase interrupted him.

"*If* charges are laid, then I will be hiring her a lawyer. I don't want her being represented by a public defender who just passed the bar."

All eyes were on her now, but Chase didn't feel the least bit uncomfortable. The cop, on the other hand, looked absolutely miserable.

"I don't understand. I thought you said her lawyer was already here. The name... it wasn't on the list."

"That wasn't her lawyer," Chase interjected. "Like I said, if she's charged then I'll hire someone."

Chase already had a specific person in mind, the sleazy lawyer from New York who had gotten ex-NYPD Detective Damien Drake out of numerous tight spots: Roger Schneiderman.

She didn't care if this was an egregious conflict of interest, either. Chase would do whatever it took to keep Bridget out of prison.

"Okay, okay," the cop relented. Both Dr. Heinlin and Chase watched as he went into Bridget's room and began speaking to the girl.

"Thanks for backing me up," Chase said out of the corner of her mouth.

"I hope you know what you're doing."

"So do I."

The cop and Bridget emerged from the room, and Chase was happy to see that she remained uncuffed.

"Two floors down, room six-twelve," Dr. Heinlin said, without skipping a beat.

The cop nodded and they started to walk past them.

Chase nearly let them go, but at the last second, she grabbed the girl's arm and said, "Sometimes it's better if you don't remember."

Bridget looked at her confused but then nodded.

She watched them make it to the elevator before addressing Dr. Heinlin.

"Do you mind if I use this room for a while?" Chase asked, indicating the room that Bridget had just vacated. "You can add it to my tab. I don't need a nurse or a doctor. I just need to rest."

"No problem. Chase, I think I know what you're planning, and I don't want to tell you how to do your job, but—"

"Then don't."

Chase spun and opened the door to Bridget's room. Inside, she found an unused hospital gown and slipped it over her clothes. Then she crawled into bed and lay on her side, her back to the door.

This was incredibly uncomfortable, and she could feel an awful pressure rising from her breast to the hollow of her throat, but it was also necessary.

It dawned on Chase as she lay there, that this was far from the first time that she'd slept in the same bed as a killer. But then she thought, maybe Bridget was the nicest of them all.

Less than two hours after she'd taken over Bridget's room, and had dozed off a handful of times, Chase heard the door open.

Wide awake now, she continued to pretend to be asleep.

"Bridget?" a soft female voice asked. Chase listened to her footsteps approach the bed. "Bridget, it's me, your lawyer. I told you I would—"

Chase kicked off the sheet as she turned and aimed the gun she'd been cradling at the woman in the doorway.

"I'm not Bridget," she said with a snarl. "And you're not a lawyer, you dumb cunt."

Chapter 55

"YOU CAN'T BE SERIOUS," FLOYD said even though he knew that for once, Tate was being just that: serious.

To prove his point, Tate showed Floyd first the photo that Chase had taken from Roger's home, the same one of the three of them that he'd seen on Henry's fridge. Next, he displayed an image of Dr. Wayne Griffith III in the morgue.

"You see the resemblance?" Tate asked, excitement in his voice. "Doesn't the girl look like Dr. Griffith?"

Floyd didn't disagree, but two photographs, one of which was of a corpse, were far from conclusive evidence.

"Maybe?"

"You're right, you're right. Coincidence—could be a coincidence."

After all the times that Tate had brought up his previous partner Constantine Striker, Floyd was finally able to educate Tate on something he'd learned from a partner of his own: Jeremy Stitts.

"I don't believe in coincidences. We have an ID linking this crime to the one in Columbus, and the MOs are identical? Sounds like a definitive link. Listen, I know the DNA came back negative when comparing the hairbrush from Roger's house and the girl who'd killed him, but what about the girl who attacked Chase or the one who killed Wayne?"

"Wayne? You think his own daughter...?" Tate shook his head. "You know what, coincidence or not before we jump to conclusions, we should contact Meredith Griffith to see if she actually has a daughter."

Floyd felt his balls rise into his stomach.

"Should we—sh-should we c-c-call her?"

Tate thought about this and then nodded.

"I'll call Meredith Griffith, test the waters. If she has a daughter, we don't know where she is. All we know was that someone with her ID was at the homeless shelter a while back and that that girl knew Roger Evans and Henry Saburra."

To Floyd, Tate's monologue sounded like something he would say as a delay tactic.

"You okay, Tate?"

Tate scowled.

"I can't believe we missed this. We have crimes committed by young women and not one, but *two* of the involved families have daughters that we don't know about? Floyd, we fucked up."

Floyd thought that Tate was being unduly harsh, especially considering the man hadn't been in the same state when they'd interviewed Henry.

Interviewed Henry...

"Shit," he cursed and then sighed heavily.

"What?" Tate asked. He had his phone out and was anxious to speak to Meredith Griffith to confirm the information that Margaret had given him.

"You didn't screw up, I did," Floyd said under his breath. *And so did Chase.*

"Floyd—"

"No, listen, when we interviewed Henry, I asked him if he knew Dr. Wayne Griffith III. I don't know why, but I just blurted his name out. And his face... Henry's face went, I dunno, squirrelly. I thought it was strange at the time, but—"

He was about to say, *but Chase didn't notice it, so I let it go,* but didn't feel like throwing her under the bus. Floyd finished his sentence with a shrug.

Tate nodded consolingly.

"We all screwed up."

He dialed Mrs. Griffith's number and put it on speaker phone. The woman answered after the fourth ring.

"Mrs. Griffith?" Tate began, lowering his voice an octave or two.

"Who is this?" came the harsh reply.

"This is FBI Agent Tate Abernathy. We met a few days ago at—"

"I remember you. You were there when that bitch Julia attacked me at my husband's funeral."

Tate looked at Floyd, silently projecting the idea that that's not the way he remembered things going down.

"I was there. I'm sorry to bother you, but I just wanted to ask you a few questions about your daughter."

The phone went silent.

Well, at least she didn't immediately reply with, I don't have a daughter, you dumb ass FBI Agent.

Seconds ticked by.

"Mrs. Griffith?"

"What about her?" There was still some bite to the woman's words, but far less chew.

"I don't recall seeing her at the funeral, so I was just—"

"She wasn't there. We—my husband and I—haven't seen her in a long time. I just don't understand what Becca has to do with any of this. Is it that bitch Julia? Did she say something? Because I've seen her lurking around, pretending to be driving by the house."

Tate raised both eyebrows.

"No, this has nothing to do with Julia. We would like to speak to your daughter. Is that possible?"

"Good luck. No idea where she is. Two years ago, she picked up and left. She was sixteen, couldn't stop her even if we'd tried."

"Was that the first time she'd run away?"

"First time? No, she ran away all the time. This time, though, she never came back."

"And did your husband and daughter—"

Meredith's sigh was so dramatic and prolonged that it sounded to Floyd like uncontrolled flatulence.

"Look, Agent Tabernacle, Becca was sick. I think she was into drugs, okay? Always dirty, forgetting to wash. Forgetting to eat. I forced her into rehab, but she just ran away from that, too. Wayne thought—shit, why are you asking about her?"

Floyd was quite certain that he hated this woman, and he didn't use that word lightly. How could someone be so callous as this? The father of her child dies, and she makes zero effort to locate her? To tell her what happened?

Tate was also disturbed by this.

"I just—I didn't see her at the funeral, that's all. Wanted to—"

"But you did see Julia, right? And wasn't she... trespassing? What are you going to do about her?"

"Ms. Griffith, I'm sorry again for the disruption that she might've caused. But Julia Dreger didn't break any laws?"

Meredith scoffed, which, while it wasn't as impressive as her sigh, had the same flatulent quality about it.

"Didn't break any laws? You mean whores are legal in Ohio? Fucking people like my husband for money? That's not breaking the law?"

Tate held his hands up, begging Floyd to help out. But there was no chance that Floyd was going to have anything to do with this piece of work.

"Again, I'm very sorry for your loss."

"Well, if you aren't going to do anything about her, then I will!"

Now it was Tate's turn to sigh.

"Ms. Griffith, I—" the phone beeped three times. "She hung up." Tate stared at Floyd. "What the fuck was that all about? Can you believe that she hung up on me?"

"Oh, I can believe it. What I can't believe, is how long Wayne put up with her. And can you blame him for seeking something on the side?"

Tate chuckled.

"Hell, no. You should have seen Meredith and Julia at the funeral, by the way. Julia wasn't doing anything wrong, and Meredith was about to strangle her."

"Not surprised," Floyd said, growing serious again. "What do you think about what Meredith said about her daughter? How she stopped washing and eating? Sounds a lot like our murderers."

"Sure does."

"You think it could be… one of them?" Floyd asked, circling back to his earlier question. "Could Becca be one of the killers?"

"I have no idea, but there is one person who might."

"Chase?"

Tate shot him another look.

"No, not Chase. The girl at the hospital who attacked Chase. Who knows, maybe we'll get lucky, and she'll tell us her name is Rebecca Griffith."

Chapter 56

"**Bridget?**"

Chase sneered.

"My name isn't Bridget. It's Chase. And you're Melissa, right? Or do you go by Teresa Long?"

"Who? What?" the pale woman looked confused.

"Did you forget that name? Teresa Long? Are you so brainwashed that you forget the name your parents gave you?"

When Melissa took a step back, Chase raised the gun.

"My name is Melissa," the woman said meekly.

"Sure, it is, and I'm the fucking Easter Bunny. What are you doing here?"

"I came to see Bridget."

Chase stood, protecting the sore half of her body by leaning in that direction.

"Yeah, I know you are. You're here to tell her to kill herself."

"N-no," Melissa said, but she was a shitty actress. One would think that a grown woman who had spent her entire adult life pretending to be someone else would be better at lying.

"Yeah, that's why you're here. But I don't give a shit about that. I want you to tell me that Brian sent you here to kill me. I want you to say the words."

Chase expected that even speaking this herself would have a haunting, chilling effect, but they seemed natural. Perhaps it was the circumstances, all the death that had surrounded with over the past few days, or maybe it was just that she was comfortable with the idea of being dead.

There is nothing.

"I don't know what you're talking about," Melissa said, unwilling to meet her eyes.

Chase lashed out and grabbed the woman by the front of her shirt with one hand and pulled her so close that their noses were nearly touching.

"After I met your piece of shit husband in County, he called you, didn't he? What did he say? Follow her? I do not know how he figured this case out before me, but he knew. And he told you to meet up with Henry, get one of his sick girls to try and kill me? Isn't that right? Typical of a man like Brian. Not willing to do his dirty work, hiring someone three people removed to try to take me out."

Chase could see in the woman's terrified eyes that what she said was the truth, that she'd nailed it right on the head. But seeing it in her eyes was one thing, hearing the words out of Melissa Jalston's mouth was another beast entirely.

"Say it," Chase hissed.

In her current state, if Melissa decided to try to shake free, or just shove Chase, she'd win that contest of strength, hands down. Chase still had her gun, lowered now, but even as furious as she was, the likelihood of using it for anything other than a threat was highly unlikely.

But Melissa Jalston wasn't a woman who stood up for herself. Brian had made sure of that. This was a woman who, like Chase's sister had been kidnapped at a young age and indoctrinated. Her entire life had been spent subservient to Brian or Timothy or both.

No, she wasn't about to stand up for herself now.

"I don't know what you're talking about," Melissa said softly. Each additional lie that came out of her mouth was spoken at a lower octave. A few more, and she wouldn't even be making sounds, just moving her lips.

"Say it!" Chase said giving the woman a rough shake, the hardest she could manage in her current condition with just one hand.

"I'm sorry, I don't understand."

Disgusted, Chase let go and stepped back.

"Of course, you understand. You know *exactly* what I'm talking about."

And yet, while they both knew that she was speaking the truth, Chase also knew that under no circumstance was this woman going to say anything to incriminate Brian Jalston. She'd proven as much when Chase had rescued her and yet Melissa, like all the other girls save Georgina, not only stuck around but visited him weekly in jail.

Chase cursed under her breath, and she tried to stem her anger.

Like Bridget, Melissa was an implement, a tool, a device that was manipulated and coerced into action.

"Kill."

The word comes from nowhere and everywhere and it fills every putrid pore and every fetid cavity.

"Kill."

Chase put the gun in her holster. Melissa didn't react. She just stood there, like some sort of automaton that had completed its coding circuit and was awaiting further instruction.

The similarities between Melissa and Bridget were uncanny.

And terrifying.

Melissa might not implicate Brian, but that didn't mean she couldn't speak. In order to get to Chase, she must have communicated with Henry, somehow. She might even know where he is.

Chase was convinced that the man with the cat was behind this and that he probably had other girls like Bridget under his control. Sick girls, girls who are already dead but who could be convinced to kill.

She had to find Henry and she had to stop him before more people died.

"Do you remember Riley?" Chase asked, changing her approach entirely. She knew that this was the most likely way to get a response of substance out of Melissa, but she also knew that her words would sting them both deeply.

"Of course. Riley's my sister."

She isn't your sister; she was brainwashed into being part of Brian and Tim's harem.

Chase looked down.

"She's dead. I'm sorry… Riley's dead."

Melissa gasped, but when she didn't say anything, Chase glanced up. Melissa's eyes were wide, but they quickly narrowed with suspicion.

"Did Brian not tell you? Riley's dead, Melissa. That's why I came to visit him in County because she was my sister, too."

Maybe it was Chase's tone, or maybe it was the sadness she felt showing in her features.

But this time, Melissa seemed to believe her.

Then she started to sob.

It took Chase a few seconds to realize that the woman was saying something between bursts of moist emotion.

"What? I can't understand you."

Melissa rubbed her nose.

"Georgina? Is Georgina… is she… is Georgina…" That was all she could manage.

Chase got the picture, but it was a confusing one. Georgina… Riley…

It clicked. Melissa was referring to her niece Georgina, not her sister. The child that Brian was trying to abduct.

"She's alive. She's with me."

Chase let her words sink in, and saw that Melissa truly cared for Georgina. And why wouldn't she? The woman had been with little Georgina for the first four or five years of her life. Hell, she'd known the girl for longer than Chase had, maybe even had a bigger impact on her upbringing, as well. And despite growing up in an ass-backward cult, Melissa and her 'sisters' had done a decent job of raising the girl. Georgina was smart, and Georgina was somehow well adapted.

And Melissa loved her.

It felt wrong—what Chase was about to do, dangle not a carrot, but an orange-haired child, was very, very wrong.

But it was the only thing that she thought would work.

"Do you want to see Georgina?"

The woman nodded vigorously, sending the tears that had coalesced on her chin cascading to the front of her shirt.

"I'll let you see her."

"Where is she?" Melissa asked desperately. "Is she here? Is she—"

Chase's voice got hard.

"I'll let you see her if you take me to Henry. If you take me to the man who convinced Bridget to try and kill me, I'll let you see your daughter."

Melissa kept nodding and crying as she spoke next, and Chase felt a pang of guilt. It just so happened to be centralized around the bandage above her collarbone.

"Okay," Melissa agreed. "I'll take you to him. But please, don't hurt Georgina."

Chapter 57

"**SHORT WOMAN WITH LIGHT GRAY** hair? Young?" Tate said, holding his hand at around waist height.

The doctor looked at the two agents, a frown on his face.

"Oh, c'mon. I find it hard to believe that the feisty FBI Agent was here, and you don't remember her?"

"I'm sorry, I just got to the ward," the doctor replied. "One of my colleagues—"

"Everything all right, Dr. Parker?" another man in a white coat asked.

"Yeah, these men are just—"

Floyd stepped from behind Tate's shadow.

"Dr. Heinlin? You know Chase—I mean, Agent Adams," Floyd said.

"Of course, stitched her up twice." Dr. Heinlin tapped Dr. Parker on the back, relieving the latter.

"Twice?" Floyd asked.

Dr. Heinlin made a face.

"She didn't... didn't tell you?"

"Chase is one hell of an agent, but communication? Not her strong suit," Tate offered.

Now, that's an understatement, Floyd thought.

"Agent Adams arrived yesterday morning, collapsed onto one of the nurses. Dehydrated, electrolyte imbalance. Her stitches had torn."

"Jesus, is she alright?"

Dr. Heinlin gestured for them to follow him as he walked down the hall.

"She'd be better if she rested. But I think we all know that isn't going to happen."

"What about the girl? The one who attacked her?" Tate asked.

"She's recovering." The doctor stopped and looked at them. "Agent Adams didn't tell you anything, did she?"

Floyd shook his head.

"I believe that the girl, who claims her name is Bridget, is suffering from a rare psychological condition called 'Cotard's'. Individuals with Cotard's can display a myriad of symptoms, but a common theme is that they all believe that they are, in fact, already deceased."

Floyd and Tate exchanged a glance as Dr. Heinlin started to walk again.

"Already dead?" Floyd asked. The claim was so bizarre that he required confirmation. It came in the form of an enthusiastic nod.

"It's extremely rare and, as such, there are only a handful of case reports in the literature. There are two rather unique features of Bridget's case: the first is that she attacked your partner. Almost all recorded cases involve self-harm and not violence against others. I believe that someone was convincing her—no, *influencing* her to behave this way."

"And the second?"

"There were high levels of a popular anti-herpes medication in her system, *extremely* high levels. A rare side-effect of this treatment can include Cotard's Syndrome."

Floyd grabbed the doctor's arm and they stopped again.

"Valacyclovir?" he asked.

The doctor's brow crinkled.

"How did you—yes, that's the drug."

Floyd turned to Tate.

"Martin wasn't giving the medicine to the girls to help clean them up, he was doing it to make them *sicker*."

Tate nodded in agreement and addressed the doctor next.

"If you pumped someone so full of Valacyc-whatever, could you make them into zombies?"

Dr. Heinlin's lips twisted unpleasantly at the use of the word, but it seemed somehow applicable.

"I doubt it. Both the side effect and the condition are extremely rare. If it were that simple, there would be many, many more people like Bridget."

"Normal people, though, right?" Tate continued. "Most people who take this drug are normal? But what about people who are already sick? People who are depressed, addicted, maybe homeless? People with other psychiatric conditions?"

Dr. Heinlin considered this.

"Maybe," was all the guarded man could offer. "Your partner is in here."

They'd reached the end of the hallway and Floyd noted that there was a chair beside the door.

"No, she's not," Tate said, pulling his face away from the glass.

"What?" Dr. Heinlin opened the door and stepped inside. Floyd followed him in. The room was empty. "She was here," the doctor said, spinning around.

"Well, she's not anymore. Floyd—"

"On it."

Floyd was already dialing Chase's number.

"She *was* here," Dr. Heinlin repeated. "She switched spots with Bridget after her lawyer visited."

"Her lawyer?" Tate asked.

Floyd listened with one ear as his call went to voicemail.

"I thought you said the only thing that people with Cotard's are interested in is self-harm? Why would she hire a lawyer?"

Floyd tried Chase again with the same result.

"I don't—she was getting better—she is," Dr. Heinlin stumbled through his words. "I—"

"Did she call anyone?" Tate pressed.

Dr. Heinlin shook his head.

"I—she—Agent Adams asked for the room, to switch them, and I-I—"

It was clear that the doctor was frustrated with himself, but the blame was ill-placed. Chase had a way with people, especially men—a way for her to get them to do what she wanted.

"She's not answering," Floyd stated.

Tate nodded.

"Where's Bridget?"

"Another floor, follow me."

As they hurried to the elevator, Floyd's phone rang.

"Chase?"

"It's Summers. Just following up."

"I'm about to get into an elevator, be quick."

Agent Summers' tone changed.

"Of course. I didn't find any additional real estate holdings in or out of state for Henry Saburra."

"Thanks."

Floyd lowered the phone, but Summers wasn't done yet.

"But I looked into the guy who was murdered? Roger Evans?"

The phone was pressed tightly to his ear now.

"And?"

"He has a hunting cabin on the southern end of Kanawha State Forest. Pretty remote, I figured—"

"Thanks. Send me the address."

This time he hung up and the elevator arrived. Floyd relayed this information to Tate as they headed down a few floors. Dr. Heinlin muttered to himself the entire ride.

The elevator doors opened but the doctor made no move to exit.

"Doc?" Tate asked. "Where's Bridget?"

Floyd didn't wait for an answer. He spotted a young police officer outside a room and rushed toward him. The cop saw him coming and leaped to his feet.

"Where is she?" Floyd demanded.

"Wha—? Who?"

Floyd scowled and pushed the officer aside and opened the door.

"Hey, you can't go in there!"

There was a young woman with shoulder-length blonde hair standing by the window. When Floyd burst into the room, she turned to look at him.

Her appearance was so shockingly normal that it took Floyd by surprise. But then he saw her eyes and the ugly purple bruises all over her throat and knew that this wasn't a mistake.

That this was the person who had attacked and nearly killed his partner.

Floyd walked right up to her.

"Where is she?" he demanded. "Where the fuck is Chase?"

Chapter 58

CHASE'S INITIAL PLAN WAS TO have Melissa drive the car. The problem was that the woman had no idea how—no one ever taught her.

Chase shouldn't have been surprised. She'd learned in the Academy that removing all reasonable means of transportation was one of the first things that kidnappers did. In this case, Brian and Timothy Jalston's home was remote, isolated, and, if Chase recalled correctly, the men only had one vehicle.

As a result, Chase was forced to drive. She kept her gun on her lap as she followed Melissa's directions, but she doubted it was necessary. Once the plan that Brian had cooked up failed, Melissa was at a loss for what to do next. Chase simply provided her with the guidance she needed and the pattern of obedience continued.

"I would never hurt Georgina," Chase said absently. She was perturbed by Melissa's comment back at the hospital. Not typically one to care what others thought, the idea that a stranger had assumed that she'd hurt a child, her niece, said something.

Chase just wasn't sure if it was a commentary on her or on Melissa.

"I know." Melissa's tone suggested otherwise, but Chase knew better than to press.

She was driving fast, too fast, and they were quickly out of the city. Chase saw signs for Kanawha State Forest and asked Melissa if that was where they were headed.

This appeared to confuse the woman.

"No, not a forest—A cabin."

Chase grabbed her cell phone and then cursed.

They were out of range.

"How did you get here? If you don't drive, how did you get out here?" Chase doubted that buses came out this way.

"I didn't. I met Henry at his house. After… it… was done, I was supposed to meet him at the cabin."

"You were going to walk?"

Melissa shrugged and a thought suddenly occurred to Chase.

"Wait, were you there? When Floyd and I came to interview Henry, were you in his home?"

Melissa nodded.

"I saw you."

"Fuck."

If I'd pushed Henry harder, maybe he would have let us inside. And if I'd seen Melissa…

At the time, Chase had been distracted, trying to help Floyd get over his anxiety.

I should have been more focused. I should have been concentrating on Henry.

She swore a second time and then fell silent.

After five minutes, Melissa said, "It's a left here."

The car jostled as Chase turned onto an even less well-maintained road. She didn't feel like talking anymore. She knew that she'd made a mistake, several mistakes, which had cost at least two people their lives: Martin, and his killer. But Chase also knew that she needed Melissa to reveal more about Brian.

She needed ammunition for when she met Brian again. If she could get to him with some concrete evidence of his involvement in this murder-for-hire scheme, then maybe he'd back off, stop pursuing Georgina.

Either way, Brian Jalston was never going to have her—he would never even get close.

"Brian told you to kill me, didn't he? I mean, not directly, but through a proxy?"

Melissa looked down.

"It's not like that."

"It's exactly like that. Brian told you to come here, to Charleston, to meet with a man who would arrange to have me killed."

"No."

"Yes," Chase nearly shouted. Melissa jumped but refused to raise her head. "Look at me, Teresa! Teresa Long, *look at me!*" And then she did. But instead of the woman's tears calming Chase, they only served to enrage her. "Stop fucking lying! Stop lying to protect him! He raped you! Brian kidnapped you and raped you! Stop lying for him!"

Melissa shook her head.

"He just told me to show your picture and hang around. That's it." She wiped her nose. "Just give Henry a picture and some money."

Henry… it is him. He's behind this. He and Brian.

But this confirmation didn't bring with it any level of pride—just revulsion.

"But that wasn't it, was it?" Chase said, her anger fading. "Because you came back. You came back and gave Bridget another pill. What were you going to do? Tell her to kill herself? Demand that she finish the job and then off herself? Just like the girls who killed Dr. Griffith and Roger and Martin?"

Melissa began to weep and held her face in her hands.

"No—I just—I was told to give it to her. That's it. I didn't—I don't know anything. I don't know what I'm doing."

Chase wasn't buying it.

"But you knew it was me? You had the photo and you saw me that day…" *The day that I saved you—the day I freed you.* "The day I killed Tim." She'd started to feel bad for the woman, but when she said this last part and Melissa gasped, Chase doubled down. "You had to know."

"I—I knew it was you," Melissa admitted at last. "But he didn't tell me what was going to happen. Brian just said that you were keeping us apart, you were trying to get him to stay in prison. And Georgina..." she trailed off.

"What about Georgina?" Chase hissed.

"He said you had her, and you wouldn't give her back."

"And I never will. Because she isn't yours. Why can't you see that?"

Melissa just shook her head.

It's not her fault, something deep in Chase's mind reminded her. She gripped the steering wheel tightly.

"What did you think you were paying Henry to do? Why did you think he needed a picture of me?"

"I didn't ask," Melissa said simply. "I just... I just do what Brian tells me to do."

The muscles in Chase's neck tensed. She'd heard this before, not with Brian's name but with a voice coming from the ether.

This sobering thought brought about another bout of silence that was punctuated by the occasional direction from Melissa.

Time worked its magic and Chase eventually calmed down. When she'd reached a near resting state, she began asking more questions.

"How did Brian know about Henry?"

Melissa shrugged.

"He didn't say."

Chase stared at the woman for a good five seconds. Melissa's cheeks were still wet, eyes moist, but she wasn't crying any-more. Instead, she appeared frightened. She looked like a frightened young girl and not a woman who had been caught soliciting murder.

Chase's car hit a nasty bump in the road, and she was forced to avert her attention. When she looked back, she didn't see Melissa, but her sister.

"What was she like?" Chase asked softly.

Melissa smiled, knowing exactly who she was referring to.

"Riley was one of the strongest women I ever met."

Chase deliberately overlooked the fact that Melissa's exposure to other women was extremely limited.

"She was... she was smart. And while Brian and Timothy sometimes get angry at us, they never got angry at her. Because they knew—they knew that she wouldn't put up with it."

This made Chase smile.

"Riley was special," Melissa continued, her voice cracking a little. "I can't—I can't believe she's gone."

Chase wanted to ask more questions about her sister but feared that she would break down. And she didn't want to cry in front of this woman. It wasn't that she was concerned about looking weak, more that she couldn't afford to appear on the same level as Melissa. This had nothing to do with pride, either—Chase still had a job to do.

A job that may require Melissa to obey maybe one or two more commands.

"What is *she* like?"

If it had been anybody else asking this question, Chase would have glared at them, but there was no ulterior motive with Melissa.

She just wanted to know how a person, a child, whom she loved dearly, was faring. And Chase, even in her darkest hour, would have found that difficult to hold back.

"She's smart," Chase said softly. "Georgina's smart, really smart, down to earth, funny. Stubborn... fuck, she's stubborn."

Melissa smiled and asked nothing further. Speaking about Georgina was painful for her as well.

"Are we close?"

Melissa stared out the window and Chase saw the woman's lips moving as if she were silently reciting directions.

"A left," She pointed at an even smaller road that was nearly completely obscured by shrubs. "There."

Chase turned onto the dirt path.

The brush was thick and just as she was thinking that Melissa must have made a mistake, they came to a clearing.

And Chase saw it: a small hunting cabin, made of wood, the lower half covered in overgrown vegetation.

Chase immediately cut the engine, opened her window and listened. She heard forest sounds, but that was all.

She looked at Melissa and was immediately conflicted. Chase didn't want to handcuff her—if she didn't come back, Melissa would be trapped. But she couldn't afford for the girl to just walk free, either.

Chase checked her phone, even though she knew that there would be no signal.

"Shit. I'm sorry," she said. "I'll be back."

Melissa didn't protest. In fact, she actually held one hand out to allow Chase easier access to her wrist. Chase loosely cuffed the woman to the door handle.

"I'll be back," she said, and then left the car, gun in hand.

But the closer she got to the cabin, the less sure of this fact Chase became.

Chapter 59

"**TELL ME WHERE CHASE IS!**"

The girl Floyd gripped by the arms looked terrified.

"I—I don't know. I don't!"

Tate peeled the two of them apart.

"What you mean you don't know?" Floyd asked. He noticed that both Dr. Heinlin and the cop had joined him in the small room, which had started to feel claustrophobic. He stepped back and let Tate take over from there.

"I—I—I just—I don't know."

"You don't know where Agent Adams went?" Tate clarified, his voice surprisingly calm. "You know who we're talking about?"

The terrified girl nodded.

"Chase... you're talking about Chase. But I don't know where she went. I've been here," she indicated the room, "the whole time."

"What about before?" Floyd asked, his anger returning "Before you attacked her?"

"I just—I don't remember. Somewhere dark and…"

"And what?"

"That's it."

Floyd wasn't sure what incensed him more, the lack of information or the woman's convalescent shrug.

"She's still recovering," Dr. Heinlin offered. "Her memory is imperfect."

"Imperfect?" Floyd gawked. "I don't—"

Tate expertly maneuvered from his position between Floyd and Bridget to between Floyd and Dr. Heinlin.

"It's best if we don't agitate her," the doctor advised.

This was the wrong thing to say—Floyd's main concern was his partner, not her attempted murderer.

"Where is Chase?" he asked the room.

Dr. Heinlin became defensive.

"She never told me anything. Just that she wanted to use the room."

Floyd's arms shot in the air. He felt a terrible sense of foreboding. Whenever Chase went MIA, bad things happened.

Mostly to her.

"Where the *fuck* is Chase?"

"Floyd, take a walk," Tate said.

"What?"

"Go, get out!"

Tate's lips were so tight that they were hidden behind his mustache.

"Fuck!" One final glare at every person in the room and Floyd finally listened to his partner. In the hall, he tried Chase again, but to no avail. Next, he called Summers back.

"Floyd? Did you get the address?"

"Yeah, I need you to give me a location on Chase's phone." When there was no answer, he said, "Summers? You there?"

"Yeah, I'm here. I'm just not sure what you're asking me."

To Floyd, he'd been painfully clear: the location of all active FBI agents could be traced through their cell phones, and he needed to know where Chase was.

"Agent Adams… I need you to track her cell."

"I—I don't have her here," Summers replied.

"What do you mean?"

"I mean, Agent Adams is not on my active list. I can't track her."

Floyd felt his vision start to tunnel.

"She's not?"

"Nope, not active. Floyd, what's going on?"

"Nothing," he said meekly.

"You want—"

"No, I—I have to go."

Floyd hung up but before he could wrap his head around Agent Summers' words, Tate came out of the room.

"Dr. Heinlin reached out to security," Tate said, his face still stern. "They have a video of Chase leaving the hospital with a woman."

"A woman? Who?"

Tate shook his head.

"Don't know."

Floyd looked skyward.

"What the fuck is this fucking case? Nobody knows anything!"

"Calm down."

Floyd glared at Tate.

"Calm down? What are you talking about? Chase has been kidnapped and you're telling me to calm down?"

"Floyd, calm the fuck down! Chase wasn't kidnapped. Get a grip."

Floyd licked his lips and stared.

"How do you know?"

"Because it wasn't the woman leading Chase out of the building, it was the other way around."

Floyd couldn't believe what he was hearing.

Chase commandeered Bridget's room after her lawyer visited and then when someone else comes, she kidnaps her and vanishes?

Something wasn't sitting right. It wasn't that Floyd didn't think Chase capable of such an act—he'd seen her do worse—but the real question was *why*. What connection did this woman have with Henry or the other girls, for that matter?

"Was the person with Chase—"

"No, she was normal. Woman in a gray suit," Tate said, predicting what Floyd was about to say.

"And was the cop around when the lawyer came?" Floyd asked, still trying to understand what was going on. "Was he outside the door when she visited? I want to know if the lawyer was the same person that Chase left with." Floyd paused. "And *when*—I want to know when they left."

"I'll ask."

Tate nodded and disappeared into the room, leaving Floyd to stew.

Chase is untraceable. Chase paid cash for her hotel room and hospital visit. Chase got me to call Summers and didn't do it herself.

Floyd shook his head.

What the hell is going on here?

Tate reemerged from the room.

"Can't know for certain, but the description of the two women is the same." As he said this, Tate reached up to run a hand through his hair. "And that was over an hour ago."

He had a dark stain around the armpit of his white shirt.

White shirt… Floyd thought… *white dress.*

He snapped his fingers.

"Let's go," he said, already moving in the direction of the elevator.

"Where?"

Realizing that Tate wasn't following him, Floyd looked over his shoulder at his partner.

"Floyd, where are we going?"

"After Chase," Floyd said. When this was insufficient to get Tate moving, he added, "Roger Evans' hunting cabin, that's where. And hurry the fuck up because we have to make up time."

Chapter 60

ONCE AGAIN, IT WAS THE smell that clued Chase into the fact that she was in the right place. And then she scolded herself for not being better prepared. When she made it to within twenty feet of the wooden hunting cabin, the reek of putrescence was so awful that it seemed to push against her like a physical barrier.

Gagging, Chase pulled Audrey's sweatshirt over her mouth and nose and relished the sweet smell of her sweat from having gone unwashed for the past two days. The small porch with rotting wooden handrails didn't appear to have an opening or stairs, suggesting that Melissa had led her to the rear of the cabin. Chase winced as she stepped up onto one of the overhanging boards and then lifted her leg high over a section of railing that had nearly completely collapsed.

She felt something stretch and pull in her neck but didn't dare look to see if her bandage was weeping blood. Tearing her new stitches now was of no consequence.

Her initial steps toward the cabin's rear door were soft and cautious. But when Chase discovered how soft and rotted most of the wood was, her approach changed from creating as little noise as possible to not wanting to fall through and twist an ankle.

The door was in a state of disrepair that rivaled the deck. It was crooked in the frame and one of its two hinges was broken. Chase tried to peer through the many gaps in the wood, but someone had applied a thick curtain or similar fabric on the inside. Her first thought was that this was to prevent someone from seeing in, but glancing around, this seemed unlikely. Not only was the cabin secluded and the prospect of a random passerby extremely remote, but the door didn't appear locked.

Anyone could just grab the rusted handle and pull it open if they were so inclined.

This could only mean one thing. The drapes or whatever they were, weren't intended to keep someone from looking in, but looking *out*.

Darkness.

No, not darkness. The notion of darkness suggests the presence of light.

There is no light.

There is nothing.

Chase sucked in a deep breath through her mouth and carefully opened the door. To her surprise, it didn't creak but moved smoothly and silently. Worried about filling the interior of the musty space with light, Chase didn't perform the standard corner checks—she just slipped in and closed the door behind her.

Then she stood completely still, trying to adjust to the darkness that enveloped her, tried to sense movement, differences in swashes of gray or black that might indicate someone's presence.

A second passed, then five. Shortly thereafter, she realized that the ground was mostly dirt—moist dirt.

Chase was reminded of something Floyd had said, relaying information from the ME about how fingerprinting these girls was next to impossible due to their skin being so pruned and wet.

I'm in the right place. I have to be.

She spotted movement in the corner of the cabin. A flicker, a disturbance in depth.

Chase raised her gun.

"Put your hands up," she ordered. Her voice cut through the din like a blacksmith quenching a new sword in water.

A humanoid shape stepped forward, and two hands shot up.

Chase immediately realized that she'd made a mistake. The arms were too thin, the hair too long and greasy.

It was a person, as she'd suspected, but it wasn't the man in the mask.

There was a shuffling sound behind her, and Chase spun her heels on the soft ground.

It was Henry. At least, she was fairly certain that it was Henry. It was difficult to know for certain, what with his face covered with a gas mask and the rest of his body concealed by dark clothing. But Chase remembered that posture, the gait.

"Don't you fucking move," she ordered, stepping back so that she could make out the girl in the corner in the periphery while keeping her gun trained on the man. He was holding something in his right hand.

A hunting knife, one that looked very much like those they'd found at the scenes of the two murders.

And the one that nearly took her life.

"Drop it," she said.

"It's not what you think."

The muffled voice did nothing to confirm or deny that this was Henry. The mask gave the man's words a strange property that bothered Chase's ears. Even though he was standing less than ten feet from her, with her eyes closed, she would have had a hard time locating the source, direction, or location of the voice.

The word comes from nowhere and everywhere and it fills every putrid pore and every fetid cavity.

Chase shook her head to clear herself of this bizarre, disconnected thought. If her stitches hadn't torn before, they did now. She felt a warm liquid begin to seep from the wound.

"Drop the knife and take off the mask." Chase cleared her throat and shrugged her left shoulder uncomfortably. "Do it."

The man raised one hand and showed Chase his palm while he squatted a little to lower the knife to the dirt, his movements slow and deliberate. His now empty right hand went to the mask and as he began to peel it from his face, Chase detected movement.

It had come from the same corner as the one occupied by the girl, but it wasn't her.

It was someone else.

Another girl who was already dead. Not much more than a corpse, she was the most decrepit yet. Skin impossibly wrinkled, every angle formed by every joint acute. Eyes so sunken that their existence was called into question. No lips, just a slit revealing more of that ubiquitous darkness within.

"Stay there!" Chase said, swallowing back bile. In addition to her sweatshirt, she used the crook of her elbow to cover her nose and mouth.

The corpse obeyed but her purpose had been fulfilled.

Chase had been distracted just long enough for the attack to come. But it didn't originate from the man who had been wearing the mask, nor the two shells of human beings.

Instead, it came from the corner behind her, the only one that Chase couldn't see.

Chapter 61

THE FERAL BLUR FLEW AT Chase's face like an organic bullet. She noticed it just in time to move her head to avoid her eyes being gouged out by the cat, but in doing so, the protective sweatshirt slipped from her face. Claws raked Chase's cheek, one of which caught near the corner of her mouth. She instinctively swatted the animal and then shrieked as the nail pulled free of her skin, taking with it a substantial chunk of flesh. The cat meowed as it struck and then rolled in the dirt, trailed by an almost cartoonish puff of wet smoke.

"Fuck!" she dabbed at her face, feeling sticky wetness.

More movement now, this time from the man.

"No!" he screamed, the pitch of his voice rivaling Chase's of moments ago. "No!"

"Stop!" Chase aimed the gun, her finger moving from the guard to the trigger. "Don't you fucking move!"

Henry, she saw now that it was indeed Henry, was in no state of mind to obey. The aghast man lunged, but not at her—for his cat. Chase sidestepped the man's oblivious approach, and if there had been any stitches remaining in her neck, they were broken now.

"Don't—" Chase grunted. She could feel blood trickling down her chest and soaking the fabric of her bra. "Don't move."

Henry dropped to the ground and wrapped his body protectively around the cat, which seemed no worse for wear.

"Fuck you," Henry hissed. "You hit Anne."

It took Chase a few seconds to realize that the cat's name was Anne.

"Fuck me?" Blood trickled from her cheek into her mouth and Chase spat onto the ground. "You tried to kill me!"

There was blood in her throat now, but no amount of spitting would clear it—it wasn't coming from her face but from the inside.

The man neither confirmed nor denied her accusation.

"You hurt Anne!"

"If you move again, you'll be—" Chase grunted and felt her legs go weak. "You'll be the one hurting."

Henry bared his teeth and his eyes fell to Chase's gun, which was now only at half-mast.

Chase should have predicted the man's next words or some facsimile of them. After all, Henry Saburra, like Brian Jalston, was a coward. They could kidnap and brainwash little girls, but when confronted by an adult? A man or woman of equal or greater standing? They preferred others to do what needed to be done, to get their wrinkled and mottled flesh dirty.

"If she shoots me," Henry began, in a voice several octaves lower than just moments ago. "I want one of you to slit your throat and I want the other to slit hers."

A sinister smile appeared on Henry's face.

Chase raised the gun and felt a rivulet of blood reach her belly button now. Her strength was waning, and she knew she didn't have long.

"Why—why are you doing this? They don't—they don't deserve this…"

Chase could feel her grip on reality fading.

"They don't deserve it? Becca didn't deserve it either. We did everything for that girl! Brought her in, cleaned her up… gave her the family that Wayne and his bitch wife Julia never did."

Chase squinted.

"What?"

She wasn't following.

"Can you believe that? They gave up on her... a doctor! A fucking doctor gave up on his child because she was sick?"

A doctor... Dr. Griffith III?

"But we saved her," Henry's eyes were wild, his face manic. "We did! Me and Roger... we saved Becca. Yes, yes —*yesssss.*"

The man was no longer looking at Chase but off to his left. She followed his gaze to a makeshift mantle upon which was propped a familiar photograph: Roger, Henry, and the girl. The former two were genuinely smiling, the latter was putting on a show.

Could it be that the girl in the photo was Dr. Wayne Griffith III's daughter? Was that possible?

There was no mention of Wayne having a child in the case file, but that didn't mean it wasn't true.

Even more alarming, however, was what was adjacent to the photo: a human skull.

"What happened to Becca?" Chase asked, her eyes moving from the skull back to Henry.

"We did everything for her," he sobbed. *"Everything.* She was abandoned by her own family — and we —*we* became her family."

"What happened to her?" Chase repeated. She spat again and Henry glared at her with a burning hatred.

"What the fuck do you think happened to her?" he shrieked. "What the *fuck* do you think happened?"

Henry started to rise, and Chase meant to stop him by flashing the gun. Only, she was too weak.

"She killed herself," Henry stroked the cat in his arms. "After everything... she just... she just came here, with *him,* and he went out hunting as he always did and she stayed here and waited for him, waited with the knife to cut up whatever ani-

mal he *murdered*. But she... she... she must have been confused — she used the knife on her own throat! God damn it, he
should never have left her! Why didn't he stay here with her!
She should never have been left alone!"

He... Roger, he's talking about Roger, Chase's addled mind informed her.

"You killed him... you killed Roger."

Henry, now standing, shook his head.

"No, no, no, no, no. I didn't do it. One of them did it," he
gestured toward the two girls huddled in the corner. At some
point during the man's frenzied diatribe, they'd both procured
similar-looking hunting knives. "It's almost poetic, isn't it?
Those knives, they're the same kind that Becca used to take her
own life. They don't want to live..." he laughed. "They don't
even think they're alive. You can do anything — no, *everything* —
you can do everything for them, and they *still* don't want to
live."

"They're sick," Chase's voice was barely audible.

In her mind, she saw two images of Bridget — one as a
corpse, the other as a blonde-haired girl — that overlapped like
a scene from a poorly made 3D film.

"I'm sick?" Henry through his head back and laughed again.
"*I'm* sick? You're the one who's bleeding." He indicated her
chest and torso, but Chase didn't look down — she didn't need
to. She could feel Audrey's now soaked sweatshirt weighing
her down, pulling her to the earth.

Chase shook her head and her world started to swim.

"I said, *they're* sick. But you..." she fell to one knee. "You're
just a fucking coward."

With this final utterance, Chase collapsed, falling face-first
into the dirt.

"Do it," she heard Henry say in his deeper voice. "Finish what you started. Kill."

"*Kill.*"

A knife.

"*Kill.*"

A promise.

"*Kill.*"

A way out.

"*Kill.*"

The last iteration of the word that reached Chase's ears was not spoken by a single person, but by three.

Chapter 62

"HER CAR ISN'T HERE," FLOYD said desperately. "Chase's car isn't here!"

There was something wrong. He could feel it. Something had happened to Chase.

And he was too late.

Tate didn't reply as he pulled up behind Henry Saburra's Mercedes. Floyd sprung from the car before it was even fully stopped and he bounded toward the cabin, only to trip on the first step that crumbled beneath his foot. He fell hard, a shock wave of pain radiating from his knee to his balls.

Then he heard a scream, and the pain went away.

"Chase!"

Floyd rocketed to his feet and threw the door open. The stench that blasted him in the face made his eyes water and his stomach revolt.

He would have vomited if not for seeing the two women on the ground. It looked as if they had been struggling over a knife, but a clear victor had since been named.

"Kill!" someone screamed from behind him. The voice was almost inhuman. *"Kill!"*

Floyd rushed to the combatants, thrusting the vagrant off the woman on the ground. Blood soaked the front of her, from neck to navel. He couldn't even tell what kind of clothes she was wearing. There was just so much blood.

"No!" he cried. *"No!"*

Floyd's searching fingers found the wound in Chase's throat and inadvertently slipped into it up to the second knuckle before reaching any resistance.

And now he did vomit, turning his head to one side and letting loose a stream of mostly lukewarm coffee.

Fury took over him and he searched the darkness for the woman who had taken his partner's—his friend's—life. But he was once again too late.

She had slit her own throat and was bleeding out.

"Fuck!"

Floyd cradled Chase's head in his hands, trying to wipe the blood away from her features but only ended up smearing it all over.

"No. *Nooo!*"

He had completely forgotten about the demonic commands he'd heard upon entering the cabin, and his eyes went wide with fear. But it wasn't a voice he heard now—it was a wet splashing sound.

Another vagrant, indistinguishable from the first, slumped on the ground, the knife she'd used to cut her throat falling from her hand.

"Tate!" Floyd screamed. "Tate, where the fuck are you?"

More scrambling noises and Floyd finally spotted Henry. The man was staring at the mantle, stroking a cat in his arms. For a split second, Floyd thought that this man, like the girls he cultivated, was ill. And perhaps he was, but his affliction wasn't Cotard's. It was something more… intractable.

"You! This is your fault!"

Henry, who seemed to be in some sort of daze, shook his head. Then his cat meowed, and the man snapped out of his trance completely and darted toward the door.

The cat, Floyd thought incomprehensibly, *this is all about the cat.*

He struggled to rise, but Chase was heavy, and Henry had a head start.

The man grabbed the door opposite the one that Floyd had come through and flung it open.

"*Tate!*"

Henry ran outside only to immediately backpedal. It was as if someone had rewound the last few seconds of real life. The only difference was that the cat was gone and there was blood, twin streams of it, dripping from Henry's nostrils.

Tate entered next, shaking his right hand.

The cat reentered the cabin, darting to a dark corner.

"Anne!" Henry shouted as he tried to grab it, but he stumbled and fell. Tate pinned him there with his foot, pressing it hard into the man's shoulder.

Anne... Rebecca Anne Griffith, Floyd thought.

"Stay down," Tate instructed.

"We're too late," Floyd whined. "Chase... Chase is... Chase is..."

"She's right there," Tate exclaimed. "Floyd, she's there!"

Floyd followed Tate's outstretched finger.

Confusion washed over him, and he looked at the dead woman he was cradling. Blood... there was just so much blood and the cabin was dark and —

"That's Chase!" Tate shouted.

The handcuff sealed it. The woman in Floyd's arms had a handcuff attached to her wrist.

...it wasn't the woman leading Chase out of the building, it was the other way around.

This was the lawyer, and that was —

"Chase!"

Lying face down in the dirt was his partner. He recognized her whitish-gray hair. Adrenaline surged, his adrenals pumping out the very last reserves of the hormone. Floyd extricated himself from the stranger and went for Chase.

He rolled her over and was relieved to find that while her sweatshirt was covered in blood there was no wound in her throat. No fresh wound, that is.

She was still breathing.

"Chase!"

She murmured something he didn't understand, and Floyd addressed Tate.

"Call 911!" he shouted. "Call 911!"

Tate shook his head.

"No signal here. You need to bring her in." Tate drove his heel into Henry's shoulder and the man wailed. "Put pressure on the wound and get her to the hospital. Go now!"

This was the encouragement Floyd needed.

He searched her pockets and found her car keys.

"Up, Chase! Get up!"

He managed to hoist her to her feet and saw that there were deep gashes on her cheek.

"You're going to be okay," he whispered. Now it wasn't time reversing itself a few seconds, but a few days. And he wasn't in the cabin. He was in an alley behind *E-Tronics*.

Only this time, Chase wasn't saying "Save her," but "Save me."

Chapter 63

"I CAN'T BELIEVE YOU'RE EATING," Floyd said.

Tate shrugged and took another bite of his sandwich.

"I'm hungry. Didn't eat at all today."

Floyd looked away. His stomach still hadn't settled from the cabin.

"I can't believe that you were right all along," Tate said, his mouth full of chicken salad.

"What do you mean?"

Floyd still couldn't look at his partner. Even the idea of food made him grimace.

"The cat. This was all about the fucking cat."

Floyd's lips twisted into a grin, and he shook his head.

Fucking Tate.

"Not *all* about the cat."

Tate took another bite of his sandwich and then pointed it at Floyd as he spoke.

"Not all about it, sure, but the tipping point? Anne… that was Rebecca Griffith's middle name, right?"

"You tell me."

Tate nodded.

"Yeah, it was. Henry was on the verge of breaking after Becca killed herself—if that's what really happened to her—but if Roger hadn't tried to gain custody of the cat? Maybe the deaths would have stopped with Dr. Griffith? Who knows?"

Floyd considered this. It was possible, sure, but realistic? There was also the dealer in Portsmouth to consider.

When he didn't answer right away, Tate flapped the sandwich more dramatically.

"Alright, I'll bite. What do you think happened? I won't laugh this time, even if you go all Berkowitz with a talking animal theory."

"What I think?" Floyd took another moment to collect his thoughts. "I think that Roger and Henry did try to help Rebecca. She was sick, had some sort of psychological disorder. Maybe Cotard's, maybe not. Maybe she was just depressed. Anyway, Henry and Roger give her the stable life she needs. They get a cat. It's her cat, or theirs—doesn't matter. They name it after her, and then…" Floyd cocked his head as something occurred to him. "You know what? I think maybe she contracted herpes, or already had it, and got a prescription for Valacyclovir and then things went south. She committed suicide in that cabin. That's when Henry started to lose it. Blamed the drug, blamed everyone, including her biological father. Wayne was a doctor after all, but I doubt as a plastic surgeon he knew much about rare psychological disorders. What? Why are you giving me that look?"

Tate was smiling from ear to ear.

"Yeah, I mean, what you're saying makes sense. Kemosabe, you may have just become the Lone Ranger," he said. "But if I may?"

"By all means."

"Can't let you have all the credit," Tate said, still grinning. "I'm guessing Henry's still working at the shelter, even after Becca dies. He comes across another girl and maybe they try to save her, too. Around the same time, the absolute numpty drug dealer is in the news for stealing the wrong drug. Still furious, Henry goes with this new girl and uses her to try to steal the drug." Now it was Tate's turn to look off to one side. "You know what? The officer in Portsmouth concluded that both died in a struggle. Robbery gone wrong. I think… I think that

Dilbert might have been right. Maybe Henry only wants the drug and then things get fucked up. Enraged, he goes back to Charleston. Still trying to blame someone, he targets Wayne. After he's killed, Roger either feels guilty if he was involved, or finds out about it, and wants to turn Henry in. Henry has no choice—"

"The cat," Floyd interrupted. "Roger wants the cat. As their only link to Becca, Henry refuses to give her up. But Roger—"

Tate hushed him and his expression grew serious.

"What?"

"Code Blue," blared over the intercom. "Code Blue—room 216."

"Chase's room," Floyd blurted and jumped to his feet. "That's Chase's room!"

Tate was at his heels as he sprinted out of the cafeteria.

There was a flurry of movement toward the end of the hallway and Floyd pushed by several nurses. Near the door, the throng of doctors was too thick for him to make into the actual room.

"Chase? Chase!"

A familiar-looking man grabbed Floyd and pulled him aside.

"It's not Chase," Dr. Heinlin informed him. "It's Henry."

Floyd made a face.

"Henry?"

When he'd left the cabin, Henry had at worse a broken nose and dislocated shoulder. Floyd glanced at Tate who shrugged.

"Suicide," Dr. Heinlin said flatly. "I don't even know how he did it. There was a cop stationed right outside his door at all times."

Floyd sighed and grabbed his forehead.

"Chase is at the other end of the hallway, room 261."

A loud beeping came from Henry's room and then Floyd saw the crowd begin to dissipate. Dr. Heinlin locked eyes with a nurse who passed by, and she shook her head.

"Fuck," Floyd muttered.

Dr. Heinlin looked at him and then at Tate.

"Let's get out of here. Let's go see how Chase is doing."

Tate put an arm around Floyd's shoulder.

"I guess we'll never know," he said, all the humor gone from his eyes now.

"Know what?" Floyd asked.

"If it was all about the cat."

Chapter 64

CHASE FELT COLDNESS RADIATE FROM the back of her right
hand and up her arm. She opened her eyes and attempted to sit
up, only to be stopped by a hand on her opposite shoulder.

"Just—just lay there, for once, Chase. Stay still."

It was Dr. Heinlin.

Chase was about to complain when whatever he'd just injected reached her brain. Her eyelids fluttered and a pleasant
calmness came over her. It didn't last long. Unaware of her history, Dr. Heinlin had likely given her a small amount of mor-
phine or similar opiate. For a normal person, the effects might
persist for hours. But not Chase. Her receptors or enzymes or
whatever was responsible for rendering the drug inert were
maxed out from years of abuse.

As the sensation passed, Chase noticed that there were two
other people in the room with her: Floyd and Tate.

Floyd looked concerned, whereas Tate was smiling. But, like
Rebecca in the photograph, it didn't seem real.

"Nice to see you again, ma'am," he said, tipping an imagi-
nary hat in her direction.

Chase didn't smile, but she didn't frown either.

"Henry, he—" Floyd began, but Chase interrupted him.

She didn't give a shit about Henry.

"What about the two girls?" she said hoarsely. "The ones in
the cabin?

Floyd averted his eyes and shook his head.

"Shit," she swore. "What about Melissa?" When this question was met with blank stares, she clarified, "The woman
handcuffed to my car?"

Chase saw the muscles in Floyd's neck tense.

"What? What happened to her?"

"Sh-she s-s-s-saved you."

"What?"

Tate intervened.

"Best guess? Henry told one of the girls to attack you and Melissa got in the way. Saved your life, but it cost her own."

Chase groaned.

"How many people have to die because they know me?" She pushed herself up. This time when Dr. Heinlin tried to force her back down she glared at him. "How many fucking people have to die?"

"Mrs. Adams, you have to be calm."

"Fuck being calm. I want to talk to Henry." Now Chase did give a shit about the man — he was the only remaining link. Everyone else who might have known how Brian had gotten in contact with him were all dead. Tate had suddenly grown uncomfortable, as had Dr. Heinlin. "What? What is it now?"

"I-I t-t-t-tried to tell you," Floyd began. "H-h-he's dead."

"What?" Chase was incredulous. "How?"

"Suicide," Tate said flatly.

Chase let her head fall back to the pillow. Selfishly, she was pissed. Rationally, she thought that maybe this was the only fitting end for the man.

"She needs her rest," Chase heard the doctor say. "Why don't you —"

Eyes still closed, Chase said, "What day is it?"

"The thirteenth. Why?"

Chase's eyes snapped open. This time when she started to rise, nobody in the world could have stopped her.

"I have to go." She started to stand and felt better than she had the last time she'd been admitted.

"Chase, you have to rest. This is the third time that I've stitched you up. You can't risk tearing the wound open again,"

Dr. Heinlin advised, but his tone suggested that his words were purely for insurance reasons and not because he expected her to obey.

"Wait, third?" Floyd asked.

His query went ignored.

"Where are my clothes?" She couldn't see her shirt or pants anywhere in the room. "Where are my fucking clothes?"

"They were covered in blood," Floyd informed her. "Completely soaked. We had to—"

Tate produced a grocery bag.

"I just guessed your sizes. The gear is probably less expensive than you're used to, too."

Chase grabbed the bag without hesitating. Inside, was a plain gray tracksuit.

"Thanks."

As she stripped down, she saw Floyd glaring at Tate. And then all of them turned their backs as if she cared if they saw her in her underwear.

"Gun? Badge?"

Floyd grabbed a case from the desk by the door.

"Found it in your car. Gun and badge are in there."

She grabbed it, but Floyd didn't immediately let go.

"What's so important that you have to rush out of here, Chase?" he asked, his eyes soft. "Henry's dead. The other girls are also dead. What's so important that you're going to risk bleeding out again?"

Chase wanted to tell him then—he deserved to know. The man had saved her life not once, but twice this week. And maybe she would have. Maybe Chase would have said, Floyd, the man who robbed me and my family of our lives is getting out tomorrow. And I have to be there. I'm not sure what I'm going to do, but as you know, I'm not much for planning.

But Tate and Dr. Heinlin were staring at her expectantly. She pulled her gun case from Floyd's hand.

"I just—I just have to go." Then to the doctor, Chase added, "Just put this on my credit card, too."

Chase opened the case, confirmed that her gun and badge were inside, and then snapped it closed. She started toward the door, only to turn back to three bewildered men.

"Thank you, thank you all."

A subtle nod from Tate and Dr. Heinlin, no reaction from Floyd.

"Oh, and Floyd?"

"Yeah?" he said, expectation on his features. Chase once again let him down.

"It's probably a good idea to keep my name out of your report—all reports, actually." Chase opened the door before turning back one final time. "Dr. Heinlin? Is Bridget still here?"

The doctor shook his head.

"Moved to a psychiatric facility, for the time being."

"And the charges?"

"None laid at this point."

"Good," Chase said. "That's real good."

Maybe not everybody who comes in contact with me ends up dead, Chase thought. But the happy feeling that accompanied this, like a drug addict's most recent hit, was fleeting. And when it was gone, the hole it left behind was always just a little bit deeper.

Chapter 65

FLOYD WAS INCENSED. THAT WAS the only way to describe how he was feeling right now: furious.

Chase had lied to him. What's worse, she'd manipulated him.

It made sense now. The lack of real investigation into her attack, the paying for everything with cash... she wasn't supposed to be here. Director Hampton hadn't let her come back on a provisional basis. The man didn't even know she had anything to do with the case.

And now, he had to write his report with more lines redacted than The Mueller Report. No, not redacted. Completely rewritten, with Chase's indomitable presence removed.

If that wasn't bad enough, Tate had "important business to attend to".

Really? Like what?

What could be more important than visiting Meredith Griffith and letting her know that her daughter died two years ago?

"Fuck."

Floyd rubbed his eyes and shook his head.

It was his worst nightmare manifested.

Chase had told him to find what worked for him. That he had to find 'something' else he falls into some fucking pit to nowhere.

It would help to know where to look, Chase. Thanks a lot. Thanks a fucking lot.

Every mile closer to Meredith's house, another gallon of sweat seeped from his pores. And then Floyd pulled the chute.

He couldn't do it. He told himself it was because he promised Julia to let her know what happened to Wayne when he found out. And while that excited him as much as a lube-free colonoscopy, it was exponentially more appealing than telling a mother her child was dead, irrespective of how bitchy the mother was and how broken their relationship had been.

Been there, done that. Got the T-shirt and decorative spoon.

"Fuck."

Floyd changed the address on his cell phone to Julia's. His anxiety, which had been ratcheted up to twelve, pulled back sub-ten.

In ten minutes, he pulled into Julia's driveway. Normally, this is the part when he'd sit in the driveway, work through his monologue, come up with contingency and redundancy plans.

But something was wrong.

There were two cars in the driveway, and he recognized both. The first belonged to Julia. The second, Meredith.

Floyd looked beyond the vehicles to the front door of Julia Dreger's home.

The door was open.

He licked his lips and slowly got out of the car. Recalling what Tate had told him about the near fistfight between the two women at the funeral, his hand went to the gun on his hip, but he didn't pull it out.

Floyd made it past Meredith's car when Julia came out of the house. She was moving awkwardly, as if heavily medicated, and staggered. The front of her blouse was covered in blood and there was a knife—not a hunting knife, but a kitchen knife—in her hand.

"Julia!"

Floyd ran toward the woman and the knife fell to the interlocking brick walkway. She collapsed into his arms.

"What happened?" he gasped. "What the hell happened?"

Julia tilted her head back and her eyes lazily drifted to the open door. She reminded Floyd of someone at that moment but couldn't quite say who.

"She came here," Julia said in an almost inaudible whisper. "She… she attacked me… just like at the funeral. And I… I…"

Floyd saw a trail of blood drops, likely from the point of the knife leading back into the house.

No, please.

He dry swallowed, then guided Julia to his car and set her behind the wheel. Her breathing was labored, but he didn't think she was injured.

"Stay here," he instructed. Then Floyd ran into the house, praying that Mrs. Griffith was alive, but knowing, based on all the blood, that she probably wasn't.

He didn't have to look too hard. And, unfortunately, his prayers were not answered.

Floyd found Meredith Griffith in the kitchen. There was evidence of a struggle—a broken coffee mug, the paper towel rack torn from the wall—but it was clear that Meredith had gotten the worst of it.

She was slumped against the custom cabinets, with several holes in her chest. She inexplicably appeared to have less blood on her shirt than Julia, but all the wounds seemed to have stopped flowing.

Floyd reached down and touched the side of her neck with two fingers. This was done solely for procedural purposes—if the knife gashes weren't conclusive enough, the open mouth and blank stare sealed it.

Like her husband, Meredith Griffith was killed with a knife.

As this realization set in, as Floyd grabbed his head and looked skyward, amazed and appalled that he had once again arrived at the scene of a murder committed with a knife, a thought formulated in his mind that he would never forget and forever regret.

At least I don't have to tell Meredith that her daughter committed suicide.

Epilogue

THEY WERE THERE, OF COURSE. Chase knew they would be, but it still pained her to see Brian Jalston's two remaining wives waiting for his release. Sue-Ellen and Portia Jalston.

Their presence pained her but their outfits—flowing white dresses—angered her.

And then she saw him: Brian Jalston.

He was no longer wearing the orange jumper, but he was sporting the same shit-eating grin. Bag in hand, he stepped outside the gates as a free man.

It was unbelievable.

Brian looked like a man finishing nine holes and greeting his wife and mistress in the parking lot.

If Chase had her way, he would never see another golf course for the rest of his—considerably shortened—life.

With her head down, and the hood of the sweatshirt that Tate Abernathy had given her pulled over her face, Chase moved swiftly through the parked cars. She waited until one of the women, Portia, handed a set of keys to Brian before she made her presence known.

"Excuse me," Chase said in a deliberately quiet voice.

Sue-Ellen turned to look at her, but Chase didn't raise her head yet. She walked by the trio and then repeated the two words, louder this time.

"Excuse me."

This drew both Portia's and Sue-Ellen's attention, but Brian, basking in his newfound freedom, didn't notice Chase.

This was a mistake.

Chase pulled the gun out of the front sweatshirt pocket, shoved Portia, who cried out, and went right up to Brian.

By the time he reacted, she'd already pressed the muzzle against the man's spine.

"If either of you come near me," Chase said, addressing Sue-Ellen and Portia, "I'll blow a fucking hole in his back. If you're lucky, he'll just be paralyzed from the waist down."

With this, Chase flicked back the hood, revealing herself.

She wasn't sure whether the women recognized her or not, and didn't care. All she cared about is that they stepped back, that they were too frightened to interfere.

Brian knew who it was. He hadn't seen her, but he recognized her voice. Chase could tell because he tensed a little.

"Open the door," she ordered, shoving Brian towards the car. "Open the fucking door."

Brian hesitated so she shoved the muzzle even harder against his back. He grunted and then pulled the car door wide. Chase reached around the much bigger man, flicked the unlock button, then got into the seat behind the driver.

Chase flicked the gun toward the women to make sure they didn't get any ideas, then pointed it at Brian again.

"Get in."

"You're not—"

"Shut the fuck up and get in the car," Chase nearly shouted. Her voice was so hoarse that she barely even recognized it as her own. "*Now*."

Brian obeyed and the car dipped as he sat.

"Now close the door."

Again, Brian did as he was told.

"Start the car and drive."

As they pulled out of the parking lot, leaving Sue-Ellen and Portia's terror-stricken faces behind, Chase reached into her pocket and pulled out a single white tablet.

The very last Cerebrum.

She looked at the pill, turning the small disc in her palm.

"Who is looking out for you, Brian? Anyone? Anyone at all?" In the rearview mirror, she saw the man's strong jaw clench and Chase held up the pill. "It isn't Riley, Melissa, Sue-Ellen, or Portia—it's none of your wives." She paused. "But you better hope it's God—because I'll never let you have her. You'll never even see Georgina again."

The irony of the fact that her biological child lived halfway across the world from her, and wanted a relationship, an uncontested one, wasn't lost on Chase Adams. But that meant nothing here.

Right now, her focus was on Georgina.

I'm living in the fucking moment, Chase thought. *I'm finally living in the moment… and I'm willing to kill for it.*

Kill.

A promise.

Kill.

A way out.

"*Kill.*"

The word had come from the nowhere and everywhere, but now it came from her.

"Put this in your mouth," Chase said, thrusting the pill forward. "And swallow it."

END

Author's Note

WELCOME BACK, *#THRILLOGANS!* IT'S BEEN a pressing few years, but I'm glad that you've decided to stick around to continue the wild ride that is Chase Adams—the (sometimes) great Chase Adams. The always determined, the smart-mouthed, the damaged, the… well, you get the picture. In some ways, Chase isn't that different from the victims in this book. In fact, I deliberately tried to draw parallels between many of the characters, even those who, at first blush, seem very different. Grief, disease, control… these are the Part headings, but they're more than that. They, like the characters, are often more similar than we might initially believe. A damaged mind, by innumerable means, can justify nearly any action. The world is real, but it is always interpreted by the gray matter between our ears. And that is up for—you guessed it—interpretation.

As much as this book is about Chase, it's also about Floyd. It's about his growth (or lack thereof) and about him being thrust into situations that he, quite frankly, detests. He stumbles, falls, gets up, falls again. And then there's Tate. I enjoyed writing Tate, and I'm positive he wasn't a flash in the pan. He'll be back. If you were really paying attention, you may have noticed the mention of another Agent, one whose series is already in the works. I'm hoping that he shows up in Direct Evidence, the next book in the Chase Adams series. About that… this summer. It will be out this summer.

You keep reading, I'll keep writing.

Pat

Montreal, 2021

Printed in Great Britain
by Amazon

84078437R00192